HOLLOW

OUT

THE

DARK

BOOKS BY JAMES WADE

NOVELS

Hollow Out the Dark

Beasts of the Earth

River, Sing Out

All Things Left Wild

HOLLOW OUT THE DARK

A NOVEL

JAMES WADE

BLACK STONE
PUBLISHING

Printed in the United States of America

First edition: 2024
ISBN 978-1-9826-0111-9
Fiction / Literary

Version 1

Blackstone Publishing
31 Mistletoe Rd.
Ashland, OR 97520

www.BlackstonePublishing.com

For Josh and Josie at Blackstone Publishing

On all levels American society is rigged . . . I am troubled by the cynical immorality of my country. It cannot survive on this basis.

—John Steinbeck

And the Lord said unto Cain, Where is Abel thy brother? And he said, I know not: Am I my brother's keeper? And the Lord said, What hast thou done? the voice of thy brother's blood crieth unto me from the ground. And now art thou cursed.

—Genesis 4:9–11

The land is in winter. An equable autumn has given way to a barbarous cold. The country's burnished bronze laminate has been in an instant discarded, replaced without ceremony by bleak, illiberal desolation.

Only the pines hold. The rest of the trees that cover the high ground and hollows are laid bare, exposed to the wanton woes of a harsh and merciless inclemency.

It is a wet cold—humid and piercing. A "mud cold" the locals name it, as the ground turns to sludge and mire and stays so for the duration of the season. Blood red clay encrusts the earth and is tracked onto porch boards and into near empty shops and is tracked along creek beds and into the darkest coves of every creature—man and beast alike.

The air is cold, but the wind is colder. There's a madness to the wind. It blows purposeless and uncontrolled. It blows beyond reason. Every leaf is torn from every branch, but still the wind rages on as if it will have the branches too. It is called a howling wind but it does not howl. It cries. It is a devastated wind and it is screaming transgressions in long, haunting tones.

Coal and wood burn continuous in the town and in the hills and thickets that surround it. Everything is rationed. Cured or smoked, canned or pickled, cut and stacked and stored for later. Life itself, a long rationing to some unknown end. Everything weighed and measured and so often found wanting. The only things in abundance are wood for the fire and cold for the winter and each is set about destroying the reserve of the other. As if the world entire is not but a god-cursed balancing act—circus performers on the high wire leaping to their death in a strange synchronized harmony.

A coyote slinks about the roadcut. Her fur is wet, and she is crouched and still, and her ovaled ears are pointed up at attention. There is a mouse sheltering within the black, wet leaves, and the coyote has fathomed out where to strike, but she does not. Instead, her ears twitch, and she stiffens. Something is coming. She darts across the road just ahead of the approaching car. The mouse survives another day.

The car is a Chrysler 72, black, with two men in the front seat and crates of whiskey and brandy in the back.

"Bad luck," the passenger says. He is slumped down in his seat and chewing a healthy wad of tobacco. He spits into an empty bean can.

"What?" the driver asks, looking over at his companion.

"That coyote was headed north. The Navajo say it's bad luck."

"For a coyote to go north?"

"For it to cross your path on its way north. Means you ought to turn around 'fore something bad happens to ye."

"That don't make no sense," the driver says, but his face is worried.

The passenger shrugs. He adjusts the tobacco inside his cheek and spits again.

"I'm just telling you what the Navajo say. Don't go sulling up on me."

"Well, I ain't superstitious," the driver says in a tone meant to convince himself of his own statement. "If the Lord means for something to happen, it'll happen—northbound coyote or no."

The passenger nods.

"I'm undecided," he says, and the driver looks at him again and waits for more, but nothing comes.

They go on in silence for a while yet. Out either window the forest is sucked away at unnatural speeds. Thick oaks and slender pines and blackgum trees stretching a hundred feet tall. Wickerwork canopies blotting out the sky, bedimming an already muted country. The rain has not stopped but neither is it falling. It appears to be hanging there in the air.

"How come?" the driver asks after a few minutes have passed.

"How come what?"

"How come you to be undecided," he says.

"They Lord, Thomas," the passenger shakes his head. "Are you that hung up on it?"

"Well."

"Alright, fine," the passenger scratches at his cheek and sighs. "I was working with this fella on a timber outfit over Louisiana way a few years back. And he was always going on—"

"What was his name?"

"Huh?"

"The fella you were working with. What was his name?"

"His name ain't important," the passenger says, annoyed. "Bob Hader was his name. And he was always going on about hats on the bed and whatnot. Real superstitious, old Bob. But I didn't never pay him no mind, until one day he come in the bunkhouse and scooped my hat off the mattress and shoved it my face—he was madder'n hell—and he says, 'Goddamnit, Dotzel, you keep leaving your hat on the bed and something bad is gonna happen to you.'"

The passenger spits in his can and wipes his mouth with the forearm of his shirtsleeve.

"Next day he got crushed by a pile of logs that come loose off a crane."

The driver frowns.

"But it wasn't his hat, it was yours," he says, unsettled.

"True," the passenger admits. "But the week before, I'd give him three dollars to take some little gal to the pictures and he hadn't paid me back yet. Can't hardly collect from a dead man, now can I? Bad luck all around, I'd say."

The driver absorbs the story. Breathes a sigh of relief.

"You lie like a damn rug," he says, looking over at the grinning man and shaking his head. "Had me half-worried and everything. I bet the Navajo don't care two shits about no coyote neither."

"Look out," the passenger hollers, and the driver rights himself and hammers on the brakes.

The Chrysler locks up, sliding to a stop and putting deep ruts in the hapless road.

Strung out from one ditch to the other are a dozen men in black coats with black wool masks pulled down over their faces. They stand silent and ghoul-like in the cold fog. They are armed.

Before them stands a tall man. He is impossibly slender. Skeletal. His coat hangs improbably from his bone-thin shoulders. But the men in the car are not looking at his coat.

The mask he wears was sculpted in Paris after the war. Constructed from a plaster cast of the man's face, then crafted with copper. It is stayed by a simple string that ties around the man's head. Most soldiers chose to have their masks painted to best match the color of their skin, but the man before them insisted on black.

And it is black that the men in the car see now. Black fabricated jaw and cheeks and black unmoving mouth. Only the man's eyes are visible, but they too are dark. Inhuman. On his forehead, blue veins bulge against his taut and pallid skin, tracing backward and disappearing under his slick white hair that is long on top and short on the sides.

It is as if been cobbled up out of some half-drawn image of a man. Cadaverous. Missing, somehow, an outer layer or casing that should have been wholly necessary.

"What the hell is this?" the driver says.

The passenger is already out of the car. He's striding toward the masked man.

"Whatever you heard, whoever you talked to, they was wrong," the passenger says. "So before you go and do what you think you're about to do, me and Thomas yonder will give y'all a chance to change your mind. And if you need any motivation to make that change, well, hell, we'd be more than happy to tell you who it is we work for."

He stops a foot from the masked man and leans around his person and raises his voice so that the men behind might hear. They are standing motionless with their weapons at the ready.

"Frog and Squirrel Fenley," he says loudly, and no one moves.

He spits. He looks back at the car and the driver.

"The Fenley brothers," he tries again. Still there is silence. No birds. No coyotes or whitetail or squirrels. The drizzling rain has stopped. There is only wind.

"Listen, fellas, if y'all don't—"

The driver sees his partner fall before the sound of the gunshot reaches the car. His eyes widen. The masked man is walking toward him and the line of men are following. They move in perfect step with one another.

The driver is frantic. He is trying to turn the car around, but the road is narrow and the ditch is deep and the vehicle careens sideways down the muddy bank, slamming hard into the red clay bottom.

Some of the bottles have broken and the car smells like whiskey and the driver is trying to scramble out but the masked man is there, his head tilted slightly to the side, his eyes watching.

"Take it," the driver pleads, grabbing at a loose bottle and offering it up like some desperate oblation to appease a vengeful god. "Take it all."

"I intend to," the man says, the molded lips of his mask unmoving.

1

Wintertide. Cold and wet. Boreal winds, and then the storm. Thunderheads what covered the county, and rain that fell laminate for hours on end. Fell hard into the night. The river ran riotous just below the town. Black water and white caps. Waves contorting and lapping at the shore where the townsfolk scurried like half-drowned rats, and the hounds baying at shapes in the rain or at the rain itself. Mutts and curs, clamoring from beneath porch fornices and back alleys and straining at the end of their runs. Whining in the dark.

The air was wet with a biting humidity. Squirrel Fenley stood outside the insurance office and took in the cold. He was dark even in the shadows. Black boots. Black coat. Curls of black hair sticking out from beneath the rolled brims of his crusher cap. His eyes were dark and short. He was short too, and slight. But if his physical stature did not command respect, all else about him did. His reputation was one of violence. Some called him mad. But those who knew him understood there was nothing mad or irrational about Squirrel. Every move was calculated. He harbored somewhere within him a constant darkness that would not permit him to back down from a fight, nor would it allow him to lose once the fight began.

The door opened behind him.

"Here you are," Eli Schaffer said.

"Here I am."

"It's cold enough to piss popsicles out here. Everything alright?"

Eli, like his brother Hank, had a barrel chest and blond hair. Squirrel had insisted Hank grow a mustache so the two could be more easily distinguished.

"The cold helps me think," Squirrel said.

Eli was already shivering. He pulled at the ends of his gloves.

"What are you thinking about?" he asked.

"About what's coming."

"Is something coming?"

"Maybe," Squirrel told him. "Maybe it's already here."

"Well," Eli nodded, uncertain. "Alright then. You want us to deal you in this next hand? Hadn't nobody touched your chips, for a blind or otherwise."

"Wentworth still in there pissing away money he ain't got?" Squirrel asked.

"Yessir. Just like you said. You want us to keep letting him take markers?"

Squirrel nodded.

Eli looked hesitant.

"But if you know he can't pay, why are we—"

"I'll be in directly, Eli."

Eli went back inside and Squirrel turned away from the door and the curtained rain fell cold into the world.

A half hour. Less. Squirrel went into the darkened insurance office and walked to the back wall and found the finger groove and slid a small section of the wall to the side and slipped through it and into a hallway. There was a thin scarlet runner on top of the wood flooring and dark geometric wallpaper that stretched the length of the corridor. There were short cavities cut into the wall every few feet and there were lanterns set on sills and about half of them were burning.

The hall spilled out into a room with no doors and a low drop-tile ceiling cut from brass. The main bar ran along the back wall, flanked on one side by a short stage. There were round tables in the middle of the room and leather booths against the wall opposite the stage. Men were arguing in a dim-lit corner booth.

"That's horseshit," Frog said. "The whole bottle would shatter."

"Not necessarily—think about a window," Hank Schaffer told him. "A bullet goes clean through, the rest of it holds together. Maybe a few little ole cracks, but it don't come apart."

"A window is bigger, but that ain't even the point. Nobody can shoot a damn bullet through the top of a Coke bottle and have it come out the bottom clean. Not from no two hundred yards."

"I'm telling you," Hollis Wentworth said, shaking his head. "There's plenty of dead Huns that can attest."

"If they're dead, they can't attest to shit, now can they?" Frog asked.

"Once I saw him throw a knife into a kraut's back from fifty yards away," Hollis added.

He was red cheeked and grinning. The blushing smile of a quick drunk.

"Did he really?" Hank asked. "Sure enough?"

Hollis nodded. He knocked back his whiskey. He was thin and gangly and unshaven. He had small green beads for eyes, set narrow, just on either side of his nose, and his fair skin was covered in dirt and freckles. His face shook slightly when he talked. The tight curls of red hair jostling atop his head.

"Threaded it through low-hanging limbs and everything," he said, blinking. "Stuck right in his back."

"Well, if Jesse Cole did it, I guess we'd all better get down on our knees and give thanks," Frog said, mocking. "You know, I don't believe half the shit they say about him."

"Whether you believe it or not don't change that it happened."

"He may be about ready to give Christ a run for his money," Hank said. "What do you think, Frog?"

"Even Jesus Christ had to take himself a shit every now and then," Frog said.

Frog was Squirrel's brother. He was aptly named, with his great wide head and oversized mouth that sloped downward in a perpetual frown. His neck was buried somewhere beneath his hunched shoulders and, unlike his brother, Frog stood well over six feet tall.

"Maybe so," Hank said, "but did he have to wipe his ass after? That's the question."

"I'm just tired of hearing about how goddamn great he is."

"Jesus?" Hollis asked.

"Cole," Frog said and spit on the floor next to his chair.

Squirrel appeared over his shoulder.

"Don't get jealous, Brother," Squirrel warned him, taking a seat at the table. "I don't have the time or the patience for another Charlie Cooper."

"Cooper deserved everything he got," Frog said, then lowered his round head down in between his thick shoulders like some mutant turtle. "Deserved it twice over, you ask me."

"Oh, you don't got nothing to worry about on that front," Hollis said. "When I told Jesse that Adaline was back, he didn't hardly say a word."

"I ain't worried," Frog said. "I'll whip Jesse Cole or any other man who tries to undercut me. War hero or not."

"Don't talk about Jesse like that," Hollis said, his courage and stupidity tracing a similar, upward path with each drink. "He saved my life over there."

"Is that how come you to follow him around like a little lost puppy?" Frog asked. "Running to him for help every time you get yourself into trouble?"

"Are we playing cards or not?" Squirrel asked and shot his brother a hard look.

He shuffled, but before he could deal, a tall, slender man stepped in from the front room, where insurance was sold during daylight hours. He took off his hat and water dripped from it and from his shaggy brown hair and he held his wet coat away from him and looked at it and shook his head.

"Still coming down, Yance?" Hank asked.

Yancy Greaves draped his coat overback an empty booth.

"The flood that was promised," he said. "I got the ark tied up around back."

"Well. Come on and get you a drink. Should we deal you in?"

"I believe I'll spectate, boys. The old lady's all over my ass about money, here lately. I'd hate to lose my whoring funds to a drunk game of cards."

Hank laughed.

"Don't blame you. Nelda's a scary woman."

"Big and scary. There ain't no better kind," Yancy said. "Hell, if a gal can't carry me out of the house during a fire, I'd just as soon not even mess with her."

"Hear. Hear. Give her big ole ass a nice squeeze for me, would you?"

"Oh, I will. And I'll tell her who it's from too. Maybe she'll take to hollering at you for a while. Give me a chance to breathe."

There was laughter in the room, but it died a quick death when Squirrel spoke.

"What'd you find out?" he asked.

Yancy rubbed the back of his head.

"You was right. He ain't nobody local."

"You get a name?"

"Nossir. Working on it. But in the meantime, we might ought to give some thought to soldiering up. I mean, the way they left them boys up on the—"

"Not here." Squirrel raised his hand. "They've got their muscle. We'll get ours."

"What are y'all going on about?" Hollis asked, well on his way to a roaring drunk. "Is somebody gonna deal the dadgum cards?"

"Come sit, Yancy," Squirrel ordered. "We're playing a high-stakes game with our buddy Hollis, here."

Yancy started to protest but Squirrel stared him into submission.

"Yeah, sit down, Yance," Hollis said. "You might be just what I need to change my luck around."

Yancy glanced at Squirrel and then at Frog.

"Sure," he said. "I'll play a few hands."

They finished a bottle of whiskey between the five of them and Eli brought them another from behind the bar and they finished it too.

Hollis was squint eyed and grinning by midnight and struggling to stare at two-pair of aces and eights with a nine kicker.

"Hey, shithead." Frog slapped his palm on the tabletop. "It's to you."

Hollis smiled wider.

"I'll be nice and check to you fellas."

"You can't check, goddamnit," Frog said. "I done raised."

"Oh, well, hell," Hollis looked at the pot in the middle. "Then I re-raise. Everything I got."

"How much is he looking at, Brother?" Frog asked.

Squirrel conferred with his ledger book.

"This is his second hundred-dollar marker. He's got sixty left on it."

"Sixty," Frog repeated. "Alright then. Call."

Frog laid down his straight, jack high. All eyes turned to Hollis, who had stopped smiling. He clutched his cards closer.

"Show 'em, Wentworth," Frog said, impatient.

Hollis was paralyzed. He wondered if the rest of the table could hear his heartbeat. Could feel it.

He took a breath in. Closed his eyes.

He sprang from the chair and it went clattering on its side and the cards fluttered behind him as he ran toward the false wall.

Hank and Eli moved to chase after him, but Squirrel halted them.

"No," he said as the outer door opened and Hollis disappeared into the night. "Let him go. It's not him we're after."

"Who are we after?"

2

Jesse Cole, awake and restless, paced the floorboards of the old cabin his grandfather built during the War between the States. It sat on a pier-and-beam foundation with a few feet of crawl space beneath the floor. Each time Jesse's boot came down on the puncheon wood he could hear the boards groaning and feel the dull reverberation below him. The windows were curtainless and even the subdued light of a new moon appeared across the room in streaks of pale blue, capturing in its sad spotlight every mote of dirt and dust.

He stared anxious at the door. In his childhood it had been a great thing—a strong and sturdy door to keep out the cold, the wet, the confusion. But somehow it had grown smaller and weaker, and he watched it now and scratched at the sides of his full beard.

He watched as the moonlight bled under the door and through the gaps and through every crack and cavity, every cleft and chasm in the wood, spilling into the cabin to stake out new territories for the night.

He walked slow in these clockless hours. Dead things called to him from dreams and bells rang where there were no towers. He would not sleep.

He nudged the door of one of the bedrooms and leaned forward and peered in. There was a small bed pushed against the wall and an egg-white dresser opposite the bed. A lighter shade of wood above the dresser where a mirror once hung. He'd shared the room with his brother, all those years ago. Now it belonged to Sarah, though she rarely used it.

In the other bedroom, Eliza lay with her back to the door, her arms wrapped tight around the girl. Sarah's head rested on the pillow she shared with her mother. He could hear them breathing. He closed his eyes and listened. When he opened them again, he studied the curve of Eliza's body. He could see her nightgown peeking out from beneath the deerskin blanket.

He remembered her as a young woman, betrothed to his brother. Light and laughing and full of a wonderment that had long since been gone from her life. Taken. Not unlike the theft of his own being, and yet here they had repurposed themselves and their devotions. She lived for the girl, and he lived for them both. Or tried.

Ten years and he could not make it feel natural. He'd thought he was doing a good thing, the right thing. He'd thought he was doing what Danny would have wanted, but often he felt like an impostor. Or worse, a thief. He turned away.

He walked out onto the porch. The storm passed and already another brewing. The country black and godless before him, and if there was some form to conclude, then surely it was the envisaged heart of emptiness. An arrant and unmixed dark.

The pots on the porch clanged against one another and against the wood and nails that held them. The trilling of insects had quieted months before—the winter swallowing them up—and so the wind's doleful moan went unanswered, passing through the thickets and hills and hollows of that sad country, rattling branches and harrying long-dead leaves, all in search of a thing it could not name. Could not hold.

Then came the lightning—one long, mute lash of purple electric in a thunderless sky. Lucent and immediate, the light spilled out over the yard and Jesse saw there the short-barreled shape of a hog.

He went back into the house and reemerged with a kerosene lamp and the hog was still there, struggling to stand. He watched it by lantern light. It came wayward and wobbling from the woods. It was upright for a minute, maybe less. Its hind legs gave out and it crumpled down in the cold, rotted earth.

Jesse descended the porch and went out through the yard and the hog tried to rise but could not. It laid on its side and Jesse knelt and listened to its labored breathing and saw the short bursts of steam escaping from its mouth. There were red and blue splotches around the pig's snout. Its eyes rolled wild in its head. Jesse could smell its bowels releasing.

He put his hand on the hog's stomach and felt its short, quick breaths. Felt them stop.

Cursed creatures upon a cursed land, and him among them.

He went inside and quietly into the bedroom closet and pulled on his coveralls and his wool knit cap and looked at his rifle for a long while before grabbing it and heading back out into the night.

3

A black Chevy Universal threw rocks and wet dirt as it slid into a turn and then accelerated. The driver was a young man with slicked-back hair and a three-day beard. His beady eyes cut from the road to the rearview and back. The sedan behind him was laying on the horn. It was a white Ford Tudor with a black stripe down the body and a large star painted on the door. In an arc above the star was the word *Texas*, below read *Rangers*.

"These sonsofbitches," the driver muttered.

He reached down and touched the sawed-off beneath his seat, then put both hands on the steering wheel and angled the car toward the side of the road.

The Ford pulled in behind.

Amon Atkins looked to his partner and nodded and both men stepped out of the vehicle. They wore brown suits, red ties, and dark cherry-colored cowboy boots. Amon stood a shade under six feet. He had dark brown hair and a narrow face with sharp features. His hazel eyes turned down at the corners so that he had often a solemn look about him.

His partner, Phil Werskey, was short and girthy with thinning auburn hair.

The two men approached the idling Chevy.

Amon knocked on the driver's window.

"What say, Amon?" the driver asked, cranking the window down.

"Merle," Amon said, his voice slow and measured. "There a reason your back end is just about dragging through the dirt?"

"Well, suspensions been acting up on me. Ain't got no money to get her fixed, what with the way everything's been going."

"I'm going to ask you to get out of the car, Merle."

"Now hold on a minute. It ain't no crime to be broke, Amon. Hell, if it was, they'd have to build four or five more jails in Smith County alone."

"You ain't poor, Nichols," Werskey said, his muffled voice coming from just outside the passenger window.

Merle leaned toward him and looked up through the glass and nodded and then righted himself in the seat.

"And it is against the law to manufacture alcohol," Amon added. "And to transport it. And to sell it. All those things are against the law. And my guess is, you have your trunk loaded down with milk crates been absent any milk for quite some time."

Merle sighed and shook his head. He laughed.

"What are you doing, Amon?" he asked, throwing up his hands. "I mean, just what in the ever-loving shit is going on here?"

"I think you know."

"What I know is that this'll cost you your job."

"It might. But I'm doing it anyway."

"So that's it, then? You're on a goddamn crusade now? Trying to be like your old man or something? The miserable bastard."

"When the law is paralyzed, justice never goes forth," Amon quoted, ignoring the insult.

"And you, Werskey?" Merle spoke louder, shifting again toward the other man. "You gonna let this crazy sumbitch ruin your whole career?"

"It ain't my career you ought to be worried about, Junior," Phil said.

"Well, now, that's where you're wrong," Merle said, still refusing to open the door. "It's corn liquor that won my daddy that seat in the first place. I don't care who says what in your little Sunday services, fellas.

Tyler, Texas, is a by-god drinking town. Just go on and ask that fella right there."

Merle pointed down the road and when the men raised up to look, he cleared the sawed shotgun from under his seat. Phil took a step back but it wasn't far enough. The blast shattered the passenger window and caught him square in the chest and blew him tumbling backward. Merle tried to swing the gun around toward the other Ranger, but Amon drew and fired his pistol into Merle's knee, the cap bone exploding at close range. Merle let loose the shotgun amid a high-pitched yowling and Amon grabbed it and yanked it through the open window.

He was quick to his partner's body as Merle screamed and cursed from the driver's seat. Phil had flopped awkwardly onto his side. Amon bent and turned him over and checked his pulse.

Amon's own heart rate had remained somewhat steady despite the suddenness of the violence, but now he could feel the adrenaline surging. A sort of rage taking hold.

"You shot my goddamn knee off," Merle screamed, dragging himself from the car. He balanced against the side of the Chevy, taking heavy breaths. He was sweating, even in the cold.

"This man had a family," Amon said, stepping out of the ditch. "Children. A wife."

"Well"—Merle was grimacing, clutching his bloody leg—"maybe I'll give her a call."

Amon's face reddened further. His finger tapped against the side of his pistol in rapid succession, as if it were tracking the meter of his contemplation.

Then the finger stopped, and Amon nodded his head and fired a round into the man's other knee.

He stepped off the road and tried to compose himself. Took a long breath. The wind was cold and relentless, and each gust filled the forest with a wretched and woeful sound—the low howling keen of the wind, the barren and abraded branches scraping against one another like deviant violins, and Merle Nichols screaming about the legs he'd likely never use again.

4

Hours to come, Jesse could feel the dawn inching ever upward from that world in the east where someplace there's a great ocean that enkindles the sun. He'd walked nearly a half mile in the cold and his hands were all but numb in his gloves when he knocked on the door.

The cabin had been built nearly one hundred years prior and in the shotgun style of that time. The family that built it was dead soon after at the hands of some disease unknown to them. Through no legal record or accounting, it was occupied now by an old man named Moss who had been like kin to the Coles for longer than Jesse could recall. Since before his birth.

Jesse knocked again.

After a while the door came open and Moss stood there holding a single-prong candelabra and his face aglow in the small dancing taper flame. He was a hearty man, once stout but softened now in his old age. He'd pulled on his boots but elsewise wore only long johns. His beard was white and gray save for a streak beneath his bottom lip that had been stained yellow by years of tobacco juice.

"I expect you're here about the hogs," he said.

Jesse nodded and walked inside and no sooner than he took off his cap a great black hog came sniffing and snorting from the back of the house, knocking into walls and furniture alike.

"Good Lord," Jesse said, jumping back.

Moss seemed not to have noticed, but he turned and looked and gave Jesse a shrug.

"What?" the old man asked. "There's a fever going around. I ain't about to leave Gloria Swineson out there with them that's infected."

Jesse shook his head.

"I wish you wouldn't name the goddamn pigs," he said.

"Don't let Albert Swinestein hear you say that," Moss warned. "That little bastard has done and changed his whole demeanor. Walks with some sort of regality to him now."

Moss set the candle in the den and poured the coffee and the two of them drank it in the kitchen without speaking and the hog laid on its side next to Jesse. The flame shivered against the far wall and that was the only light.

Moss finished his coffee and stared into the emptiness of his cup.

"You have any of that serum left?" Jesse asked him.

"I do. Serum. Virus. About fifty cc's. Enough for two, maybe three little ones. But it won't be enough."

"What makes you say that?"

"I seen a passel of 'em yesterday," Moss said. "Whole herd just riddled with it. There ain't nothing to be done."

"There might be," Jesse said. "We ought to at least go out and see. There's people depending on that meat."

Moss eyed him, curious-like.

"Word going round at the farmers exchange is that you ain't selling much pork as it is," the old man said. "Been all but giving it away."

"Me getting by with less is better than them trying to get by with nothing," Jesse told him.

"What's Eliza have to say about that?" Moss asked.

Jesse clicked his tongue.

"That may be a harder sale," he said. "Still, we ought to go take a look. See just how bad it might be."

"Too early to argue with you, I guess," Moss said. "And there ain't no getting back to sleep now."

They pulled on their caps and Moss his own pair of coveralls and he told the pig to stay, and the two men went out into the cold. Jesse carried the rifle, a buck knife, and a tow sack that held three and a half gallons of corn. Moss wore a satchel filled with medical supplies. Over his shoulder rested a thin vanadium pole with a small, looped rope at the end.

They hadn't gone a mile down the old Coushatta trail, when Jesse knelt in a wide berth of fresh rooted dirt under an old oak that stood lonely in the pines. He leaned the sack against the tree and untied it. He scattered half the corn and stood and called out in a series of yips and squeals.

Moss unburdened the satchel. He opened the kit and pulled out each bottle and set them one beside the other: Lysol, water, virus, serum, and lastly, a wooden box with velvet lining that held the shape of the glass syringe. He loaded the first dose of serum, and when he stood, Jesse was shoving the pole at him.

"Here they come," Jesse said.

The hogs came wild and trampling through the brush. There were at least a dozen and they pulled up at the sight of humans. Another six or seven followed behind.

"C'mon now and get this corn," Jesse told them, shaking out the second half of the sack.

The hogs gave a weary approach but were soon eating and snorting and burying their noses in the soft, wet soil.

Jesse watched them. The long bones from their jaws pushing through the skin and forming bladelike tusks. The tufts of greasy black hair standing and clumping on their backs. Half the pigs had a cut on their right ear—two straight notches, two crops, and one underhack. It had been the mark of Jesse's father, then his brother. Now it was his.

He counted the hogs and the brands and the dissident pigs with no markings. It was a good mix of both, and he watched them closely. A few stumbled, others were broken out in splotches, and still others stayed back from the rest and refused to eat.

"It's got damn near a quarter of them," Jesse whispered.

"I'd say there ain't much helping it," Moss nodded. "But being as we're here, what do you want to do?"

"Is this the bunch you saw?"

"It is," Moss said.

"And you don't think hooking one and taking a look at him will do any good?"

"I don't."

Moss coughed and most of the hogs retreated into a mott of twisted oaks, their black eyes watching from the brush and the briars beneath. A few fled the area altogether.

Jesse shot him a look and the old man shrugged.

"I saw a pregnant sow or two in that bunch that still looked alright," Jesse said. "But if they catch it, or if there's others to pass it to the shoats as soon as they're born, it'll decimate the herd."

"Your call," Moss said.

"What would Danny have done?"

"Fever touches a hog, it's dead in a week. Your brother would have done what he needed to do to try saving the rest. And I would have told him it was too late. Not worth the trouble or the bullets."

"But he wouldn't have listened."

"I kindly doubt it."

"Well," Jesse said. "I guess let's set back and see if they come finish this corn."

They backtracked fifty or so yards through the woods and then sat on either side of a black willow and looked to the east for some sign of light, but there was none.

Jesse looked again at the rifle. It had belonged to his brother.

"He sure was a good'un," Jesse said, and he saw his brother's face grinning somewhere in that outer dark. "Ole Danny."

"He was," Moss confirmed.

"Did he ever say anything to you?" Jesse asked. "Ever—I don't know . . ."

"He didn't come around much, after you shipped out," Moss said, not wanting to linger on the subject. "I hadn't seen him in nearly three months when Edith got sick."

Jesse wanted him to say more. Something that might give him some understanding, even after all this time. But the old man stayed quiet and Jesse was left still searching for answers to a question he wasn't sure how to ask.

The hogs had returned. Their black shapes barely made out, moving against a black background. The two men crept closer until they could see well enough to favor the sick from the rest.

Moss looked at Jesse. They both looked at the rifle.

"You want to give it another try?" the old man asked.

Jesse nodded.

He raised the rifle and lined up the sight behind the shoulder of one of the splotch-marked hogs. He took a breath in. The world hummed around him. The ground felt uneven beneath his feet. The sight began to sway all over the pig's body. He blinked and then blinked again but his vision was a blurry mess. When he exhaled, his finger moved away from the trigger. He lowered the gun. He was trembling.

Moss nodded and patted him soft on the back.

"My daddy used to love eating squirrel and dumplings," Moss whispered. "Would take me hunting for the little bastards ever' chance he got. But after he come home from Antietam, we never did eat it again."

He took the rifle from Jesse.

"You're alright, son," he told him. "Cast your burden and I'll sustain ye."

Moss raised the gun and began to fire at the diseased pigs. Jesse looked away.

When the shooting stopped, all else stopped with it. No sound save the rolling wind like an ocean tide, hounding at the trees, and then away. The branches settled uneasy, waiting for the next wave to come. And always it is coming.

5

Amon's commanding officer was little more than a voice on the end of a telephone line. Sometimes a signature, scrawled sloppily at the bottom of a letter. Despite his every directive coming from Austin, Amon had never been to the capital city. He'd never been west of the Brazos River.

"You knew who he was," Wolfe said, the most recent voice on the line. "But you did it anyway."

"I did," Amon acknowledged. "I don't believe getting elected—or in this case having your old man elected—makes anybody less of a criminal."

"That's fine and well, Atkins, but your beliefs don't take precedence over your assignment."

"I was under the impression my assignment was to arrest bootleggers."

"Bootleggers," Wolfe said, agitated, "related to the shootout at the Keller Orchard."

"I have a witness who says he saw Merle Nichols fleeing the orchard the night of the incident."

"That witness withdrew his testimony."

"After intense pressure from local authorities."

"Even more reason to leave it alone, Atkins. Don't you understand? You can't go riling up the locals in all these little shit towns. They protect their own. We do our job the best we can, then it's on to another little shit town. And if we do our jobs enough, we get a desk in an office in a city that serves a good steak. That's the game. Open and shut."

"It is a corrupt game then, sir. With all due respect."

Wolfe sighed.

"I don't know what to tell you. If it makes you feel any better, Ma Ferguson wins this next election, she'll get rid of us all anyhow. In the meantime, you're being reassigned."

Amon had expected as much.

"Where?" he asked.

"They're sending you to Enoch to look into a murder down there."

"What's it look like?" Amon asked, flipping open a notebook and switching the phone to his left hand so he could use the pencil with his right.

"Gentleman named Charlie Cooper was found with a gunshot wound in the back of the head," Wolfe told him. "Suspects are brothers, Frances 'Frog' Fenley and James 'Squirrel' Fenley. Cooper was a resident of Nebat City, but the murder took place in Enoch—smaller town the Fenleys operate out of. They run a local gambling and bootlegging outfit, but that's not your purview. You're there to arrest them for murder and make the charges stick. There's a telegraph with a list of contacts, persons of interest, a widow, so on and so forth. The sheriff's boys have a spot for you in their annex."

"If it's common knowledge that these men are criminals, why not just arrest them and go from there?" Amon asked. "Why do they need the Rangers?"

"To tell you the truth, Atkins, the public's losing interest in the Volstead Act. Nobody wants to see folks locked up over a bottle of whiskey anymore."

"It's still the law."

"Not for long," Wolfe said. "Most laws aren't much more than a verdict of the times. Opinions and postulations that seem to matter in the moment. But murder, hell, that's still a commandment. Anyhow, sheriff down there says he's shorthanded."

Amon sat thoughtful for a moment.

"What do we have connecting them to the deceased?" he asked.

"Rumors and reputation, mostly. And Frog Fenley has taken up with the poor departed Mr. Cooper's widow."

"Motive."

"Indeed it is," Wolfe said. "Anyway. You leave first thing."

"What about the trial?" Amon asked.

"What trial?"

"The murder trial. The trial to hold Merle Nichols accountable for killing Phil Werskey, a decorated Texas Ranger and my partner for the past four months."

"The DA isn't bringing the charge."

Amon was quiet for a while.

"How can that be?" he asked at last.

"Nichols and his lawyers are claiming self-defense—and your blowing his knees off helps that argument."

"But I'm a witness. I can testify to the truth."

"No, you can testify to cover up for yourself and your partner. That's what the defense will argue. And there's not a jury in Smith County that will side with you against any of the Nichols clan. The DA would lose, and he'd lose a lot more than just the trial."

"This is an abomination."

"It may be. But you're lucky to still have a job. You crippled a senator's son, for god's sake. They wanted you gone, but I convinced them otherwise. You're a good lawman, Atkins. Smart. Capable. But you have to follow orders. Stick to your assignment. Connect the Fenleys to the murder and then make the arrest. Understood?"

"Yes sir."

"The state still has a lease on your place in Tyler for another month. I don't anticipate the investigation in Enoch taking longer than that, so your family ought to be fine until you get back."

"No sir," Amon said. "My family goes where I go."

Wolfe was quiet for a beat.

"I'd advise against it," he said. "You're going to a dangerous place, run by dangerous people. And the only place we could find you is a loft above a barbershop with one bedroom and a kitchenette."

"We'll make do," Amon dug in. "They go where I go."

"Suit yourself, Ranger."

Amon hung up the phone and stared at it.

He sat with his guilt. The living room around him was spare but warm. Photographs hung from the walls and the picture window adorned with lace curtains looked out into the garden. He stood and walked to one of the frames and straightened it a half inch. Inside was a picture of the two of them, his father and grandfather. His grandfather sat in a chair and his father stood to the side and back and rested his hand on the older man's shoulder. They both held their hats just below their chests and they both wore the badge. They gazed at him from the past. Judging. Taking account.

Amon could not recall his grandfather save for a few flashes of memory. Photo-like evocations of strawberry ice cream, an old pair of boots, sunlight shattered on the surface of a lake.

It was said he'd been a kind man. *Perhaps he kept all the kindness to himself,* Amon thought. His own father had shown no such good nature. William Atkins was hard at every edge and in the center too. Gruff in speech and demeanor. Bad Bill, they called him. He rode in and out of Amon's life, from one assignment to the next, crisscrossing the great state of Texas as if he alone would undue all its injustices. And yet no amount of arrests or executions could content him. He saw the country around him becoming less stable. With the explosion of oil, there were wildcatters and corporations alike taking advantage of a burgeoning industry that operated under little to no regulation. Murder rates were on the rise across the nation, and the Jim Crow South sat like a powder keg resting near an open flame.

He became convinced that none of his efforts had meaning. That, indeed, meaning itself was merely supposition to appease the ignorant. There grew in him a deep sorrow—a depression which young Amon took upon himself to cure. But just as his father could not rid the earth

of its ills, neither could Amon mend the brokenness in the old man.
Though this did little to stop his trying.

He stared at the photograph.

"I suppose you would have just marched on up the steps of the
capitol and handcuffed Nichols and his boy right there on the Senate
floor," he thought.

His father's face was emotionless. Eyes looking out from some
inaccessible place, holding naught but contempt for the world
without.

Amon served as a police officer in Dallas, where he lived during
his early twenties before joining a new batch of recruits to the storied
Texas Rangers.

At the time, the most well-known law enforcement outfit in Texas
was embroiled in scandal. Rangers had killed more than five thousand
Hispanics with little cause and in doing so had lost much of the public's trust. Part of the reform effort was to recruit men of "high moral
character," and Amon was at the top of the list. His service record was
dignified and distinguished.

For nearly a decade Amon served as a Ranger in towns and outposts
around North Texas, and he was proud to do it.

But soon politics crept into the organization again and by the early
1930s the Rangers had gone public in their support of Governor Ross
Sterling, who many believed would lose his reelection bid to former governor Miriam Ferguson. There was also the matter of local corruption,
which Amon saw rising significantly. There seemed to be a never-ending
turnstile of people operating above the law, and he felt his confidence
in his own agency waning.

He'd only known Phil Werskey a few months, but Amon believed
the two of them shared in the principle of justice over jurisdiction. Phil
had been a fine Ranger and fine man and now he was dead, and the
guilty would go unpunished in this life.

"We're not staying here, are we?" his wife asked.

Cora stood in the doorway. She was tall, though not as tall as Amon,
and thin. She had light skin and brown hair and her face was short and

mouselike. She wore a blush dress. A string of pearls given to her by her mother rested against her collar bones. He could see the muscles in her slender neck, prominent and pulsing the way they often did when she was worried or upset.

"It's because of that business with Merle Nichols, isn't it?" she asked.

"Yes," Amon nodded. "They're reassigning me to Enoch."

"Us," she said. "They're reassigning us."

She had been with him since the beginning of his career. Longer. They met as students at Texas Christian University, one of the few coed schools west of the Mississippi. Amon was studying law and Cora taking nursing classes. She was from a prominent family in Dallas—a soft-spoken girl, but quick to laugh and full of an elegance Amon had not seen elsewhere.

"Will you tell Joseph or should I?" he asked.

"He loves it here, you know."

"I know."

"There are other kids like him in the school. And a teacher just for them."

"I know, Cora," Amon said. "But this is my assignment."

"And our friends are here, and the garden parties, and the teas."

"There'll be garden parties in Enoch," he said, unsure.

She stared at him with a raised eyebrow.

"Well, there will be gardens. And it won't be for long."

"How long?"

"No more than a few weeks," he said.

They'd waited until graduation to marry, with Amon planning on law school afterward. But for reasons unknown to his new wife, Amon had abandoned this pathway, opting instead to enroll in the police academy in Dallas. Her family was not pleased with her prospects shifting so suddenly from marrying a lawyer to now being wed to a city patrolman, but Cora loved Amon with an unworn heart. Passion meant far more than practicality. And if she begrudged him this now—with their years spent in different towns, and her at home pinching pennies and praying for his safety—she did not show it.

"Oh fine," she said, her face softening. "Take us to the woods."

"We'll make do," he promised her.

"We always have," she said, and her face softened, and she went to him and he pulled her close.

Cora had learned that his promises were not merely words. While her family placed great value in wealth and status, Amon had a nobility about him that was sculpted from his discipline, not his lineage.

Yet, it was lineage that held sway over much of their lives. She soon came to understand the strange and strained relationship between father and son. Everything Amon did appeared to be in service of his father's approval, though such a sentiment never came. It remained forever pending.

And now the same pursuit would take them onward to Enoch, the latest in a line of rural Texas towns. She'd hoped Tyler would be a permanent home, but somewhere in her heart she knew better. She knew there was a reason she hadn't bothered to touch up the paint on the front door or grease the squeaking hinge in the pantry.

"I'll get the trunks," she said, and he kissed the top of her head, and she left him standing there, staring at the picture of his father.

6

The morning sun was fresh and the cold lingering on the fogged window glass. Sarah opened her eyes and looked at the pane and the obscured light from without. She rolled over, still heavy with sleep, and saw her mother watching her from the wooden chair across the room.

"What are you doing?" Sarah asked, yawning.

"Looking at the most beautiful girl there ever was," Eliza told her.

Both the girl and her mother had round faces with full cheeks and waves of blond hair, but Sarah's eyes came from her father—big and brown and aflame with some far-off desire that knew neither form nor function, yet on it burned.

Eliza feared those eyes. They were the only part of the girl that proved Daniel was anywhere within her, and Eliza worried what that inner fire might do to her daughter.

Eliza studied the girl's shape—broad shoulders and long torso, like all the women in Eliza's family. At fourteen she was nearly a woman grown, but Eliza pushed away the thought. There was still time.

"I need to pee," Sarah said, sitting up and making to stand.

"Wait, wait," Eliza rushed to the bedside with a pair of slippers. "The floor is cold. Put these on."

"I'll put on my boots," Sarah told her.

"You're not going outside," Eliza said. "It's near freezing. Just use your pot and I'll take it out when you're done."

Sarah looked uncomfortable, but she slid her feet into the slippers and knelt and slid the chamber pot from under the bed and turned to look at her mother who sat unmoved in the chair.

"I'll bring it to you when I'm done," Sarah said, and for the briefest of moments her mother hesitated before standing and smiling encouragingly as she left the room.

After she was finished, Sarah moved the pot aside and stayed in the bedroom for a few minutes longer. She went slow across the room to the window and used the sleeve of her nightgown to wipe at the condensation. But the outside world was blocked by a thin lamina of frost and her mother was calling from the den.

"Sarah," Eliza said, and the girl could hear the eagerness in her voice. A desire that neared panic. "I thought we might play rummy after breakfast. I've got us set up right next to the fire. Nice and warm. Sarah?"

Sarah closed her eyes and turned from the window, waiting for her mother to call again. Instead she heard voices outside and sprang from the bedroom, forgetting the pot. She grabbed her boots, hurried them on, and went out onto the porch without a coat before Eliza could stop her.

The two men were coming up from the tree line, dragging a dead deer behind them.

The sunlight had finally broken through the pine thicket and somewhere out there, past the furthest ridge in the county, the prospect of the world was afire.

"Good morning, Miss Sarah," Jesse called. "You'd best get the boiler ready. Old Moss here decided we ought to eat good this week."

"Much obliged, Mr. Moss," the girl said, as Eliza came onto the porch with an oversized quilt and tried to drape it across Sarah's shoulders.

The girl shrugged it off and Eliza frowned.

"You're more than welcome, darling," Moss said. "And getting prettier every day, looks like. Thank the good Lord you look like a Felker and not one of them slop ugly Coles."

Sarah laughed to appease the old man.

"Descended from the ugliest puffer fish you ever seen," Moss continued on.

"Puffer fish?" The girl asked.

"Oh sure," Moss said. "You hadn't ever seen how Jesse's cheeks get red and puff out when he's mad?"

Moss puffed his own cheeks and put his hands up on either side of his face like flapping fins.

"Come inside, Sarah Bear, it's too cold for you to be out here without a coat," Eliza pleaded.

"Well, at least somebody's telling the truth," Moss said, turning loose of the deer leg and breathing heavy. "I'm gonna go on home and warm up. Catch me a nap. You done wore an old man plum out."

"Suit yourself, old-timer," Jesse said. "I'll save you a piece of backstrap."

"You damn right you will."

Moss dawdled off toward the trail.

"Say," Jesse called. "You don't let that pig in the bed with you, do you?"

Moss shrugged.

"Times is tough," he said. "Pigs is warm."

A half hour later Jesse squatted before a great iron cauldron and grunted and lifted it up and carried it across the yard. Eliza and Sarah had stacked stones into four piles in a square shape about a foot and a half off the ground. They lit a fire in the center of the stones and had it burning proper by the time Jesse arrived with the pot and placed it atop the rocks and the girls began filling it with water. The gray stone coping of the well rising up from the earth, surrounded on all sides by black morning trees.

"Come help me," Jesse said, and he and Eliza went to the corner of the house and lifted the rain barrel from its trestle and carried it to the cauldron where they poured in what must have been a dozen gallons of rainwater.

"It'll take months to fill this thing back up," Eliza said. "What if there's a drought?"

"The way this winter is going, it'll take about ten minutes," Jesse told her. "Besides, we got bigger problems."

"How bad is it?" she asked.

"It ain't good. It's gonna spread, and when it does we won't have the meat to eat, let alone to sell."

"Is that what you've been doing with all those pork loins?" she asked, sharp. "Selling them?"

He sighed. Scratched at his beard.

"You help folks when you can," he told her. "They'll help you when they can."

"You sound like your brother," she told him.

"That's because he's the one who taught me. He used to say charity's not just for folks who have plenty. Just like courage ain't just for them without fear."

"Oh yes, he knew all about courage, your brother," Eliza said, crossing her arms.

He never knew how to respond when she spoke of Danny in this way. He understood her anger. Her frustration. He knew both emotions were born from her grief, but it troubled him all the same.

"Sarah said y'all got a little from the garden before the frost took it."

"A little ain't enough," she told him.

The water was boiling within an hour and they took the small deer and heaved it into the cauldron and then back out again and Jesse went to scraping away the hair with a forge-hammered butcher knife. In time the carcass was strung up and gutted and the insides spilled into a tin washtub that was then carried into the kitchen, where Sarah washed the organs and Eliza trimmed away what little fat there was to make tallow.

In the yard, Jesse took a short-handled axe and set about his own trimming, chopping hickory logs into smaller kindling and dragging up dead moss and other lesser sticks and branches to make a new fire. He used a wheelbarrow to take the haul to the smokehouse door and then dragged the wood in and arranged it just so in the brick-circled pit in the middle of the room.

The trimmed meat was heavily salted and again transported by tub and then hung on nails from the blackened smokehouse walls.

He looked at the black burn marks and layers of ash across the bricks.

"I'll get it going for you, Jess," Danny told him, and Jesse not but seven or eight years old. *"But then I gotta go help Momma. It's your fire after that. You gotta keep her going."*

"For how long?" Jesse asked.

"As long as it takes."

He stood and stared at the memory for a moment more, then lit the fire and walked out and closed the door behind him.

He went inside and pulled off his bloody clothes and put on new ones and took a long, deep breath.

Eliza came to the door.

"I'm sorry," she said, and the sentiment caught him off guard.

He turned to look at her.

"You don't deserve any of this either," she told him. "And you're doing everything you can to help us. You always have."

He could sense the tide about to turn. It did.

"But your notions of right and wrong are going to leave us with nothing," she went on. "And now there's talk that Percy Preston's gonna shut down the mill."

"Well, it's his mill. I imagine he can do what he wants."

"A lot of folks will be hurting if he does."

"A lot of folks are hurting now."

"There's not but ten dollars in the can, Jesse."

"I know it," he said and went to the kitchen.

He took up a burlap sack and sniffed at the smoked pork inside.

"Medicine takes money," she said. "And not just for the hogs. Did you see the bank sent another letter about property tax?"

He pushed past her and went out into the cold.

She followed him onto the porch.

"You're acting like I'm the crazy one for worrying about how we're going to get by," she said, and he stopped and turned to her from the yard.

"You're not crazy, Eliza. Not at all. But I'm telling you it'll be alright. We'll find a way."

"Where are you going?" She asked. "I thought you were off today."

"Preston hadn't turned the lights off yet," he told her. "I'll go ask Dalton for extra shifts. He always liked my old man. Danny too."

Her face was forever worried, but she softened it now and looked at him with some version of kindness. They were, if nothing else, partners in their own survival.

"Did you sleep?" she asked.

"I closed my eyes."

She nodded.

They looked at one another and the trammels of encumbrance surely settled behind their tired stares. A sorrowed pairing of propinquity and heartache. Once they'd been happy in life. Before the war. Before a great many things. Once they'd known the marvels of sum and substance, when the weariness of disappointment had come infrequent and unaccused.

He searched her eyes for some semblance of the woman he remembered. An adoring mother and consummate homemaker. She had been radiant. Danny at her side, and their two precious daughters. Jesse had not begrudged them that domesticated happiness, but neither had he aspired to it. His life was immune to routine.

One day fighting with the boys from across the river and the next sharing a drink with them. Playing cards or stealing cigarettes. He'd sometimes pick a trafficked spot along the thoroughfare and play his banjo or his father's fiddle to make a few dimes. Dimes he would then spend on Adaline Brookshire—her face forever in his memory even when all others had faded.

In those days survival had been manifest—plain and palpable and never in question. But such times existed only as vapor. Other lives lived. Died.

"I'll be fine," he told Eliza and tried to muster the appropriate levity. "*We* will be fine."

7

1916

It's autumn, and the night is cool. Adaline Brookshire sits atop a stump Jesse pulled up for her, and she's taken off her coat and laid it across the lap of her dress. A green dress. And black hair, and green eyes, and pale skin polished by the moonlight. He glances at her as he gathers wood, and she is too lovely for a steady heart so his beats desperate and erratic.

He builds for her a fire and the wind comes for it and puts it to heel and he cusses and apologizes for the cussing and throws on more kindling.

"This ain't much for a first date," Adaline tells him, but she's smiling when she does.

"Sure it is," Jesse says. "We got smoked pork, a deck of stolen Luckies, and a demijohn full up with blackberry wine. What else could we want?"

"There's a dance tonight," she says.

"Where at?"

"Dizzy Alderman's barn."

He spits.

"I ain't much for rich kids," he tells her.

"You think the Aldermans got money?"

"Got more than me."

"My folks got more than you. Does that make me rich?"

"You're rich no matter what," he says.

"What's that mean?"

"It means your smile is priceless."

"You're a regular cake-eater, ain't you?" she says and shakes her head.

"No, ma'am. Just like the way you look. That's all."

"I hope they like it in New York."

"You're going to New York?"

"Soon as I get the chance," she tells him. *"I'm gonna be a singer."*

"A singer?"

"That's right."

"In New York?"

"Uh huh."

"Well. I guess I'd better start packing."

"For what?"

"I'll need clothes and a toothbrush in New York, won't I?"

"Oh, you're coming with me?"

"Course I am."

"But you won't take me to the dance?"

"If you want to go that bad, I'll take you."

"Are you a good dancer?"

"Sure, I am."

"I don't believe you."

"Well, now we got to go. There ain't no way around it."

"You hush."

"I'll pull a move right here by the fire if I have to."

"Stop it."

He grins.

"How come you want to go to that dance and not stay up here in the woods with me?"

"I don't know."

"Yes you do," he says.

She blushes.

"Fine," she says. "Because Dizzy dumped me this summer and I want to show up hanging on your arm."

"Well, hell," he tells her. "That's all you had to say."

"Really?"

"Sure it is. Anybody dumb enough to let go of you deserves to see the repercussions. Let me put this fire out and we'll get down there."

He moves to kick the dirt.

"No wait," she tells him. "I like it here."

"You sure?" he asks, hesitating.

She nods.

"Dizzy can't see this far, you know," he says.

"Just hush up and kiss me."

8

Amon's first impression of the town was the great Naked River. The commerce of Enoch offered respite from the forest for those who desired it, but still the town relied on the bounty of the woods and hills that surrounded it. And so too it relied on the river. And the river always there, running down from the hills and through the wilderness and alongside the town and onward into the ever after.

And since the Second Day hath it run, Amon thought.

He stopped the car in front of the barber shop and pointed up to the second story.

"There she is," he told Cora. "And an entrance, there, in the alley."

"There aren't any windows," she replied, but then clapped her hands onto her thighs and smiled. "Less to keep clean though, I suppose."

"There's one, I think," Amon said, leaning to look. "That small one in the alley is ours, maybe."

"What about you, Joseph?" Cora turned and looked in the back seat at her son. "Excited to see your new room?"

"It's only got one bedroom," Amon said, and his wife sighed.

He could feel her suppressing the disappointment.

The boy didn't acknowledge either of them. He was tall for his age, his brogan shoes swinging just above the floorboard of the car's back seat. He had yet to fill out his long frame, and his ears and nose were bigger than his face. He wore overalls that didn't reach his ankles and a newsboy hat made from slate-colored wool. He sat with his hands folded in his lap, face against the window, looking out across the street at the cobblestone steps that led down to the water.

"At least we won't have far to go for a haircut," the boy's mother continued on, but he didn't hear her. He didn't hear anything at all.

His father's face appeared in the window and then the door was opening and Amon was reaching out his hand.

The boy took it. He felt something.

He pulled back his hand and looked in his palm and there was a piece of hard candy and he looked back up at his father.

Amon put his finger to his lips and then pointed at Cora and shook his head. He smiled.

Joseph grinned back and put the candy in his coat pocket.

The three of them stood next to the car and looked up at the loft apartment. Amon wore a long gray duster over his suit. Cora in a shawl that clasped at the top of her dress and a fleeced jacket over them both. And Joseph all but disappearing in his oversized wool coat with two missing buttons.

"I'll help with the trunks," Amon announced. "Then I need to drive over to the annex and get acquainted."

"They can't give you a day?" Cora asked. "Just to get settled in, I mean."

"I'll be back around sundown," he said. "Mr. Bennett said he would make himself or his son available if you need any help."

"They gave you a day in Tyler," she said. "They gave you two, if I recall."

"This isn't Tyler," he told her.

"No," she said, shaking her head. "It certainly isn't."

First Street ran alongside the river, elevated a dozen feet above the bank to protect from flooding, and in rapid succession the storefronts and shop signs and carefully placed adverts were stacked atop one another for a quarter mile stretching north to south.

The only medical doctor in Enoch was Gabe Withers, who held a lease on an office across from the filling station at the end of the main drag.

Amon drove the thoroughfare and turned west away from the river and up the block to Second Street, where the buildings began to thin. The Nebat County courthouse and jail were both located in the county seat of Nebat City, and the small township of Enoch was equipped only with a gaunt one-room structure built in a long rectangular shape with brick and mortar at the foundation and pine slats for siding.

There were four desks, two on either side of the room, all facing inward. Two of the desks were occupied by the deputies assigned to cover the eastern portion of the county. A third desk belonged to Sheriff Cheatham himself, though the political nature of his office meant the sheriff spent most of his days in Nebat City, where the county's power structure was constantly being shaped and reshaped by those select few men who stood to gain the most from each decision.

Amon stood in the small doorway and the deputy nearest him looked up and nodded.

"You're the Ranger, then?" he asked.

"Yessir," Amon said. "Amon At—"

"We got the letter," the deputy cut him off and put his head back to the papers in front of him.

Amon took his post at the fourth and final desk and looked toward the back of the building, where sliding iron bars ran from one wall to the other and a second set came up perpendicular from the back and formed two makeshift jail cells. One was empty and the other occupied by a soiled drunkard who wrapped his hands around two of the long vertical bars and pressed his face between them.

"Davis," he hollered at the other deputy. "Let me outta here. I got somewhere I need to be. You can't keep me in here like this. I've knowed you since we was little. Hell, we're practically brothers."

Davis, a blond, curly-haired man with a resting smile, looked up from a catalog and shrugged his shoulders.

"We ain't brothers, Max," he said. "And if you hadn't been pissing on Mrs. Perkins, you wouldn't be in there and I wouldn't have to listen to you cry about it. We can hold you for one more hour, and that's what we're gonna do."

"I weren't pissing on her," Max argued. "It ain't my fault if she got splashed a little bit. She needs to be more careful is all."

"You were on the sidewalk," Davis reminded him. "And where is it you gotta be so bad, anyway? You ain't got no job."

"Well, I can't tell you," Max said, crossing his arms defiant. "And I thought this was a free country. A man ought to be able to piss where he damn well pleases. Ain't that right, fella? You, new fella, ain't that right?"

Amon looked up.

"Freedom requires protection from those forces that would wish to upend it," he said. "The law is not established to curtail your freedom, sir, but to enhance it."

Max scoffed.

"'The law is not'—would you listen at this, Davis? Would you just listen at it? This old boy sure as shit don't know how things work around here, does he?"

"That's enough, Max," the first deputy, a man named Boyd, said. "Just set there real nice and quiet-like and reflect on all your misdeeds."

"I ain't believin' this," Max mumbled, but he did as he was told and retreated to a short wooden bench mounted against the back wall of the cell.

"Say, Ranger," Davis said, leaning back and kicking his feet up on his desk. "Word around the campfire is you're here for the Fenleys."

"That's enough from you too," Boyd snapped.

Boyd was olive-skinned, with dark hair and dark brown eyes. He was muscular. Square jawed and tight lipped.

"What?" Davis asked. "I'm just trying to work on my—what'd that letter say? Interagency cooperation?"

"That's partially correct, deputy," Amon replied. "I am here to investigate the murder of Charlie Cooper. The Fenleys are believed to be involved."

"Well, gosh, that sounds exciting," Davis said, feigning enthusiasm. "Maybe you can show us how to be real lawmen, like you. Or would you rather we just shined your boots?"

Amon frowned.

"This is not the first time I've been assigned to work with local law enforcement," he said. "And it's not the first time a local lawman has been insulted by my being here."

"Insulted?" Davis asked. "Are you insulted, Boyd?"

"Just shut up," Boyd replied.

"Let me tell you something, *Ranger*," Davis said. "When the oil come in up in Kilgore, so did every swinging dick thinking they was gonna get out of the depression. And a good many of them never had any intention on working a rig. A bunch of pimps, gamblers, and kids with guns thinking they'd be the next comic book outlaw. When the governor turned the spigot off, they all needed somewhere to go. Now, Nebat City's got a sheriff, a dozen deputies, a constable, and a handful of feds. All Enoch has is me and Boyd. So, where would you go if you was up to no good?"

Davis looked over at Boyd, who shook his head.

"We worked our asses off to clear this place out," Davis continued, "until there was only the Fenleys and a few whores around. And we'll get them too, soon enough. But we did it all without so much as a penny or a pistol from the fat cats in Nebat City. So we sure as shit don't need help from some jackass out of Austin."

"I'm not from Austin," Amon said. "And you, Deputy Boyd? Do you feel the same on the matter?"

"This ain't Tyler," Boyd grunted. "We do what we can with what we got. Same as the rest of the folks in this town. That's all I got to say on it."

Amon drummed his fingers on the desk.

"Well, I appreciate your passion," Amon said. "And I certainly appreciate all the work you've put in to clean up your community. But you've still got suspected murderers operating in the area. And I still have a job to do. That's why I hoped, Deputy Davis, that you might join me today. Visit with some of the locals and show me around until I can get my bearings."

"What, like a chauffeur?" Davis asked.

"No, Deputy, like you said: interagency cooperation."

Boyd snorted out a laugh.

9

The walk was long, and Jesse checked his watch every quarter mile or so. When he emerged from the trail and onto the old logging road near the north edge of town, he could hear the river running and he could smell all that the thick winter air had to offer. The smell of wood pulp and smoking stove pipes. The smell of pine and cedar in the hardwood forest. The earthen smell of wet soil and algae spores disturbed by the rain and by the wind.

He headed south and could just make out the buildings in the distance when he heard a car engine and moved off the road. He looked north until the slick coupe came roaring into view. It flew past him, splattering mud as it went, and then slid to a stop several yards ahead.

Jesse walked unhurried up to the running car and stood near the driver's window.

"What say, Jesse Cole?" Squirrel Fenley asked. "You look like somebody done licked the red off your candy."

"Squirrel." Jesse spit and looked down and couldn't see where it landed for the wetness of the ground below.

"Say, where's your old buddy, Hollis?" Squirrel asked him.

Jesse looked up and cocked his head.

"Hadn't seen him."

"Well, you do, you tell him he'd be smart to come find me before I find him. You hear?"

"He in some kind of trouble?"

"Just business," Squirrel said, noting Jesse's interest and trying not to smile. "You come across him, I'll be out at the Taggert place. Got some fights lined up."

"Will do."

"Talked to McElroy over at the butcher's," Squirrel said as he put the car into gear. "Told me there's some sort of swine fever running around."

Jesse nodded and looked away.

"Must be bad for business," Squirrel went on.

Jesse didn't answer.

"You gonna head up to Washington, DC, with the rest of them boys in uniform?" Squirrel asked. "Try to get more of what you're owed from ole Uncle Sam?"

Jesse shook his head.

"What's the matter? You don't agree with the cause?"

"It's just hard times," Jesse replied. "All around."

"You know, you can always come work for me."

"We'll manage."

"That's what I figured you'd say. But things got a way of changing," Squirrel said, looking down the road. "Anyway, I ain't too hard to get a hold of."

Again Jesse didn't respond.

Squirrel began to drive away and then hollered a reminder.

"You tell Hollis, now."

Jesse stuck his hand up and stood there until the car was out of view and then walked on.

On the north end of town, he passed a mischief of children who called out and named for him his own purported military exploits, though such legends predated most of their births.

"Killed a hundred Germans . . ."

"Saved the whole village . . ."

"Two hundred, it was . . ."

"Got any jerky today, Jess?" the youngest boy asked.

Jesse stopped.

"Not today boys," he said, "but you ought to get Doc Withers to look at that thing growing behind your ear."

He bent at the knee and performed the silly illusion his brother had practiced on him countless times. The boy grinned and took the nickel, but the other children were sullen, so Jesse emptied his pockets and gave them a nickel each until he was gone of nickels and the last few had to settle for pennies.

"If I see you tomorrow," he said, "I'd best run in the other direction before y'all have me waving Hoover flags."

"What's going on at the mill this morning?" one of the older boys asked him.

"I guess I'd better go find out," he told him. "Y'all go on and work on your fastball."

Eliza had not been the only one to hear the rumors. Jesse knew well that the mill's days were likely numbered. The colored workers had been furloughed. Skeleton crews manned the machines. Still, the mill had always been there and a great part of him could not imagine a world without it.

It was built in the 1850s, when the newspaper wars reached Texas, and for generations the Preston Paper Mill looked down on the river town of Enoch. It was constructed on a short, flat hill above the Naked River. Each morning the sun rose, and each morning it sent the shadow of the mill reaching out over the town—the unconsumed carbon from the mill's smokestacks drifting over the tops of buildings like a mutant fog.

Before they were teenagers, any good son of Enoch could spot the difference between a single- and double-felted press. They could speak confidently of fiberboard and linters and deinked pulp. They knew the sound of a pounding Jordan, the smell of ammonia and sulfur and sawed wood. When they came of age, the boys were sent to work in the wet end, where bleach covered their clothes and filled their nostrils and the wood pulp lay in powdered piles like fresh snow.

It was the mill that welcomed them home from France—its vacuum boxes and granite rollers filling their ears with the steady hum of industry and blocking out the low zip of bullets passing, the whistling mortars, and trembling earth.

The war lingered. The tunnels and trenches and stacks of ammunition and stacks of bodies and dirt turned to mud by blood and not rain. The stink and rot and other ill imaginings of a grotesque god. And when they returned home, they were fewer, and the sickness they brought made them fewer still.

The mill welcomed them all the same. Even as the Depression came crawling across the country, the mill still stood, still sang unto the pines with the melody of machines. Everything was loud. The gears and compressors and great growling engines. The hiss of the steam joints, the howl of exhaust fans, and the endless stacks of paper—chopped and prepped and bleached, then pressed and dried and packaged. So incredibly, mercifully loud. She pacified them, their mother the mill.

Jesse came to the crossroads and turned east and began the quarter-mile climb to the mill's front gate. He was not yet halfway up but already he could see them standing there. They swayed about in their winter coats and the cold blown in from some far-off place where they imagined it was never warm. They stared at the locked gate, their lunch sacks and tin pails tucked under their arms, and they smoked cigarettes, and their faces were stern and unaffected.

Jesse reached the top of the hill and pushed past them and stood in front of the gate. The newly placed chain hung from the fence and drooped across the gate, threading through the top of a Closed sign. The bottom of the sign caught the wind and flapped outward and then clanged back against the iron to which it was tethered. Over and over, it beat against the fence, tin against metal, in a cold, chaotic anti-rhythm.

He turned and looked across the river. The sun was blood red and thin puffs of clouds turned carmine and crimson as they passed along the horizon. "Red sky in the morning," the men said, each nodding, each aware of the coming storm.

Such a prognostication was but one in a long line of prophetic notions handed down as some form of ancestral divination, and yet this greatest tragedy before them had not been foretold. And so there they stood like failed conjurers. Carnival-act sorcerers who had played their only trick. And one by one they broke ranks and descended the bald hill—some into the town, and others back into the forests and hollows that covered much of the county.

Someone patted Jesse's shoulder. Darby Langford. He had been a friend of Jesse's brother. They stood together, both men staring up at the mill as if someone might emerge from one of the garage bays or run out onto the iron catwalk and call to them that it had all been some terrible mistake. That the whole of their world had not once again shifted beneath their feet.

"Dead when it still looks living," Darby said, turning to go. "Like the rest of us, I'd suppose."

Jesse waited until the last man had gone. He followed the fence line around to the north side of the compound, where the administration building sat empty. There was a smaller entrance there and it, too, had been chained off.

A plump security guard was walking the perimeter.

"Scooter," Jesse called.

The man stopped and stood looking and then came over to the gate.

"Jess," Scooter said. "What are you doing here?"

"I'd ask you the same," Jesse told him. "What's a shuttered mill need with a guard?"

Scooter looked unsettled. His cheeks were red and droopy, but his eyes were big to the point of bulging.

"Mr. Preston don't want nobody busting in," he said, lifting his head to reveal the roll of skin beneath his jaw. "He aims to sell off a bunch of them machines. Don't want nobody fiddling with them."

"Can you let me through for a minute?" Jesse asked.

"You know I can't," Scooter said.

"C'mon, now, Scoot. I ain't even gonna go inside."

"Where are you gonna go?"

"You know where."

Both men stared across the north lawn to where the bare and thorny limbs of rosebushes pressed in a row against the easternmost fence, over-looking the river.

"Oh, Jess, I—" The man appeared pained.

He looked around. It was just the two of them.

"Please don't take long," he said, unlocking the chain.

Jesse thanked him and squeezed through the gate before it was all the way open. He left the nervous guard loitering by the entrance and walked across the lawn and stood near the rosebushes and looked out at the sleepless river running brown and sallow and bloodless before him.

Was this the last thing you saw? he thought.

He knelt. Touched the cold earth. He watched his breath dance out in front of him—hot energy alive on the cold, thick air. He watched it appear and disappear and he opened his mouth wide to breathe out and watch it again. After a while the cold of the world seeped into his lungs and cooled the fire within and now the phantom smoke was gone and the inner workings of the man were made invisible once again.

A cherry laurel stood up out of the mud, its leaves a sour yellow from the abundant rain. It had a smell to it. A fragrance he couldn't name other than to say it smelled like a cherry laurel.

He nodded at Scooter and thanked him and passed back through the gate and started down the hill.

10

As Davis drove, he pointed out various landmarks, histories Amon did not care to know—where the county's record hog had been shot by a child, where an unfaithful husband had been shot by his wife—but mostly he pointed to other roads and spoke of where they led, as if every road in Enoch led away from the town rather than to it.

They stopped at a crossroad and Davis pointed.

"That there's the Preston Paper Mill," Davis said. "Up yonder on that hill."

"I've read it's the largest employer in Enoch."

"It was. Until this morning," Davis told him. "Percy Preston decided to close the doors. Probably taking his money up to Dallas or the like. It's folks in the rural areas that always get forgot."

Davis continued on with a half-cooked theory of regional economics being controlled by an elite society but Amon wasn't listening.

A bearded man in a coveralls came striding down the hill. Amon was watching him.

The man stopped twenty yards from the car and stared back.

Amon felt a sudden unease. He moved his hand slow across his lap until it rested on the heel of his pistol.

"Who is that?" Amon asked Davis, who looked hurt for a moment that the Ranger had not been listening to his theory that connected all the presidents to a secret organization based beneath Mount Rushmore.

"Huh?" Davis asked, leaning forward to see around Amon. "Oh, that's Jesse Cole."

"Who is Jesse Cole?"

Davis seemed to give the question real thought.

"Well, he was born and raised here, far as I know. Fought in the war. Brung home a fistful of medals. Married his brother's widow. Took in their daughter."

"What happened to his brother?"

"Took the coward's way out. Ball and pistol," Davis said. "Right up there on that hillside."

Amon turned to look at Davis and when he looked back the man was disappearing down the road. Amon took his hand off the gun.

"Why would they operate out of such a conspicuous location?" he asked. "This secret society."

Davis turned the car in the opposite direction.

"Throw folks off the scent," he said. "The most obvious place is the last place anybody thinks to look."

The first house they stopped at belonged to Yancy Greaves. A simple place on the west edge of town with an unkempt yard and a short fence. Paint peeled off the porch boards and the door squeaked as it opened.

A big woman in a boxy oversized dress stared up at Amon with an already distrustful look.

"Good morning, ma'am," Amon offered. "Is Yancy Greaves about?"

"You ain't Ralph," was all the woman said.

"No ma'am, I'm Amon At—"

"Ralph ain't been by in damn near two weeks," she lamented. "Now, you tell me what'n the hell I'm supposed to do for two weeks without no milk. The little'uns ain't got much else to drink. The biscuits are drier than dirt. You just tell me, why don't you?"

"I'm not affiliated with Ralph or the milk company, but I am a member of the Texas Rangers, and if your husband is home, I would very much like to ask him a few questions."

The woman stiffened.

"Ain't home," she said and slammed the squeaking door.

Amon had his list of names and worked quickly down it. Most would not speak to him. Others lied. One man spit on his boot.

"Not everybody's as keen as you and me to go locking up the Fenleys," Davis told him as they sat in the idling car. "Times is tough, Ranger. The Fenleys got almost as many folks on their payroll as the president. And Lord knows how hard it is to find work."

"Breaking the law is not work, it's crime."

"Maybe. I imagine a lot of the people who work for the Fenleys would agree with you."

"But they do it anyway."

"Some of them. Others do things like cook or clean or tinker with their cars. It's not all moonshine and stickups."

"Doesn't matter. If you take a criminal's money, you're dirty."

"Tough to get by on righteousness, Ranger. There's enough deer and rabbits and squirrels, even birds if things get bad enough. Folks in this county won't starve. Not for a while. But sooner or later, money becomes as necessary as food and water. The bank owns a quarter of these houses and more than half the land on account of property taxes alone. And they ain't accepting hides to pay down debt. Can't get by on just the old ways no more."

Amon was quiet.

"That," Davis continued, "and there's plenty of distrust around the government in these parts."

"I'm not in the government."

"No, but you work for the government. And like you said, if you take a criminal's money," Davis told him with a wry smile. "Where to next, Ranger?"

"Let's just keep working down the list. I'm not quite tired of having doors slammed in my face."

Their last visit of the day was with Charlie Cooper's widow. She opened the door before Amon could knock, as if she'd been watching from the window. Amon explained who he was and why they were there, and the woman invited them into the sitting room at the front of the house.

She wore a dark green dress that laid loose against her cream-colored skin. Dark hair. Green eyes. She was thin but not overly so. Amon took her for athletic. In fact, he took her for one of the prettiest women he'd ever seen.

"It's a fine smelling perfume, you've got," Amon commented, though in truth she had applied far too much, and he found it overwhelming.

"Thank you, sir," she said, and already her eyes were welling up with tears. "It was Charlie's favorite."

"We're not here to upset you, ma'am," Amon said, glancing over at Davis. "I want to bring your husband's killers to justice. And I was hoping you could help."

"Alright," she nodded, sniffling and pulling the lengths of her black hair off her shoulders and behind her back. "I'll try."

"What can you tell me about the Fenleys?"

"The Fenleys?" she looked surprised.

"Frog and Squirrel," Amon said.

"The Fenleys are two of the best fellas I've ever knowed."

Amon looked again to Davis, who shrugged.

"Would they have any reason to hurt your husband? A gambling debt, maybe?"

"Gambling? Hurt Charlie? No, no, of course not."

"And what about the talk of . . ." Amon hesitated. "Is it true you and Frog Fenley have taken up together?"

"What?" the woman appeared in genuine shock. "Frog comes by to check on me now and then. Plenty of folks do. I hadn't took up with none of them."

Amon frowned.

"Ma'am, why stay in Enoch?" he asked. "Why not go back to Nebat City?"

"That's where me and Charlie lived, but it ain't where I'm from. I'm from right here."

"Here in Enoch?"

"Here in this house," she said. "You're setting in what used to be my daddy's favorite chair."

Amon scribbled in his notebook.

"Listen," she said, nodding to herself as if something had just come to her. "I know Frog and Squirrel got a rough reputation. But I don't believe they had a reason to kill Charlie. Truly, I don't. Far as I'm aware, they didn't even know each other."

"Well," Amon closed the book. "That's all for now, ma'am."

He stood and waited for Davis, who seemed to have nearly nodded off. When the deputy snapped out of it and scrambled to his feet, they headed for the door.

"I'm stationed here at the sheriff's annex if you need anything," Amon said, turning back from the porch and touching his hat.

"Boy, she sure is a pretty one," Davis said as he drove them back to the annex. "Not too bright, though."

"Smart enough to fool you," Amon told him. "That was an act. She's hiding something. It may just be covering for the Fenleys, or it may be more. But it's something."

11

Jesse stopped in at the farmers' exchange and traded a half pound of salted pork for a block of cheese, a sleeve of crackers, and a jar of milk. He sat near a handful of other men in the feed aisle with his back against a grain sack and used his pocket knife to carve off slices of cheese. No one spoke.

He ate the cheese with the crackers and washed it down with the milk, and an old man the others called Oren passed him a jar of mustard, which he spread on a few more bites before sliding it back.

"I heard Percy Preston ain't in the papermaking business no more," the old man said, and a few of the men mumbled curses under their breath.

"News any better on your side of the river, Oren?" one of them asked.

The bearded old-timer worked his gums up and down a few times with his mouth closed and then opened it.

"The blue tick had puppies, John's done and gone off to Austin, and Ms. Leena's about wore me out running back and forth hauling lamp oil."

The first man laughed, happy for the distraction of someone else's woes.

"Just hold out a little longer, Oren. Electricity's gonna be ever'where before you know it. Ain't even gonna have no need for oil."

"Har," Oren said. "Ye go on and put electricity on a cut from a cat-fish, see how that does you. Coal oil and camphor, boys. Cures what ails you. Always will. Besides, they ain't about to make no cars that run on electricity, is they? Oil'll be around a lot longer than you and me."

"Well, we'd better hope there's a bunch of it in the ground too. Them fools out in Kilgore went to drilling every piece of wet dirt they could spit on. They got derricks in a cemetery in Gregg County."

"The hell you say."

"I swear it. The Rangers had to come in and declare martial law to get them to stop the pumps—and not just the ones overtop Meemaw's headstone neither. Governor said he'd just as soon have the oil stay in the ground. Said these no-sense fools are driving down the price. Drilling and drilling and drilling some more. They don't know no better. Like trying to keep rabbits from fucking. I imagine they'll all get together and give him the boot. Let Ma Ferguson back in there come this time next year, for all the good that'll do."

"Yessir." Oren nodded. "Times has changed, I'll allow ye that. They got tractors do the plowing now. Half the state flooded, the other half dry as a banker's sweat rag. And for the life of me I can't remember it being this cold for this long. 'Course I got old bones."

The younger man lit a cigarette and folded up the edges of the empty butcher paper that had held his sandwich. He took a few long drags and tipped the ash in the paper.

"What do you figure it'll take to pull us out of all this, Oren?" he asked.

"What are you asking me fer?" the old man challenged.

"Hell, I don't know. Just making conversation at worst. At best, I figure you've been around, seen a thing or two. You might have some sort of wisdom the rest of us hadn't run across yet."

"Shit. Ain't nothing wise about getting old. And there's only one thing'll turn this mess around."

"What's that?"

"The war."

"What war?"

"The next one that's coming," Oren said. "And that's the only wisdom I got fer ye. They's always one coming. Shapes everything, good and bad. Ye want my estimation? War's always right around the corner and getting ready to turn."

"Well, I don't know who the hell we'd fight. The Republicans, maybe."

Some of the men chuckled.

Oren smiled and nodded and worked his gums.

"They'll always be somebody spoiling fer a fight," he said. "Just ask that old fig tree from the Bible."

"Whatever you say, Oren," the man nodded. "You're a good'un anyhow."

"What about you, Jesse?" the same man asked, and all turned toward this hero of the Great War to see what hope he may offer. "You reckon our luck's gonna turn?"

Jesse twisted his package of crackers closed and wrapped the remaining cheese in its wax paper and put them in his sack. The milk he finished.

He stood and they were all watching him. Hopeful and longing.

"Goddamn," he hollered, crouching and pointing at the ceiling.

All the men flinched and turned up their heads to see but there was nothing.

"See there," Jesse said, deadpan. "Things is looking up already."

He left them hooting and hollering and shaking their heads.

Hollis Wentworth lived on a small piece of land just above Ballard Slough, his cabin backing up to a generations-dry rivulet that had once been a branch of Buck Creek. Jesse knocked on his door and no one answered and he knocked again. He came down off the porch and went around the side of the cabin and looked at the outhouse and the woodlot. In the corner of the yard was a sheet-metal garage with no flooring and a burlap sack hanging over a crudely cut hole in the wall.

Jesse pulled back the sack and slipped through the hole. Inside the garage was what looked to be a roughshod museum of rusted metal and old tools. There were lengths of old nickel sheets, scattered nails and screws that ranged from an inch to an arm, and a month's supply of empty Van Camp's cans. There were vice grips, sawhorses, and an old crank radio. Oil cans, basswood boards, and coffee-stained diagrams of submersible vessels from Bushnell to Hunley.

In the middle of it all was a six-foot-tall oblong shell made from oak and covered with pine tar pitch. Jesse walked up to it and stood for a while, then bent down and picked up one of a half dozen hammers and beat it on the side of the structure.

"That you, Jess?" an echoed voice called from within.

"You better hope it's me."

Hollis emerged from the opening in the top.

"Goddamn," he said, scratching at his ear in the manner of a junk-yard dog. "Liable to deaf me like that."

"How come Squirrel Fenley's hunting you?"

"What?"

"Don't lie to me," Jesse told him, throwing an empty can Hollis's direction.

Hollis ducked.

"I just wanted to play some cards is all."

"How much do you owe?"

Hollis looked away.

"I took a few bad beats—"

"How much?" Jesse asked again.

"Two hundred dollars."

"Jesus Christ, Hollis."

"Naw, I done and got it all sorted out," Hollis announced. "I'm on the graveyard shift tonight. I figure I'll ask Mr. Dalton if he can advance me."

"He can't."

"I just figured I'd ask."

"Dalton can't give you an advance, because Dalton ain't the mill foreman, because the goddamn mill is shut down."

"Oh."

"Yeah. *Oh.*"

"Well that ain't no good."

Hollis looked around.

"When do you think it'll open back up?" He asked.

"About the same time Heaven goes quiet for half an hour."

"Shit," Hollis said. "What do you think them Fenley boys will do to me?"

"I don't know, but I can't imagine they're in the tickling business."

"What should I do?"

Jesse thought for a minute. He looked around the garage as if some solution in the shadows might step out and make itself known.

"Let me think on it a little bit. See if I can't work something out."

"You'll do that for me?"

Jesse looked at him. Hollis Wentworth. He'd been drafted into Mc-Mahon's Fifth, same as Jesse. They'd been together in the Argonne Forest. The bloodiest fighting of the war. Of any war, to hear some tell it. But it wasn't just the fighting. Or the fear. Or the rivers of piss and shit and tears in the trenches. By the blood of the covenant, they were brothers.

"You know I will," Jesse said. "We'll go talk to them tomorrow. Just lay low until I come get you."

Jesse tossed the wrapped cheese up to him. Hollis caught it and peered inside the wax paper.

"You ain't got any crackers to go with it, do you?" he asked.

Jesse shook his head and pitched him the sleeve of crackers.

"Thank you, Jess," Hollis said, and Jesse nodded and held up his hand as he walked away.

Hollis came down from the hull and stood in the opening of the garage and watched Jesse go out across the yard and down the double-rut trail until the trail disappeared and so did he.

12

The rain came again. An afternoon thunderstorm that beat down on Jesse as he made for home. Minutes only, but he was soaked in full, the water fountaining down from his hat, his boots sluicing through the red mud with each step. He squinted his eyes and looked to the sky as if he might take measure of his assailant or perhaps might spot the faintest light boring through the dark. But the sky was gray and the clouds legion.

He passed beneath the serried pines and across fields of broomstraw and buffalo grass. Thick cedar rows filled with refugee birds. Waxwings and warblers. Huddled sparrows and puffing cardinals.

It was early evening when he arrived back at the cabin. Sarah sat in the oak rocker nearest the window and listened to the radio. Orchestral sounds crackling like firewood through the RCA speaker box. She smiled at Jesse as he came in.

"Where's that one out of," he asked, slapping his wet hat against his leg and hanging it on a nail by the door.

He shook out his coat and folded it and laid it overback the empty rocking chair nearest the wood-burning stove to dry.

"Chicago, I think," she said. "Did you ever go there?"

"No ma'am. Just New York."

He warmed his hands by the stove.

"And France," she reminded him.

"Right. And France," he said. "Where's your momma?"

"Out back. Talking to Edith."

"She didn't ask you to go with her?"

"She did," Sarah nodded. "I stayed out there a while, but it got too cold. She sent me back inside as soon as the rain started."

"You need me to build this fire up any?"

"Nossir, I'm alright."

"Alright," he said and started down the hall.

"Hey, Jesse," Sarah called, and he stopped. "You want to play a few hands of rummy or something?"

He looked at her and his brother's eyes were staring back.

"You might could talk me into it," he said.

She grinned and hopped down from the chair and went to the kitchen and opened the nearest drawer and fished out a deck of cards. She was shuffling them before he could get his boots off.

After the first few draws, she'd already made a few sets and laid them perfectly aligned in front of her.

"Why does Momma talk to Edith like she does?" the girl asked, feigning interest in the cards she held.

Jesse frowned.

"Some people—it makes them feel better to talk to loved ones, even after they're gone."

She wasn't satisfied with his answer and he could tell.

She made another set.

"You been practicing your fiddle?" he asked.

"You changing the subject?"

He laughed.

"I guess you've been smarter than me for a long time now."

She smiled, pleased with herself.

"It'd be nice to use these smarts somewhere other than here," she told him, her voice becoming hesitant, fearing she may have pushed too far.

"Sarah," he said, and his shoulders dropped. "I swore on your daddy's grave that I'd take care of you and your momma. But that don't mean making her decisions for her. If she wants to teach you here, it's not my place to stop her."

"But I don't know anyone my own age," she argued. "When I go into town with Momma, I can see them whispering about me."

Jesse looked at her, his eyes apologetic.

"She's doing what she thinks is best," he said.

Sarah put her cards on the table and crossed her arms. She turned her body toward the window.

"You think the train in Nebat City goes to Chicago?"

He looked at her—the ardent glow of the lantern there on her face like a flame burning before a mirror.

"Why would you ask that?" he questioned, not unkind.

"I don't know," she shrugged. "I was just wondering."

He started to press for more but the door opened and Eliza came inside, dripping wet and shivering.

"Come here," Jesse said, rising and pulling the door closed behind her. "By the fire."

She let him lead her to the chair and she sat and Sarah covered her with a quilt.

"You alright, Momma?" Sarah asked.

The woman did not answer. Instead she pulled the quilt around her and buried her head in her hands.

"Let's give her some time," Jesse said, and the girl nodded.

He walked with her to her room and they sat together on the edge of the bed.

"She's getting worse," Sarah said.

"It's just the time of year," Jesse assured her. "Plenty of folks get down when the weather turns like it has. It'll be better come spring."

"Sometimes she cries all night."

"I know."

"Other times," Sarah said, "she seems happy, but . . ."

"But what?"

"I don't know. Like she's not here. Not truly."

"Why don't you leave the worrying to me, yeah? You're too young for all this mess."

She pursed her lips.

"I won't be young forever," she said.

"No," he told her. "I guess you won't."

In the back of the bedroom closet was an old oak trunk that had come from Ireland during the Great Hunger, and he opened it and dust slid silent from the crevices of carved wood. The inside was lined with yellowed paper and on the paper were repeated scenes of an angel and a devil mid-dance and blossoming flowers at their feet.

The trunk had once held his great-grandfather's every possession as he fled across the sea and held thereafter his grandfather's nautical charts and fishing ledgers from his time in Galveston, but it contained now just a few tokens of his own father's remembrance. A woolen ascot cap. A pair of suspenders with a torn leather tab. A paper sack half filled with shotgun shells. An old comb. A short stack of leather-bound books. And a photograph of Jesse's family taken in front of the mill during a company picnic.

He studied the picture. He remembered his father as a dull and ornery man, but here he was smiling, holding baby Jesse as young Danny balanced between his mother and father. In the photo his father was wearing the cap from the trunk and Jesse picked it up and placed it on his head. He adjusted it one way and then the other, but it was too big and wouldn't fit. He took it off and stared at it.

"I only ever saw your brother wear it," Eliza said from behind him. "It fit him well."

He didn't turn around. Instead, he put the cap back in the trunk and closed the lid.

She put her hand on his shoulder. She didn't know why. She couldn't remember the last time she'd touched him at all.

"I remember," Jesse said. "He was wearing it the day I left. Sarah toddling around at his feet. And Edith, she could barely lift her head."

"She was two months," Eliza said, closing her eyes and forcing a smile.

"I should've seen it then."

"Seen what?"

"He was quiet. All morning he barely said a word. Downcast. Like he just—I don't know," Jesse said, shaking his head. "Then there at the door, right as I was leaving he came up and shook my hand and he said to make him proud. I told him I would. And that's when he pulled me close and whispered something in my ear. *If we can't protect the ones we love, we're lost.*"

Eliza watched him. Waited for him to say more. But he was lost in the memory and said nothing.

"Do you know what he meant?" She asked.

Jesse shook his head.

"No. I've thought about it more times than I can count. Best guess is that whatever sadness or sickness—however you sort it—the thing that took him, it was already alive in his head that day. Already starting to wear him down. If I'd seen it—"

"Stop." Eliza was shaking. "Stop talking about him. Stop feeling sorry for him."

Her voice caught. She felt so suddenly weak. She stepped backward into the room and sat on the edge of the bed.

"He left us," she said, unsure if there were any tears left to cry. "He left his family."

Jesse frowned. His instinct was to comfort her, but also to defend his brother. He did neither. He sat there in silence until she stood and retreated from the room with her hands over her mouth, shaking her head.

He watched her go, then turned back to the trunk and opened it once more. He held up the picture and looked at his brother's smiling face.

"I'm trying to protect them, bud," he said. "I'm trying to make you proud."

It had been Danny who taught him to shoot. Their father working graveyard at the mill. Sleeping during the day. Jesse and Danny had run wild through the hollow. Backwoods, thickets, and river bottoms. Hunting and fishing. Playing make-believe soldiers. They were princes of pines.

Danny had been sandy-haired, fairer skin than Jesse, and with bigger features. Broad shoulders. A wide face and big brown eyes. He had large ears and a bashful, childlike smile. But his temperament was far from that of a child. While Jesse had been untroubled by his own existence, Danny found it overly cumbersome. He seemed to notice, even feel, all of the world's troubles. It's injustices.

It had been Danny who first stood up for Hollis Wentworth.

The Wentworths and Coles were both working class, and while neither family had an abundance of prestige in the region, growing up, it was only Hollis who caught the teasing. His father was a drunk and a gambler and his grandfather had been an eccentric—a young widower who fancied himself an inventor, though he had no true inventions to his name. Hollis had never met his mother, but the rest of the children in town seemed to know all about her and told him as much.

Gertie the whore, Gertie the whore, left little Hollis at his daddy's door.

They had chanted it from the dugout during a baseball game once. Danny, playing shortstop, threw down his glove and walked across the field and punched the loudest boy square in the mouth. The chants stopped after that, at least while Danny was around.

"Some folks have to be watched over," Danny told his little brother, when Jesse asked him why he'd done it. "Others have to do the watching."

Jesse had heard those words throughout the war. Had lived by them. And even now, with Eliza and Sarah, he heard them still.

Jesse reached back into the trunk and pulled out one of the books. A Kipling novel. *The Light That Failed.* He opened it and the medals slid out.

Distinguished Service. Victory. Congressional Medal of Honor.

He grabbed them in his fist without ceremony and closed the trunk.

13

It was near dark and bitter cold when Amon arrived home. He noticed how quickly the sun vanished in these deep woods. No boundless vista wherein the earth's edge may be glassed out on some distant ridge of the Revelation. When the failing light made its retreat, there was no dial with which to measure its descent. The transformation was sudden and soundless. The light exists. The light is gone. And in its absence the yellow pines and green needles and brown moss, and all of them black in the night, and the night black around them, and the way forward was never certain. The darkness was the Great I Am, suffocating and expansive and swallowing of the world.

And what Delphic happenings might go unaccounted in such blackness? Amon thought. *What is here that I cannot see?*

He removed his hat and gun belt and made to hang them on the nail by the door but there was no nail and so he pressed them to his chest and stood frowning.

"Where's the hammer?" he asked. "I'm going to put a peg by the door."

"No, you're not either," Cora warned. "Mr. Bennett said no new holes in the wall. Find a place that already had a nail and put it there. Or quit wearing a hat and gun."

Amon smiled and shook his head and tossed his hat toward her. She caught it and placed it atop her head and struck a pose.

"Well then," she said. "How's the future look at the end of the day?"

"Complicated," he told her, laying the gun belt on the kitchen counter. "What's for supper? I'm as close to starving as I can get without falling in."

She plopped down a bowl of pintos in a thin brown broth with steam coming off the top.

"Beans. I couldn't get down to the store today, what with all this." She gestured around at the trunks and boxes. "But I did go through the trouble of heating them up for you. Now, complicated how?"

"Oh?" he asked as he sat and scooted his chair up to the table. "Hot beans? I ought to get my dinner jacket."

"You don't have a dinner jacket, and don't change the subject," she said. "Complicated how?"

He shoveled a spoonful of beans into his mouth and talked while he chewed.

"I think one of the deputies is on the take," he said. "Fella named Davis. He seemed too upset by my being here. Too angry. I'm not sure about the other one. Boyd's his name."

She pursed her lips.

"What?" he asked, swallowing.

"Unless their names are Fenley, does it matter?" she asked.

"I'm just feeling things out," he said. "That's all."

"Fine. Just don't go feeling on something that'll get you in trouble."

The beans were gone in a few quick minutes, and he stood and thanked her and kissed her on the head. He went into the bedroom, where the boy was sprawled on the floor rolling wooden cars back and forth and into one another.

Amon watched him for a while and when the boy looked up and noticed him Amon knelt to his son's level.

"Joseph," he said, his mouth moving slow and exaggerated. "I missed you."

The boy smiled and threw his arms around his father.

"You like it here?" Amon asked, motioning around the room and giving a thumbs up and then a thumbs down.

Joseph feigned a thoughtful face, then tilted his head to the side and shook his hand in front of his face.

"Just alright, huh?" Amon laughed. "Well, we can work on that."

Amon sat on the edge of the bed and picked up the book next to him.

"*The Secret of the Caves,*" he read out loud. "The Hardy Boys doing any good in this one?"

Joseph wasn't looking at him, he was back to the cars, and Amon reached out with the book and tapped his son's head. The boy turned and Amon held the book in front of him.

"Good?" he repeated and repeated the thumbs up and down.

Joseph thought for a moment and then made a series of gestures with his hands.

"No, no," Amon stopped him and pointed to his own mouth. "Try oral only, son."

Joseph shook his head.

Amon gave him a sympathetic look but insisted.

"It's the only way to assimilate, Joseph."

The boy looked confused.

"It's—" Amon started then slowed and began again. "It's. Good. For. You."

Joseph shook his head again.

"Let him do his signs," Cora said.

She came into the room and crossed her arms.

"The experts say not to baby him," Amon told her. "Alexander Graham Bell said that the only way to be a true and productive American is—"

"He's seven, Amon," she stopped him. "He doesn't need to be productive. He needs to be a child. And he was born in Grapevine, of course he's American."

She shook her coat down over her arms and balanced uneasy against the bed to pull on her boots.

"Where are you going?" he asked.

"Like I said, I been busy moving us in all day," she said, brushing past him. "I need to go to the market and get a few things."

"Don't spend too much."

"Hah," she called over her shoulder as she left the room. "As if we had too much to spend."

"Count the blessings, dear," he said, playfully, and he could hear her laughing.

"What should I do with the rest of my fingers?" she asked, and then the door closed and she was gone.

Amon looked down at the boy.

"I think your mother won that round," he said, standing and patting his son's head.

He knelt alongside the wood-burning stove and looked at the shape of the floor as it sloped rearward into the back corner of the room. He opened the stove and stoked the logs. The flames rose before him in aspiration of some higher, unconfined existence, but he denied them such, swinging shut the door and leaning the iron prod against the wall.

In the dark of the morning, Amon stirred from his sleep. It took him a few seconds to know where he was. Even in familiar places such misshapen hours had long haunted him. Purgatorial hours between night and day. A time of merciless judgment. He would lay awake and think of his son. His father. All the desperate issues of his mind. Recent nights, he'd see Phil Werskey's wife and daughter alone in their weeping. He'd never met them, but he could see them nonetheless.

He lay there for a while, trying to quell his thoughts. At long last, he rose and took up his Bible from the nightstand and went into the kitchen and put fire to the lamp and set it in the middle of the table and pulled up his chair.

The chapter was marked.

And again, departing from the coasts of Tyre and Sidon, he came unto the sea of Galilee, through the midst of the coasts of Decapolis. And they bring unto him one that was deaf and had—

"What are you doing, Amon?" Cora asked, her eyes heavy with sleep interrupted.

"Couldn't rest," he said, closing the book. "I may go down to that hotel and see if the café is open yet."

Her arms were crossed, and she was frowning, but she nodded all the same.

"I'm going back to bed," she said. "Lock the door if you leave."

14

It was well before dawn when Jesse set out. He took the mule but he didn't ride it. Instead, they walked side by side in the dark, both of them grateful for the company. It was almost an hour to town on foot and he thought the sun might be up when they got there but it wasn't. He tied Cecil on the south side of the building, out of the wind, and patted the animal's neck and went inside.

The shop was dark, but the streetlight gave off enough glow to see inside. There were rows and rows of eclectic wares. Pots, pans, boots, and coats. Tackle boxes, guns, and ammunition. Flatware, dishes, and painted serving platters. Jewelry in a glass case. Rubies and emeralds and small diamonds. Family heirlooms. Artifacts and treasures stolen from Indians. Knives from the Alamo. Bayonets from the Revolution.

Jesse rang the bell on the counter. From somewhere in the back of the shop a dog barked.

"I'm coming," the proprietor called from his cot. "Let me get my boots on."

A few minutes later the man sidled up from out of the dark and hit a switch and the lights buzzed on. He was short and bald and wore wire-rimmed spectacles. The dog followed at his heels.

"It's a bit early, ain't it, Jess?" the man asked.

"If you don't want folks coming in, you ought to lock your door."

"I can't do that," the man said, shaking his head. "Half my trade comes through in the midnight hours. Desperate for money. 'Course most folks is desperate these days. What can I do you for?"

"How much can you give me for these?" Jesse asked and he laid the medals on the counter.

The man took a step back. So did the dog.

"Lord a'God, Jesse. Them's your war medals."

"I know what they are. I need to know how much you'd give for them."

"I couldn't," the man stammered. "I wouldn't. It ain't right."

"Don't start your routine, Sid," Jesse told him. "You got things in here that cost more than blood. Things that come in here by way of entire nations disappearing."

The shopkeeper scoffed.

"Now I run an honest business here," he said. "And it ain't up to me who or what comes through my door."

"How much?" Jesse was growing impatient.

The man huffed and puffed but he took up the medals and gave them a look and turned them every which way and mumbled something here and there.

"Oh, I don't know, Jesse. This sure don't feel right, but I guess you must really need it. I could go ahead and give you thirty dollars for all three."

"Thirty dollars," Jesse repeated.

"Gold's down to seventeen dollars per troy ounce," the man said. "Now, you just take a guess what that means for bronze."

Jesse shook his head.

"Give me fifty," he said.

"Fifty dollars? Lord, Jesse, they'd institutionalize me. They'd come down here sure enough and throw me in the back of a wagon and haul me off. Fifty dollars," the man said again.

The man waited and Jesse didn't speak and after the while the man shrugged.

"I suppose I might could go thirty-five," he said.

He left the pawn shop with the money and checked in on Cecil and went next door to the hotel and gave a nickel for a cup of coffee in the café. The dining room was at the front of the hotel, separated from the rest of the space by two large alabaster pillars with volute spirals at the top their columns like coiled snakes. The carpet was red and almost all the furniture—upholstered chairs, mahogany tables, and lengths of white linen—had been brought by wagon sometime before the Civil War.

There were a handful of other customers about. Locals and travelers alike.

Jesse sat next to the window and drank his coffee and watched the morning crawl up over the trees on the far side of the river. It was a sour sun. Pale yellow like stained ivory. It kept its distance, daring the land to survive. The Cimmerian land. Dark and brumal. Diseased.

He imagined dead hogs littering the thickets. And the smell of them. Smell of death like a foul feast. In his mind the buzzards were descending in waves of black, and more circling still. No light against which to pair them. No light to the sky. His thoughts had taken him now and in his dislocation the hogs were gone and there was only the dead and the dead called to him.

He was shaken from the blackness by a pounding on the window. Hollis Wentworth stood outside.

"Stay right there," Hollis called, his voice muffled, and he took off for the door and came inside and strode across the dining room with a look of discontent.

"You give up your medals," he shouted at Jesse before he'd reached the table.

Heads turned.

"To hell with the Fenleys," Hollis proclaimed. "It ain't worth you selling your medals to that cheap bastard, Sidney Hearne."

"Hush and sit," Jesse said, yanking Hollis down into the chair next to him. "I thought I told you to stay put?"

"You ain't the only one that had the bright idea to sell off them hunks of metal they give us."

"Alright, so why are mine any more important than yours?"

"Because I'm the one them sorry sumbitches are after. Not you."

"Well, it's not enough anyway," Jesse said. "But maybe we can work something out with them."

"I know it ain't," Hollis slumped his shoulders and put his elbows up on the table. "I don't imagine that greedy old cuss would give a nickel to see Jesus in a marching band. And for all we done for this country. Fifteen dollars he says."

"He only gave you fifteen?" Jesse asked.

"What?" Hollis lifted his head. "How much did he give you?"

"Thirty-five."

Hollis leapt from the table and again was shouting.

"That no good grifting bastard," he said and all but ran from the hotel and back into the street toward the pawn shop.

Jesse watched him from the window and when he turned back to the dining room one of the patrons was standing next to the table.

"Mind if I sit?" the man asked.

"I don't mind enough to stop you," Jesse said.

"You're Jesse Cole, aren't you?"

"I've been accused of it a time or two."

"Amon Atkins," the man said, extending his hand. "Texas Ranger."

Jesse tilted his head suspicious, but took the man's hand and shook it.

"I think we might be able to help each other out," Amon told him. "I couldn't help but hear that you all might be in a bit of a situation with the Fenley brothers."

"I'm starting to mind," he said.

"What?" the man asked.

"You sitting here," Jesse told him. "I'm starting to mind it."

"Alright, I'll make it quick," the man said. "I'm here to make a prosecutable case against the Fenleys. And, once I've done that, to arrest them. Can I ask if you knew Charlie Cooper?"

"No."

"No, I can't ask, or no, you didn't know him."

"Both."

"Do you know his widow?" Amon asked. "She was raised here, like you."

"What do you know about where I was raised?" Jesse asked, frowning.

"I've asked around about you," Amon said. "I know you're a war hero."

"I was in the war. That don't mean I'm a hero."

"I know you're an honorable man," Amon said, undeterred. "Taking in your brother's family."

"They took *me* in," Jesse said, crossing his arms. "What else do you think you know about me?"

"I know the mill shut down. I know folks need money." Amon leaned across the table until Jesse could see himself reflected in the Ranger's eyes. "I could have my office compensate you for your time."

"What time?"

"Any time." Amon shrugged. "Any information you give us that leads to an arrest. It might not be much, but it's something."

Jesse drank the last of his coffee and set the cup on the table. Amon watched him. His eyes shifting from Jesse to the mug and then back.

"Who else?" Jesse asked.

Amon paused, confused. He gave a slight shake of his head.

"You said you're here to arrest the Fenleys," Jesse said. "You and who else?"

"I'm working with the local deputies, but I'll call in more Rangers when the time comes."

"You better," Jesse said, and he wiped his mouth with his napkin and set it on the table in front of him and stood.

"And I suppose you wouldn't do it just because it's the right and moral thing to do?" Amon asked.

Jesse stared down at him, taking measure of the man. He was tall, but slight. Narrow shoulders. Thin wrists. But there was something in his downturned eyes that Jesse recognized.

"That's what the government told us about the war, you know," Jesse said. "Did you fight?"

"I did not," Amon answered. "I served my country by keeping the peace in Dallas."

"Well, I sure appreciate you not letting the kaiser take the Trinity River," Jesse said, touching his hat. "Have a good one, Ranger."

Jesse walked away and Amon followed after him.

"I could use a man like you," he called. "A soldier."

At the hotel door Jesse turned.

"I don't want to get involved."

Amon put his hands up.

"That's fine. But if you change your mind, I'm at the annex during the day, the loft above the barbershop at night. Come find me anytime."

Jesse didn't respond. He pushed the door open and went out onto the street. Still cold, but not yet raining. The day's trade had begun and there were a few dozen townsfolk about. He headed toward the side of the pawn shop to untie Cecil but stopped a few feet short of the alley and stood looking down the street.

A woman had come out of Mott's Mercantile carrying two grocery sacks and she was loading them into the back of an idling car. Jesse couldn't see who was driving but he knew the woman like he knew the sun. He longed for her warmth. Even now. Even after all this time.

Her black hair was pinned up and her bare neck set white against it save for those few raven-colored wisps that fluttered loose in the winter's blow. She was a memory come to life and it unnerved him. Like a dream he'd already had. She wore red rain boots and a long gray coat and even at a distance he could make out the stern angles of her face. Or maybe he just knew they were there. Knew them from his every recollection.

His mind had gone strangely blank. He just stood there, staring. And he was staring still as she climbed into the car and it drove away in the opposite direction. The only feeling left to him was the need to be someplace he couldn't get back to—couldn't even say where it was.

15

1917

The summer is sweltering and the red dirt and the small rocks along the bank are hot on his legs and he looks at her in the river. She is singing a song about a tenant farmer whose fields are on fire. Her black hair is outspread over the surface and moving with the current even when her body does not. Her shoulders are bare and wet and he watches her and listens to her voice and forgets much of the rest of his life and the rest of the world and what day it is.

She stops singing and stares back at him.

"What about when I'm old and wrinkled?" She asks, as if she's reading his mind.

"Well, I'll be old and wrinkled too."

"I don't care about what you'll be. You ain't no top prize as it is," she tells him. "I'm talking about me."

"I'll still love you."

"You don't know that. And it's dumb to say things you don't know when you don't know 'em."

"I do know it," he says.

"Lord."

"What?" he asks.

"Nothing. I just realized something."

"What?"

"That I'm gonna be stuck with you forever."

He laughs.

"Hell, it ain't like nobody's tying you to a chair or nothing," he tells her.

"I know. But I've done asked the river and the river says we'll always be connected."

"Oh, you asked the river?"

"I did."

"And it told you the future?"

"The water don't lie. It's the closest thing to truth there is."

"Does the water have a read on who's gonna win the pennant?"

She closes her eyes and strokes her arms out to the side, her head tilted back.

"Boston," she says, nodding.

He shakes his head.

"I better send Danny down here," he tells her. "He's about to marry Eliza Felker. He ought to check with the river first."

"Eliza Felker," she says. "That girl's wanted babies since we were six."

"And Danny's wanted a wife since he was five. I guess they're a good match."

"What about us? Are we a good match?"

He feigns thinking hard about his answer.

"I guess we'd be pretty smart to listen to that old river," he says. "Been here a lot longer than us."

"And if the river said we're no good for each other?" she asks. "What then?"

"Well . . . It'd take a long time to empty the bastard with a bucket, but I imagine I'd try."

She splashes him.

"Get in here," she says.

"Yes ma'am."

16

It was raining again, watering a country that didn't need it. Rain drops fell thin and cold and the sky like soot. Trees gray behind curtains of showers. Wet and frozen fields and animals gone forth with wet coats.

Hollis Wentworth followed Jesse down the road. He stared at the soggy ground as they walked. Pulled his tattered coat tight around him.

They moved off the road and went on foot, cold and wet through the woods, and in doing so cut down the distance, as the hollow and the ridges above it were connected by a dozen or more game trails and old wagon roads and narrow forest paths cut by entire civilizations of men now gone from this land.

"It's colder than a goddamn frosted frog," Hollis complained. "And here we are walking through the Argonne all over again."

Jesse shook his head.

"What?" Hollis asked. "Marching through the woods to go find trouble. This don't remind you?"

"Nothing reminds me," Jesse lied. "You complaining, maybe."

"Shit."

The rain let up and the winter sky cleared. The small day moon hung pale and bloodless and jays and wrens and warblers alike all flit-ted among the bare branches of an orchard as the men passed. There was no wind.

They passed along the bridge at Blind Cove, whereon a pair of young boys were skipping rocks across the slime-topped surface, their lines sitting in the bloated brackish backwater. The cove was little more than a flooded crater full up of red dirt and detritus, and what mutant fish might linger in such a slop-mattered underworld were sure to be some breed all their own.

"Simpler times," Hollis commented, and both the men looked down at the boys as if they might see in them the shade of their former lives, and both men became at once lost in the longing for the days of cane poles and smooth stones.

The Taggert spread sat just off the market road that ran beneath Har-matia Hill. The house—such as it was, a series of cobbled wood and tin and hazard-stacked stone—was dwarfed by the giant garage behind it. And Ansel Taggert himself a part of the aesthetic in his mechanic's dusting jacket, often found smoking one cigarette while rolling another.

The old man had not intended on becoming the sole automobile technician for nearly every bootlegger in Nebat County, but his tucked away location in the hollow made for a more advantageous stopping-off point than did the open and exposed shops in town or along the highway.

On this day, despite the cold, old man Taggert stood barefoot and shirtless in only his overalls. His grown son Coy sat on the porch behind him, scraping a hooked boning knife down the length of a basswood branch. Taggert produced from his front pocket a tobacco-filled pouch and satiated himself with a handsome chew and turned and tossed the pouch to Coy who did the same.

"Jesse Cole," Taggert noted as the men approached.

"Christ Almighty, Mr. Taggert, you ain't got no coat?" Hollis asked.

"The Lord made me and he made the cold," the old man said, as if that alone explained things.

Coy spit and shook his head.

"Old man ain't got no goddamn sense," he said.

"You watch that mouth, boy," Taggert scolded him. "'Fore I bloody it."

"We need to visit with Squirrel a minute," Jesse said.

"Fightin'," was the extent of Taggert's reply.

Once an old barn, the garage had been built out and extended and now sheltered a half dozen cars and parts of cars and still a few wagons as well. The big sheet-metal doors were slid half open and there were fires built in the gaps and the whole place took on a tint of smoke. There were tools Jesse recognized and some he didn't. A crankshaft grinder, jacking skates, a gantry hoist, a large pile of rubber bumpers, and a half dozen stacks of Dunlop twin wire wheels.

These things and more were relegated to one side of the garage, while the other was open for any and all manner of gambling. There were card games and dice, two billiards tables, and a makeshift bar. But the main attraction was the canvas boxing ring in the center of the action.

Frog Fenley lumbered about the ring, tucking his chin so far down into his chest that despite his considerable height he still needed to look up at his opponent.

That opponent was a big-eyed kid, athletic but lanky, and from what Jesse could tell he was just running around the ring, trying to avoid Frog's reach.

"Yonder's Squirrel," Hollis said, and Jesse turned from the fight and saw Squirrel at a short table near the back, scribbling in multiple notebooks.

If he was surprised to see them there, he didn't show it. He looked up once as they approached and then went back to his bookkeeping.

"Change your mind already, Cole?" Squirrel said without greeting.

"We got fifty dollars here," Jesse told him. "We'll get you the rest as soon as we can come by it."

Squirrel didn't look up.

"I don't do installments, boys," he said. "And fifty ain't two hundred."

"What'll it take to get Hollis square with you?" Jesse asked, leaning on the table with both hands.

Squirrel stopped writing. He looked at Jesse's hands first, then at his face.

"I'm willing to work it off," Hollis volunteered.

Squirrel gave him a contemptuous look and turned back to Jesse.

"Your buddy here owes two hundred dollars. That's what we'll take. Nothing more. Nothing less. No interest. No installments. That's as fair a deal as you're liable to get from any bona fide criminal in the county."

"I can give you a few hogs."

Squirrel appeared amused.

"Hogs?"

Jesse nodded.

"I can bring you some meat pigs, or get you a boar and a sow if you want to breed them yourself."

"Do I look like I'm in the hog-fucking business?" Squirrel said. "The price is two hundred dollars. Nothing more, nothing less."

A man in a straw hat struck a small ringside bell with a hammer and the dozen or so men watching the fight groaned in unison.

Squirrel smiled.

"C'mon, Squirrel," Jesse said. "There's got to be something."

Squirrel, acting agitated, put down the notebook and closed it and leaned forward over the table. He drummed his fingers.

"I guess there is one thing. Seeing as how I'm in a generous mood," he announced. "Come work for us. If you really want to vouch for Wentworth, that's fine with me. Half these still hands I got bottling for me can't clip their overalls, let alone drive a car. You make some runs for me, we'll see about squaring things up. I can even throw a little cash your way to sweeten the deal. Outside of that, it's the afore-mentioned two hundred—unless you're ready to hop in the ring with Frog, yonder."

As if it were choreographed, Frog came out of his guard and feigned a right cross. When the kid moved to block it, Frog put his weight behind a left hook and Jesse could see a foot of daylight between the canvas and the kid's shoes as his body rose up with Frog's punch and then crumpled down in an unnatural position.

Jesse rubbed the back of his neck.

Max Doughtry, a town drunk who'd been fired from the mill some three years ago, was being held back by his compatriots as he yelled at Frog for being a cheat.

"I ain't paying you shit, Fenley," he hollered, turning his ire toward Squirrel. "You hear me, you sorry sack of shit. Not a goddamn dime. You're a cheat. A no-good lying cheat."

Max continued to kick and scream as he was dragged from the garage by a group of men who implored him to be silent.

"Times are tough. People are desperate," Squirrel said, unfazed by the commotion near the ring. "Where else you gonna find the money, Cole? Must be expensive, inheriting them mouths to feed."

Jesse's face tightened. He pointed his finger at Squirrel.

"You don't do that," he said. "You don't bring my family into this."

"*Your* family?" Squirrel asked.

"I'll do it," Hollis said, stepping forward with his chest out. "I'll work for you until my debt's cleared."

Squirrel's boredom turned quickly to disgust.

"I don't want you," he said. "I want him. Cole goes or there's no deal."

Hollis bit his cheek. He looked at Jesse.

"You ain't got to do this, Jess," he said.

"I had a couple boys get bushwhacked down in south county," Squirrel said, not waiting for an answer. "Held them up just outside the Neck, took a half dozen cases they was carrying. I imagine the folks down there are getting mighty thirsty. You take a shipment for me today, and when you get back we'll talk out all the details of your pending employment."

Jesse was quiet for a while. He turned and looked at the ring, where the kid was only now trying to stand but couldn't. He'd take a staggered step or two and then his knees would buckle and he was back on the canvas. Jesse thought of the struggling hog.

There was blood on the kid's face and blood smeared onto his chest and patches of his hair were matted together with blood and the fight was long over. Everyone else had dispersed to the gaming tables or gone outside to smoke and take the air. The boy was alone—lost in every way. There was hurt and confusion in his face and Jesse had seen such faces before.

Entire towns crumbled under the weight of war, and he had not been there to witness their disfigurement, only the desolation that remained after. Saviors descended but came too late. Pinchbeck liberators who offered bread while starved bodies lay dead in the rubble of their old homes. Orphans tottered about with no direction, no intention. Punch-drunk children of the Great War who would grow to fight their own, if they grew at all.

He watched the boy stumble around the ring. Jesse's own heart hammered in his chest like a battle drum. Graves upon graves.

"If you're trying to think of some other way, there's not one," Squirrel said.

"What will you do to him?" Jesse asked. "If I say no, and we can't get the money."

"Nothing good."

"You wouldn't kill a man over two hundred dollars," Jesse challenged.

"I'd kill a man over two hundred pine needles if there was principle in it. Now make the goddamn call and quit wasting my time."

Hollis stood there, a blank expression on his face, despite the man across from him openly considering his murder. His arms were crossed and his torso pitched backward as if he were leaning against the air.

The drums beat louder, and Jesse could feel his hands shaking in his pockets. Then his mind went quiet save a single moment. *If you're staying, I'm staying.*

"Fine," he whispered. "One run. Then we talk."

"Glad to hear it," Squirrel clapped his hands together then reached into his shirt pocket and pulled out a small ledger and tore a page from it. "Have Ansel or Coy bring you a car around and help you load. Here's a list."

"Your boys—the ones that got held up," Jesse said. "Did they say who it was?"

Squirrel shook his head and waved off the question.

"Probably just some local river rats on a drunk. We'll find them and deal with them. But here's this to take," he said, unhooking from under the table a sawed-off shotgun that Jesse realized had been pointed at them since they'd walked up. "And I might give some thought toward carrying a pistol if I was you."

"Pistol?" Frog asked, his big frame appearing to their side. "Don't everybody know Jesse Cole can kill off a whole army with nought but sling and stone?"

"Frog," Jesse said.

Frog ignored him and passed a sweat towel down his face and opened his eyes and mouth wide and shut them and toweled himself again.

"Take?" he asked his brother.

"About a hundred and eighty dollars," Squirrel said. "They all bet on you to end it in the first, they just didn't have much to bet."

"Shit, that won't hardly pepper the eggs."

"How much does the kid get?" Jesse asked, and Frog looked at him and spit.

"He gets however much we say, soldier boy."

"He gets five dollars," Squirrel said. "And the right to say without lying that he lasted more than one round with Frog Fenley. That'll give him a reputation, get him more fights. More money."

"Yeah, and what about *my* reputation?" Frog asked. "I could've ended that boy ten minutes ago."

Squirrel stood from behind the table and glared at the big man.

"If I say to wait a round, you wait a round," he snapped. "If I say to let one of them sissy boys from Longview knock you out, you'd by God better be face down on that canvas."

Frog looked away, his large frame somehow disappearing into itself. He appeared small.

"It was fixed?" Hollis said before Jesse could stop him.

"Yes, it was fixed, you ignorant hillbilly," Squirrel said. "It's all fixed. Every lazy, lackluster step you take on this earth is part of a swindle that's been running long before you were ever born. You can make a dozen decisions a day and live to be a hundred years, but in the end you're only ever the rube or the racketeer."

"Come on, Hollis," Jesse said, pulling Hollis away before his curiosity got them into more trouble. "Let's go get us a car."

17

The coloreds in Nebat County lived south of Enoch where the river bent east for nearly two miles and then righted itself to the south, and they lived along the neck of that great bend in log cabins, some still with thatched roofs, and in small houses with board-and-batten siding, and they lived close to one another and kept mostly to themselves.

It had not always been so, but in the decade past there were many instances of racial violence and most often the victims lived in isolated parts of the county. Rather than own large tracts of land, even those who could afford such banded together and formed their own community and called it Revrag, which was the backward spelling of Garver, after the town's founder, John Garver. But for those in the area, black and white alike, the community was known by its geographic feature and thus referred to as the Neck.

Colston Garver, whose father had built the town and rid the Neck of the Klan, took great pride in the ability of Enoch's black community to fend for itself. There were many, he knew, who sought integration and equality, but Garver himself favored independence. He was quick to point out to his peers that this did not mean he feared white men, but rather he held himself above them.

Still, it was not entirely uncommon for others to enter the Neck. There were several black men who worked at the mill, and some hesitant friendships with whites had been formed. There was also trade—certain items hard to find in one community or thought better gotten from the other, though Garver kept a close eye over who and what was allowed to pass. And certainly there were those few angry confederates who might venture into the Neck on a drunk and looking for trouble. Finding themselves immediately outnumbered, such men would hurl a threat or slur and quickly retreat north to the safety of Enoch proper.

Garver kept a rotating watch of men along the only entry point to the Neck. A single road coming south from town and ending at a single wooden gate that led into the neighborhood. Some said they felt the small village was more a fort than a community. Garver didn't mind such talk. His primary goal was keeping his people safe.

"The army used forts to keep out the savages," he'd told them. "And these are savages that surround us now."

The alternating sentries sat alongside the road in a makeshift deer blind fashioned from wooden tent poles and draped hides that hung loose enough to filter out the smoke of fires when they were necessary. And on this cold January night fire was indeed a necessity and it was Garver himself who fed the flames throughout his watch.

It had been a quiet post but as morning began to break, he looked out at the unpromised coming of the dawn and there in the early gray light stood a motionless figure in a black mask with a line of dark-clad men at his back. They appeared as suddenly as timber ghosts. Haints for the haunting. Like something conjured up in a nightmare from childhood that stays in the memory for a lifetime, even as all else fades.

Garver noted their numbers. Their weapons. He also noted the deathly quiet of the woods around them. He could hear only his heartbeat as it thumped against his chest plate, perhaps to warn him. Perhaps trying to escape.

"You lost, friend?" Garver called, steadying his voice.

"No more than the rest," the masked man replied, and his voice was muddled—hoarse and strained—and the painted lips of the mask forever at rest.

"You got business here?" Garver asked.

"I do."

He had moved onto the trail and the men followed in step behind him.

"With who?"

"The fire brigade," the man said.

"Then you must be lost."

"Very well," the man told him "Then I have business with Colston Garver."

Garver shook his head.

"You ain't got no business with me."

"We have a deal to make, you and I."

"If it's labor, I don't work for whites. If it's liquor, I don't sell to whites."

The man nodded as if he approved of such terms.

"You have a fine camp here, Mr. Garver," he said. "A close, tight-knit community. Even your houses are so very close together. You have done well for yourself and your people. And I cannot blame you for your position. However, there are some things that defy race."

"Not in these woods," Garver told him.

"I'm told you once made the finest corn liquor in the county."

"Like I said, I don't sell to whites. Even them that's painted up in black masks."

Garver felt his own defiance growing. If this queer creature wanted him dead, he would have come shooting, not talking.

The man in the black mask ignored Garver and stayed with his own line of questioning. "But six years ago, Frog Fenley beat one of your men near to death until he divulged the secret to your distilling success. Did he not? And now he goes around saying he has the best whiskey formula in the region. An ingenious method known only to himself and his cohort. Isn't that right?"

Garver crossed his arms but didn't answer.

"In fact," the man continued, "despite your very loud, very public decries of any commerce involving whites, you now provide the Fenleys with corn from your fields. Do you not?"

"I made the decision that was best for my people," Garver said. "Folks like us can't go to the law. And I don't aim to see the Fenleys or anybody else hurt these families."

"My people," the man repeated and laughed behind the mask. "A modern-day Moses. Just be weary of the idols, Mr. Garver. As to our deal, from now on, you sell to me. My employer and I will handle the Fenleys and you will be paid handsomely for your talents."

"I know who you are," Garver said. "And I know who you work for. So you go on and tell that old man that I ain't making no deal with the devil."

The man laughed. A choking, corrosive sound.

"I have seen the devil, sir. And I can assure you, I am not him."

"You not welcome in the Neck, mister," Garver warned, reaching for the shotgun that rested against the blind. "Not today. Not ever again."

The masked man drummed his bony fingers together.

"If you insist," he said, stalking back toward the woods, his long legs bowing out and striding like a mutant insect. "*Ave atque vale*, Mr. Garver."

Garver stood and watched the stranger go. Only when someone from inside the gate yelled 'fire' did he realize that the line of men had vanished as quickly as they had appeared.

18

When Amon arrived at the annex that morning, there were two boys and a girl standing and staring up at the roof.

He parked the car and got out and stood. He followed their gaze above the small building but saw nothing save the same gray clouds that seemed conjoined to each passing day.

Then a cry came from somewhere beyond the annex.

"Annie, Annie, over!"

A baseball soared overtop the roof and one of the boys caught it and the other two children giggled and he quieted them with his finger to his lips and began to creep toward one side of the annex with the ball in hand.

"Hey, kid," Amon called and the boy stopped and stood straight. "You can't play here. There's bad men that get brought right up these steps. It's dangerous."

"Aw, c'mon, mister," the girl said. "This place is the perfect size."

"Yeah," the boy with the ball added. "Tony and Mae can't throw it over the buildings on Main Street."

"The hell I can't," argued a small boy who, along with two other children, came around from the backside of the annex.

"He says we can't play here," the first boy relayed to the group as he moved off the dead grass and onto the blacktop, waving for them to follow. "And we can't go back to the mill or Tony'll have bad dreams about the boogerman he thinks he saw up there."

"I did see him," the small boy said, running to catch up with the others as they moved on down the street in search of a more fertile frolicking ground.

Boyd and Davis arrived one after the other, passing the children on their way in.

"That's some fine police work there, Ranger," Boyd said. "I feel safer already."

Amon held the door open for them and forced a smile.

"I'm gonna head down to the thoroughfare here after a while and stick close to them boys putting together the camp revival," Boyd said, leaning backward and stretching with his hands at his waist. "Last time a traveling preacher come through here, him and his acolytes stole a box of hymnals and a wagon full of lumber."

"You want me to come by and spell you this afternoon?" Davis asked.

"Nah, there ain't no use in both of us being cold," Boyd told him and turned to Amon. "What about you, Ranger? More folks on your list?"

"Headed to Nebat City," Amon said. "Gonna talk to some of Charlie Cooper's neighbors out there. See if anybody is willing to say they saw him with the Fenleys."

"And if they ain't willing?"

"One step at a time, Deputy," Amon replied. "This is how it goes. Documentation. Compiling evidence. Can't go in guns blazing anymore."

"You know, Jack Duverney was the only Ranger I ever knew," Davis said. "And when he thought somebody was causing trouble, the only thing he'd compile is a tall enough tree."

"But you did," Boyd said to Amon, ignoring the other deputy.

"I did what?" Amon asked.

"You went in guns blazing. Got your partner shot and killed on some backroad in Smith County. Didn't you?"

Amon was quiet for a minute.

"I did," he said, chin raised, teeth gritted. "And I'm not going to make the same mistake."

"Speaking of Duverney," Davis went on. "I think he worked a case or two with your old man, Atkins. Didn't they call him Bad Bill?"

"They still do."

"He got more cutthroats off the street than syphilis."

Amon nodded.

"Didn't he go crazy or something?" Davis asked.

"Something," Amon replied, and Davis became aware of the nature of his question.

"Sorry," the deputy mumbled.

"He put a slug in a fella that was already handcuffed and on his knees," Boyd said. "Shot him right in the back of the head."

Davis looked at Amon for confirmation.

"Seven children had gone missing in Wichita Falls," Amon said. "My father was there, working the investigation for nearly a month. Talking to the families. Grieving with them. But the trail went cold, and they were ready to call it quits, when a tornado came through. Big one. Tore up all sorts of things in town. Took a man's shed, lifted it right off the ground. Underneath, there was a bunker. It had this big heavy door on it."

Amon stopped and shook his head.

"They'd talked to the man already. He was a strange one and some folks had whispered this or that, but he'd let them onto the property and let them look around. They looked in the shed, but it was small. Too small for that many kids. There were reel mowers and shovels and all sorts of things piled in there, covering up that door. But those things got thrown around in the twister, and when the weather settled, there it was. My father and his partner opened that door. Took both of them to do it. They found . . . only two of the children were still breathing. And the things they'd had done to them. Unspeakable."

"So, yes," Amon nodded. "My father's partner had cuffed the man, but he shot him anyway. And once he was dead on the ground, he shot him again. And again."

Both deputies were quiet.

"They tried to take him off the road after that," Amon told them. "A forced retirement. But he wouldn't have it. His partner testified that the man was trying to escape. That my father didn't know he was cuffed. I doubt it would have mattered one way or the other. The folks in that town saw my father as a hero. He stayed on the job. On the road. His whole life he'd been looking for that door, and once he found it, he was convinced there were more. That there'd always be more."

There was silence in the room. A car passed outside.

"Well," Davis said at last. "To hell with any man who'd hurt a child."

They all three nodded, then went their separate ways.

19

It was midday when they hit the blacktop in south county. The Taggerts had outfitted them with a five-year-old Model A Ford. It wasn't as fast or showy as some of the Fenley fleet, but it had a brand-new Kingston heater that made Jesse and Hollis feel like they were in the lap of luxury.

The rain had long since passed, but the gray sky lingered and without the wind the world felt stale—ensnared in some cold, persistent gloam.

"I don't care for a dark day," Hollis said. "Surely I do not."

He looked at his pocket watch.

"Here it is, a quarter to noon, and nearly dark as coffin air."

"Just keep looking out," Jesse told him.

"For what?"

"Anything."

Hollis gave a half salute and looked for a few seconds out the window and then turned back to Jesse.

"I was out at Concho Calhoun's a couple weeks back," he said. "And this fella come in there looking for a drink. So Concho gets him one, and the man throws it back and asks for another and Concho tells him, says, 'Let's see some money first, mister.' Well, of course the old boy ain't got not a dime on him and he gets to telling all sorts of tales about how he's out of a job and this and that. Concho says to him to go on and get the hell out, and the man's begging and he says, 'Please sir, will you at least give me a few pieces of bread for my wife and children?' Ole Concho looks him dead in the eye and says, 'I got a stale loaf you can have, but I don't want your goddamn wife and kids.'"

Jesse shook his head, but he smiled, and Hollis was slapping his own knee.

"Did any of that happen?" Jesse asked.

"Naw, I heard that one at Bennett's place a while back, but he used a barber instead of a barkeep," Hollis said. "I wouldn't mind going to Concho's though. I hadn't been out there in a while."

They came first to a well-frequented café between Enoch and the Neck. It was an older building, but new weatherboard had been put up in the last few years and new steps leading to the main door. In front of the café was a dirt lot half filled with trucks and coupes and a wagon whose mule was tied to a pole nearby. The door was around the side and Jesse took his hat off when he entered. Hollis followed suit.

It was counter service and there was a young boy in a paper hat taking orders.

"Who do I talk to about deliveries?" Jesse asked.

"Depends on what you're delivering."

"Well, it ain't nothing that goes on hamburgers."

The boy nodded.

"Davey's out back. Y'all can go on."

"Quite a few folks in here," Hollis noted. "Y'all giving away milkshakes or what?"

The boy leaned around the two of them and looked into the dining room.

"If they find a slip of paper in their burger, they get it free, plus a dollar" he said.

"Anybody found one today?" Hollis asked, eager.

"There ain't no paper, mister," the boy said. "Just something we tell folks."

Hollis deflated.

They collected a few glances as they walked through the dining room and out the back door. Out back, there were overfull barrels of trash and a few ruined tablecloths wadded up next to them. A short-haired man in wire glasses had a dead calf strung up from a pole and both hands inside the carcass, fishing for some organ or the other. He turned when he heard the door.

"Gentlemen," he said, and there was a cigarette between his lips that bobbed up and down as he spoke. "What can I do for you?"

"Kid up front says you're the fella to talk to about deliveries," Jesse said.

"That would depend on what you're delivering."

"Kid said that too. We're with the Fenleys."

"The Fenleys, huh?"

"That's right."

"Well, I hate you drove all this way, but we're all set in that department."

"What do you mean?" Jesse asked him.

"I mean we don't need any alcohol. If that's plain-speak enough for you."

"We were told your last shipment never made it."

"That's right."

"So we got you covered. Crates are out front in the car. Want us to pull it around back?"

"Like I said, I ain't interested."

"I'm not following here, Davey. Let's go back to that plain-speak you mentioned."

The man wiped his bloody hands on his apron and took a drag from the cigarette and took it from his mouth and flicked it away.

"I'm not getting in the middle of some fucking whiskey war," he said. "All I know is a fella come in here wearing one of those masks—you know, the ones they give the poor bastards who got their faces blowed off in the war. And he said I'd be working with him from now on. Naturally, I told him to fuck off down the road somewheres."

"I'm guessing he didn't."

"What he did was hand me a slip of paper with my address on it,"

Davey said. "And a list of names—my wife, my children, even my mother. So, I'd appreciate y'all telling Frog and Squirrel that it ain't nothing personal. But I got a family to think about."

"And you think the Fenleys wouldn't go after your family?" Jesse asked.

"I imagine they would. But there was something about this old boy—I can't put it into words. Let's just say he convinced me that whatever the Fenleys are, he's worse," Davey told them. "And there's something else."

He pulled a folded piece of paper from his apron and passed it over to Jesse.

"He gave me this," Davey said. "Said to pass it along to Frog and Squirrel or whoever come by."

Jesse looked at the string of numbers and letters listed on the paper.

"Coordinates?" he asked.

"That's right."

"To what? This looks like it would put you somewhere out near Dover's Point."

Davey shook his head.

"I don't know and I don't want to know. Like I said, I ain't got nothing against y'all, and I'm sorry you come all this way. If you're thinking of smacking me around, it won't help. I'm dug in on this one. And Scotty in yonder may be young, but he don't need to be a crack shot with the scatter gun he's got hanging under the counter."

Jesse shook his head.

"No, we ain't here for that. We'll take your message to the Fenleys. They may have a different thought on the matter."

"They're welcome to it. They know where to find me."

Jesse rubbed his hands together in the cold.

"Say there, Davey. We got a handful of joints we're supposed to stop off at. You imagine they'll have the same story as you?"

"I don't want to put words in nobody's mouth, but that's the talk. This new outfit has everything from here to the Neck."

"And I guess you wouldn't give us a name?"

"Couldn't, even if I wanted to," he said. "Just a man in a mask."

"We'll leave you to it, then."

"For what it's worth, fellas, I appreciate the way y'all went about all this."

"Yeah, we're regular aristocrats," Jesse said, closing the door behind him.

They walked back through the dining room and out the front door. They piled into the car and Jesse started it up.

"What's next on the list?" he asked, putting the car in gear.

"Why don't we just go back, Jess?" Hollis asked. "Hell, you heard the man."

"Yeah, I heard him. But we need to hear it from the others too. I don't imagine Squirrel Fenley's willing to take Davey's word for it."

"What about them coordinates he give you?" Hollis asked.

"What about 'em?"

"You ain't the least bit curious what's out there?"

"Sure I am," Jesse said. "A man likes to have some idea of what he's getting into. What he's coming up against. But that ain't what we're down here for."

"Well, it's not but a few miles out of the way."

Jesse looked at his watch. Looked again at the slip of paper. He closed his eyes and kept them closed and then opened them after a while and looked over at Hollis.

"Pull that shotgun out from under the seat," he said. "If we're gonna do something stupid, let's commit to it all the way."

20

Amon drove west through the county with the tarnished sun behind him. No warmth to it. No reprieve. Boundless acres of forests and fields ravaged by the winter. Red weathered siltstone and red dirt and copper clay, all of it mud slick and treacly. And soon the gray clouds retook the sky and all was brought somber once more. The land, like the nation upon it, in a state of perpetual gloom.

The first marker of Nebat City was a Baptist church on the east side of town. Amon slowed the car and looked there at the day's breadline.

In sad, swaying rows they shuffled forth, rawboned and ragged. Gaunt, skeletal figures with lantern-jawed faces and eyes drawn deep and hollow in their sockets. Their mouths hung open and their dry tongues flicked out at the smell of the soup and sustenance.

The boys in tattered shirts and girls in their flour sack dresses. The younger children wore clothes passed down from their siblings, their thin arms disappearing into oversized sleeves. No one spoke, just stood waiting. Waiting for food and waiting, many of them, for something else altogether.

Soldiers, from the Great War. Farmers. Factory workers. Schoolmarms and ministers and men who had spent the whole of their lives without asking a single thing of the world save rain and sun. Proud men and strong women and children much older than their age, and all of them silenced by the roaring rapacity of a foundering nation.

They cast their caverned eyes downward at their own thin, patched boots, and the heady scent of earth and pine blew cold from the north country and down through the trees wherein those sorrowed souls closed their pitiful coats against the wind and turned away from it—as if hiding their faces from the coming storm might spare them its wrath.

Amon drove on.

He parked slantwise in front of the sheriff's department and looked up at the gathering clouds and went inside.

A short, round secretary who looked annoyed by his presence led Amon back through the building and into the sheriff's office.

Sheriff Cheatham was a hefty man with pockmarked cheeks hidden beneath a reddish-blond beard.

"Cooper?" the sheriff said after Amon introduced himself and gave his purpose for the visit. "You're gonna want to talk to my deputies over in Enoch. That's where the murder happened."

Amon nodded.

"Yes sir," he said, "but I looked at the coroner's report and it appears Mr. Cooper had been deceased for some time before his body was found."

The sheriff stared at him.

"So," Amon continued, "it seems possible the body could have been moved."

"Alright," the sheriff said, shrugging. "The murder happened somewhere. Maybe in Enoch. Maybe not. Either way, the Fenleys are the only suspects we have, and my deputies in Enoch know more about them than anybody here."

"I understand that, sir," Amon told him. "I was just hoping to get any information I could from your office. A case file. Even just your theory as to what happened."

"A theory?" the sheriff laughed, his red, bulbous nose turning near purple. "Sure. I'll give it to you. Charlie Cooper was a lowlife. A con man with delusions of grandeur. Dreg of society, really. How he landed that pretty little girl, I'm sure I don't know. But then, that's what got him killed."

"The widow?" Amon asked.

"That's right," the sheriff nodded. "Old Charlie had something Frog Fenley wanted. Fenley shot him in the head and took it. 'Course, there's no bullet. No gun. And nobody who seen Charlie or Frog—or apparently any other soul, living or dead—on the night in question. So, like I said before, if y'all want the Fenleys out of the way, you'll have to come up with something a hell of a lot more compelling than Charlie Cooper."

"The widow says she isn't with Fenley. You think she's lying?"

The sheriff shrugged and scratched at his large nose.

"Could be," he said. "But from what I know of Frog Fenley, I'm not sure it makes a difference. I wouldn't put it past him to have killed Charlie before ever even talking to the gal. Just to remove him from the picture."

"So you believe the Fenleys are as bad as people say?"

"Oh, I imagine they're quite a bit worse. You'd have to be, wouldn't you? To kill your own parents."

Amon frowned.

"You hadn't heard?" the sheriff asked. "The Fenleys showed up in Texas when they was ten and eleven, if I recall. Maybe eleven and twelve. Squirrel being the older. They got caught holding up a church service in Texarkana. A *church service*, if you didn't hear me. They was gonna steal the offering plate and whatever else, I guess. Anyhow, the sheriff up there at the time, fella by the name of Bell, he asked them where they was from and they said Faulkner, Tennessee. Well, come to find out, about a month before all this there'd been a double murder in Faulkner, Tennessee. A real no-good sumbitch named Earl Fenley and his wife, Tottie, had been found just stabbed all to hell with a bowie knife. Whoever done it had tried to cover it up by setting the house on fire."

The sheriff paused and leaned forward and took a pack of cigarettes out of his desk drawer and put one in his mouth and lit it and went on.

"Neighbors there in Faulkner didn't seem real sad about the whole ordeal. Earl Fenley had himself a reputation as a card-carrying degenerate.

Used to get drunk and get in fights. Destroy property. Beat on his wife and two boys."

He tipped the ash from his cigarette into a painted tray and leaned back.

"Now, the boys said they didn't know anything about all that. They didn't have a knife on them or can of gasoline or the like. They said they must have run off before it happened."

"Nothing came of it?" Amon asked.

"The authorities got together and talked it out. Turned the kids loose to an orphanage somewhere outside of Dallas. Not a month or two later, they run off from there too. Nobody seen hide nor hair of them until they was eighteen. Showed up in Enoch with a bag full of money and bought that farm. Rest is history."

"But you believe they did it—killed their parents?"

"I was born at night, but not last night. I can handle a coincidence, just not a bushel of them all at once."

"Do they, or did they ever, come into Nebat City?" Amon asked.

"Every now and then, I'll get word they were here," the sheriff answered. He was looking past Amon. Staring at something only he could see. "The one thing I never understood is why they killed their momma. Drunk bastard beats on you? Alright. Fine. Knife the sumbitch. But by all accounts, Tottie was a sweet woman. That's always stuck with me. That little bit of it."

The secretary opened the door, seemingly breaking the sheriff out of his trance.

"Sheriff, Judge Reese wants you over at the courthouse," she said.

"He say what it's about?"

"He said it was about his reelection campaign, but not to tell you it was about his reelection campaign."

The sheriff laughed.

"Wouldn't trade her for all the deputies in the world," he told Amon. "Good help is hard to find. Let me walk you out."

Amon went alone to the last address of Charlie Cooper. It was a small clapboard house with peeling paint. Visibly leaning. There were other houses along the street. Each one appeared more tumbledown than the next. Ramshackle structures with broken windows and sagging roofs.

He walked up to the Cooper house and knocked on the door, but no one answered. He peered into the front window. Darkness. He knelt to where the bottom of the door met the threshold and ran his finger along the small gap between the two. A trace of something rust-colored in the dirt and dust. He squatted there for a while, rubbing together his forefinger and thumb.

After a while he walked back out to the car and he saw a woman's face in a window across the street, but when he crossed and knocked on the door, no one answered.

21

They kept on the farm-to-market road until the city maintenance ended and the red dirt paths took over, meandering in no discernible pattern through the pine thickets of south county. Jesse turned the car slow onto a rock trail that ran westward up a ridge known as Dover's Point on account of a pilot named Dover had crashed into it while testing a plane for the military in 1915.

Less than a half mile up the ridge, the trail grew too narrow for the Ford. Jesse inched the car forward and back until it was facing out the way they'd come and the two of them climbed out and continued on foot.

The ridge was slightly cambered, higher in the west, and sloping away to the north and south, where the smallest gap in the canopy signaled the presence of deep gullies and shallow washes. There were thickets you could see beyond and thickets you could not, and all the while the two of them walked, they never touched dry ground.

The two men moved quick up the steep trail and Jesse stopped once and looked back to measure their progress and then went on.

"Just up yonder," Jesse said as they rounded a short switchback.

The sky above was skull colored. A stale, enigmatic gray.

They were some sixty yards from the summit when Jesse dropped into a crouch and pulled Hollis down with him.

Hollis looked up and followed Jesse's gaze to the summit of the ridge, whereon a cherrybark oak had fended off all comers to create space for its thick round trunk and long loping branches.

From one such branch hung the days-dead remains of two men. Dark shapes of men, turning slow in the breeze. Some macabre, necromanced puppetry. Forgotten marionettes in the cold wind.

"Shit fire," Hollis said.

"How many shells do you have for that shotgun?" Jesse asked.

"Enough to pull the trigger twice and take off running," Hollis told him.

"There's something around their necks.".

"I ain't no expert on hangings, Jess, but I believe it's a couple of fucking ropes."

"No. Something else—a sign maybe. Come on."

They approached cautious-like, crouched and quiet. They could smell the bodies. The rank of death.

"Buzzards been at 'em," Hollis said, studying the hanging flesh and chunks of meat and muscle missing from the limbs of the dead men. "Surprised they ain't here now."

"Heard us coming, I guess."

"Or got run off by whoever is waiting in these woods to shoot our dumb asses."

"Or that," Jesse admitted, and both of them looked out into the dark woods where nothing moved.

"There's your sign." Hollis pointed, and sure enough both dead men were adorned with splinterwood signs that hung from smaller lengths of the same rope used to display their corpses.

On one was written "Squirrel," on the other "Frog."

"I guess a strong message is a clear one," Hollis said. "We ought to get word of this back to the Fenleys."

Jesse toed the wet dirt beneath the bodies.

"They already know," he said. "Squirrel lied to me. Sent us down here just to see if whoever did this was still around."

"Should we cut 'em down?"

"No. We'll tell Boyd and Davis. Let them handle it," Jesse said. "I'm not getting no further into this mess than right here, right now. We'll figure out some other way to pay them bastards. I don't care what they say."

Hollis opened his mouth to argue, but he stopped. Closed it again.

"Is that something burning?" he asked.

Jesse looked.

Great plumes of thick black smoke were rising and fanning out above the distant tree line to the southeast.

Jesse looked back from the top of the ridge and could see a handful of miles to the break in the trees where the river ran. He tracked its winding path with his eyes until it converged with the smoke-filled horizon.

"That's the Neck," he said.

"What's the odds on Garver and his bunch just burning a bunch of trash piles?"

"Ten minutes ago I might've believed something like that."

"But not now."

"No. Not now," Jess said. "Come on. Let's go."

Hollis sighed.

"Out of the frying pan," he said and followed Jesse, who had taken off at a quick jog.

Jesse whipped the car around the tight curves that bent south through the trees. With the crates of booze in the back, the weight distribution was near even and the car hugged close in the corners but never fishtailed and Jesse pushed the six cylinder to its limit on each short straightaway, the car lurching forward out of the turns and slinging red mud in its wake.

"You sure are driving fast toward something that ain't our problem," Hollis said, steadying himself in the passenger seat.

Jesse ignored him. The closer they got to the Neck, the more encompassing the smoke became.

"Hell, the whole place is burning," Hollis said.

Indeed, the air itself seemed afire, the cold wind crashing against the infernal flames, pushing and tossing them across the rows of houses that had now been reduced to kindling. Pine logs incinerated. Old clapboard buildings that might as well have been made of gasoline.

There were men with water buckets, but they stood trancelike and stared at the fire, knowing the truth. There were children crying and other children who were quiet and hidden behind the skirts of their mothers, peering out at this thing they'd never seen and thought perhaps they were not meant to look at.

There were maybe sixty people in all and some of them turned to look as Jesse got out of the car.

"What happened here?" He asked, but no one answered.

A man came coughing and choking and crawling out of the smoke and two others helped him away from the fire and sat him up against a stump and the man shook his head and tried to speak.

"Colston still in there," he managed, pointing. "Still in there."

The ash fell like rain and was frozen before it touched the ground and Jesse was shaking but not from the cold.

"I told you," Hollis whispered, maybe to himself. "I told you it was the same."

A half dozen men were running back into the burning houses and Jesse found himself alongside them.

"Colston," they called, and Jesse called too.

The flames forked and spiraled and moved unlike any Jesse had ever seen. The fire itself was wholly unnatural, as if it were being driven by a force outside itself. The great rushes of heat threw the men backward, sent them scrambling for any semblance of shelter.

"Here," came a voice from amid the chaos. "I'm here."

Jesse saw a hand reaching from a pile of coal and rubble and black-burned wood whereon a long beam had fallen overtop. He crawled to it and took off his shirt and used the shirt against the hot wood to try to lift it but he could not.

The man was mumbling beneath the wreckage. He spoke of black masks and golden lions.

Jesse strained against the log and it would not budge, and then Hollis was at his side.

"Give it again," Hollis said, his own shirt in his hands, and the two of them lifted the beam and threw it aside and began picking away the lesser wood and burnt remnants of the structure that had been.

They pulled Colston Garver out and he managed to stand despite the calamitous look of his burned limbs and charred face, bits of which seemed to flake away even as they stumbled forward out of the fire and into the cold dead grass beneath the pines. Several people rushed to him and poured water on his being and Jesse watched in horror as the man writhed and screamed and steam came hissing from his body.

Two men had attached chains to cars and were driving in and out of the burning hamlet dragging makeshift sleds with sad piles of smoke-stained clothes and furniture and cups and plates which rattled and cracked and went bouncing into the ash-laden mud. What few items could be salvaged would forever be tainted by the fire. By the smell of it. By the memory.

One of the cars caught fire and a man dove from the driver's seat and rolled onto the ground as the burning automobile continued into the trees, flames like streamers in the wind, a warhorse of the mechanical future.

It crashed into a tree and men rushed with their buckets to put it out before another fire could start.

Many women knelt in prayer and they rejoiced with raised hands and grateful tears when the gunmetal sky opened and let fall the pounding rain.

"Praise God," they cried, and the men cried too. "Praise God."

The flames licked for hours yet. The coal smoldering for days. And in those days to come, as the damage was surveyed and the desolation accounted, still they thanked God for sending the rain.

22

1918

Spirals of razor wire run alongside corpse-piled trenches and bodies left tangled in the wire like the trappings of some demonic holiday. Tanks and gas and screaming men and screaming horses. Flares and fires burning in the loud night across black mud fields littered with the hollow vessels of extinguished souls. The smell of smoke and shit and burnt powder. And Hollis has pissed himself. Jesse can see it. Neither say anything. Hollis is shaking. There's the whistle. Over the top.

Hollis is crying and he can't make it out of the trench. Jesse grabs him. Hauls him up. "Stay down," he tells him, but Hollis is looking at something far away. Something from his childhood. "Stay behind me," Jesse yells, and they move forward. The fighting looks heavy off to their left. The spent payload of a half dozen mustard canisters give the field a pale, stinging veneer. The lines have broken on both sides. Men are scattered. Blinded by the night and the gas and their own fear. A Hun rises quickly from an unseen position and is immediately shot and killed by his own comrade who is too startled to take a closer look. Jesse fires and watches the comrade fall away into the dark like the target at a carnival booth. Twenty more yards and now they are alone.

"I don't think I want to be here anymore, Jess," Hollis says loudly, and Jesse shushes him.

Then a low whistle, and Jesse hits the ground. He cocks his head and there is Hollis, still standing upright. He's dropped his gun somewhere and his arms are straight down at his sides. Jesse launches himself. He tackles Hollis as the mortar round explodes.

They make the village by sunrise. There are others. They nod and touch their helmets and the small motion is an acknowledgment, an announcement, like the birds calling out to the morning that they'd survived another night.

23

Jesse dropped Hollis as near to Old Moss's cabin as the car could make.

"Tell him you need a place to stay for the night," Jesse said. "I'll be by later to check on you."

"Let me go with you, Jess," Hollis said. "It's my fault, anyhow."

"No. If things go wrong, I need somebody to look after Sarah and Eliza."

"C'mon now, goddamnit," Hollis argued. "Eliza don't even like me."

"Well then, you'd better hope nothing happens."

Jesse left Hollis standing near the trailhead and drove away. He headed north toward Harmatia Hill and in time came to the turnoff to the Fenley's farm and took it and followed the little road up to the house. He parked the car off to the side of the farmhouse and went up onto the porch carrying the shotgun and knocked on the door. He was covered in soot and ash and mud. A fire-born golem come crawling from the flames.

Frog opened it and gave him a once over.

"You look like shit, Cole."

Squirrel came up behind him.

"You don't need drivers," Jesse said, throwing the keys down at their feet. "You need cannon fodder."

Squirrel feigned remorse.

"You got it all wrong," he said. "Yes, I might've held back a bit ear-lier. But there's a war coming, Cole, and I need soldiers. Ain't that what you are?"

Jesse shook his head.

"Your war's already started," he said. "You knew those two boys were dead down there. Why lie?"

"Would you have gone if I'd told the truth?"

"Who is it you're fighting?" Jesse asked, ignoring the question.

"I was hoping you'd figure that out today. Guess I was wrong."

"So that's it, then. We were bait."

"Well, hell, it's not like I was throwing you to the lions, Cole. You got a reputation as a fella who can handle himself. Or am I wrong about that too?"

"I'm out," Jesse said. "Car's around the side. Cases are still in it, except the one we left in the Neck."

"The Neck?"

"Whoever's coming for you, they already got to Garver. Burned them out. Me and Hollis left them some whiskey, for all the good it'll do."

"Garver alive?" Squirrel asked, his face unchanged.

"Barely."

"It's just some greedy bunch, probably from across the water. We'll be just fine," Squirrel said. "So long as you and the boys hadn't forgot how to pull a trigger."

"I'm out," Jesse said again and leaned the shotgun against the door jamb.

"Hold on there, haas."

Squirrel tossed an unzipped canvas bag at his feet. Jesse could see stacks of banded bills. He stared at the money but didn't pick it up.

"Aw, I was just playing hard to get," Squirrel told him. "There's plenty more where that come from. Why don't you go on and take it. Call it a down payment."

"I don't care about your money," Jesse said. "I'm not playing a part in this."

Squirrel sucked his teeth.

"I'll tell you what, Cole," he said, nodding. "You go on home. You can even keep the car. And you take tonight to think things over. But while you're thinking, just remember it's more than money on the line. Hollis still owes. You vouched for him. That means you owe too."

Jesse didn't answer and Squirrel didn't say anything else. He kicked the keys out onto the porch and slammed the door.

Jesse looked at the keys and at the bag of money and he was a long time looking. Finally, he turned and descended the steps.

It was a long walk in the cold. The highway was crushed rock—a tar-bound macadam, twisting through the pines and hills and sandy sloughs. It began to rain and sleet and great balls of hail clattered down to plague the earth. He turned onto a decade-old pipeline road and then a muddy cut-through and soon he was back in the damp woods, where the hail could not easily reach, where each path narrowed until the widowed branches overhung the trail like endless gallows and on he went among them. On into the dark.

24

There was hardly a sun to set. The sky shifting to darker shades of gray.

Eliza covered herself in a deerskin shawl and came to the top of the porch steps and gathered her skirts about her and sat down on the pine boards with her feet resting on the top step. She brought her knees to her chest and held them there and looked out at the country before her.

The cabin had been built on the west edge of a clearing with dense forest at its back to block the afternoon sun. From the porch she could see down the trail and a few of the ridges and, when the light was good, the deep roadcuts and the cross-bedding of red clay on top and gray papered lignite below.

She sat there a while until it was full dark and then stood and walked around to the back of the house and followed the short trail between the smokehouse and the garden and sat on the little oak bench that faced the grave.

They'd buried her on their own. Back then, the funeral parlors were full up with bodies—overrun by the dead. The Enoch cemetery had coffins stacked along the fence line for months. Some of which held the gravediggers themselves. It was a horror. An indignity. And even surrounded by the destitute and dying, the interment industries of this great country found cause to price gouge. They used supply and demand as an ethos, as if its principle were some alternative morality which thereby absolved them of their greed. Even the cheapest of pines boxes became unattainable.

Like many in their line from other places in other times, Daniel and Eliza had seen to the inhumation themselves. She remembered the day. Despite her longing to forget, she would remember it always. An unseasonably warm day in March, and a day that raged with sunlight and it shone there on Danny in the yard as he set about passing the serrated blade in exchange with the hewn oak boards. She remembered the sound, the back-and-forth rhythm of which drew down on her sanity with every stroke.

Hours she spent rocking—the cadence of the creaking chair matching the grinding of the saw teeth. Forward and back. Forward and back. Forward and back, until Eliza could no longer withstand the onslaught of metered sound.

She rose from the chair and crossed the room to the crib. Forward and back. She pulled the muslin cloth away from her daughter's face and covered the small ears with her hands so that she might not hear the construction. Might not frighten at the sound of such confined eternity. The child was unmoving. Unbreathing. But still, Eliza held her hands over either ear.

"Hush now," she spoke, closing her own eyes so that she might share in the vision of the dead. "It's alright."

When the coffin was finished, she took the body and laid it in. Once the lid was closed, it seemed so small. So impossibly small. Eliza was shaking.

But it had not been the box that did her in—not the box itself. It was the world in full bloom around her and those few but prominent things worth seeing, worth smelling, worth reaching out to touch. The honeysuckle and blackberries. The smell of the trees in the new spring sun and the new blossoms and the bluebonnets and winecups and Mexican hat flowers. The spotted fawns on awkward, uneasy legs. And the brilliant rays of light in the forest—light that could bend and dance in the wind and explode through the great canopy of limbs and branches like a thousand speckled suns. She belonged in this world of light. Not beneath it. Not in that cold dark.

Daniel had used the rest of the wood to build a bench where Eliza could sit and speak with her daughter and Eliza sat there now, all these years later. There was no stone to head the grave, just a twine-bound cross driven deep into the dirt.

"I hope you're not too cold," she said. "The spring will come, or it will be the first one that never did. You'll see. The flowers will come back, and the sun. You'll see. I'll be right here with you."

She took off the shawl and laid it out in the mud beneath the cross and nodded and went back to the cabin.

Hours to come, Jesse had not returned, and Eliza braided onions and picked nervous at her teeth. Sarah counted out the winter crop. Potatoes, carrots, and beets, all of which were cleaned and stored in the pantry. When the food was put up, they set to their needlework, and the fire in the stove warmed the cabin and gave it the scent of smoke and pine, and the blankets covered them in their chairs and draped down over their legs.

Eliza checked the window periodically and at last she saw him coming slowly down the drive—his strides purposed, his face sullen. Whatever news, she could tell it would not be welcome.

He had the same look the night he'd first returned to Enoch.

Jesse Cole, the great war hero. It was a strange thing for Eliza. For years it was Daniel who had been loved by the people in Enoch. A fine man with a fine family. A good job. He had been the chosen son. Not Jesse, with his long hair and mischievous grin, running roughshod through the county in the company of degenerates and drunkards.

But whatever he had been, he was not that anymore.

Daniel was six months in the ground when Jesse returned. Eliza was the first one to see him. Sarah was asleep and Eliza heard movement outside the cabin. She might have shot him, she thought now. She might have shot him right there in the dark. Instead she'd leveled the shotgun and told him to get off the property, but when he spoke, she knew it was him.

"Something happen to the old door?" he'd asked her with great concern and confusion in his voice. "Danny replace it or something?"

She lowered the gun.

"It's the same door as far as I know," she told him.

"Seems smaller."

In those first weeks, he would sleep in the old barn. He ate supper with Eliza and Sarah, and once the latter was asleep, Eliza would join him on the porch and sometimes they'd talk, trading stories, losing themselves in safe memories. Jesse spoke often of his brother and he spoke of him as if Daniel had been some mythic hero, and each time, it made Eliza uncomfortable but she said nothing.

Other times they would sit in silent agreement and listen to the sounds of the night. And always Jesse would be the first to rise, and always he would nod at her and then move slowly down the steps and out across the yard. Night after night she watched him disappear out there in the dark.

Each morning he returned and often carrying firewood or wild berries or flowers for Sarah. He mended the roof and hauled in a new washtub and took a job at the mill.

On the fourth week, under a new moon, Eliza sat with him on the porch, and when the time came that he rose and nodded and made to leave, she grabbed his hand instead. He looked down at her.

"Do you think your brother would want you to take care of me?" she asked, her voice trembling.

He nodded.

"Then take care of me," she said.

She led him inside. Led him to her bed. It was perhaps out of pity or proximity or even the desire to anger ghosts, but in the moment her lust was real.

He was desperate and passionate and quick, and afterward he wept silently next to her. They were, the two of them, lost and alone.

They were married the following day at the courthouse annex. A pairing of convenience, if not compatibility. And for a time they lived as such, in the absence of love or joy but in the presence of one another. An existence of shared responsibility, with the common thread of familiarity and their great love for Sarah. Perhaps, Eliza hoped, this would be enough to keep the specters of the past from their doorstep.

But Eliza could see now on her husband's face as he came into the cabin that something had changed. He again had the look of a lost soldier, unsure how to march forward.

25

Amon returned to Enoch with no better idea of how to proceed. *Rumors and reputation.* He spent the hour-long drive trying to decide if this entire assignment was simply a punishment. A warning. He'd clashed with leadership before, but the Volstead Act had changed things. More federal presence. More revenuers on the road. The Rangers were no longer the authority they had once been. And if things progressed politically the way they were expected to, the Rangers would soon cease to exist altogether. He wondered what his father might think of such a thing.

The old man had given his life to the idea of law and order—the notion that those who forsake the law praise the wicked, but those who keep it work against them.

"Whatever evil stands against us, we do not stray," Amon remembered him saying.

Do not stray.

His father had said it often. Written it. Mumbled it in his sleep. And for those days of his life Amon was witness to, the old man indeed stayed the path. It cost him a wife. A daughter. Only Amon stuck by his side.

In the end, it was Amon's own family that had finally pulled him away. His own wife and child and career.

He switched his headlamps on in the early dusk and found himself imagining Joseph in the uniform. His father and his father before him. Rangers all. Maybe it was for the best if they were disbanded. Perhaps his disappointment could be circumvented.

Disappointment.

He felt a sudden anger at himself for even the thought. His son would not be a Texas Ranger, whether the agency survived or not. He would not be a great many things, and this was his lot and Amon wanted to accept it—tried to. He had been angry with God, though he never told his wife. He thought he was being punished. Tested. *Fine*, he thought. *I will pass Your test. I will never abandon my son, the way my father did. The way You did.*

It was full dark when he parked in the alley and climbed the stairs and Cora was waiting with supper and Joseph ran to him with a great beaming smile that washed away the worrisome drive. Amon picked up the boy and kissed his wife and they sat together at the small table in the small kitchen and, for the moment, his inner voices were silent.

They ate hamburger steaks with boiled potatoes and carrots that had been soaked in butter and sprinkled with salt. Cora brought a basket of rolls wrapped in a towel, and they ate those with the rest of the butter and sides of honey. There was no milk, but they drank tall glasses of cherry Kool-Aid that left their upper lips stained red.

"Y'all enjoy it, tonight," Cora said. "It's canned ham and beans the rest of the week."

"I don't get paid until next Friday," Amon told her.

"I know. We'll figure it out. You just worry about doing your job and getting us out of here."

"I'll try. It's been slow going these first couple of days."

"Well, pray on it," she said. "Double check everything. It'll come to you."

There was a knock at the door and the two of them turned to look and the boy sat trailing his fork through the honey.

Another bang at the door before Amon could get to it.

"Ranger, it's Deputy Davis," Davis said. "It's colder than the taxman out here."

Amon opened the door and Davis gave him a quick nod and ran across the room to the stove and stood beside it.

"Ma'am," he said to Cora, twisting his body in different directions to warm himself. "Sorry to intrude."

"What can we do for you, Davis?" Amon asked.

"Apparently, hell's done come off its hinges down in south county. The Neck's been burnt up, and there's two white men hanging from a tree up on Dover's Point. I'm headed down there, thought you might like to ride with me."

Cora shot Amon a look.

"I'm not sure this has much to do with my investigation," Amon told Davis. "Where's Deputy Boyd?"

"I went by his house first, but he wasn't there," Davis said. "And it might have more to do with you than you think. At least that's what the signs say."

"The signs," Amon repeated an hour later, his flashlight pointed up at the chunks of wood and the near-frozen bodies hanging from the big oak limb.

Davis was shivering next to him.

"Told you," the deputy said. "Frog and Squirrel. You figure it's them taking credit for killing these fellas?"

Amon shook his head.

"I kindly doubt it."

"So what then? Like a warning?"

"That's what I would guess," Amon said. "And I'd also guess once we identify these gentlemen, we'll find they have a connection to the Fenley operation in some way or another."

"Alright, well, let's get the poor bastards cut down and loaded up. We can do the rest of our guessing somewhere with a fire."

"I'd like to visit the Neck," Amon said.

"That's a bad idea, Ranger," Davis told him.

"It wouldn't be the first one I've ever had."

"Colston Garver and his bunch don't too much care for our coming around. Wouldn't take help if it was offered to him."

"Why?"

"Thinks blacks can do everything on their own, I guess."

"I'm sure his community's past experiences with law enforcement have nothing to do with it," Amon said, raising a brow.

"Whatever the reason. We ought to just let Garver handle it."

"I'm not asking, Deputy," Amon told him. "You're welcome to stay in the car and keep company with the dead."

They could smell the smoldering structures before they could see them, and when they did arrive, it was to utter and unwavering desolation. Photographs Amon had seen of townships leveled during the war had been more forgiving.

Davis stopped the car in the middle of the road and the two men got out and looked at the dozen or more houses that had been consumed entirely and many more with walls caved in or charred beyond any integrity.

What Amon didn't see were any of the Neck's inhabitants. He walked near the first row of burnt houses but found the site was still quite hot and so he stopped and stood and for a moment, wondered if there had been anyone left alive.

A twig snapped. Amon turned and there were three of them with shovels.

One stepped forward, a giant hulking man with a fearsome look.

"We help you with something, mister, or you just come to see for yourself?"

"I'm a Texas Ranger. Law enforcement," Amon said. "Just wanted to know what happened. Where is everyone?"

"Gone," the man said.

"Gone where?"

"Don't take no offense, Ranger, when I don't tell you."

Amon nodded.

"What are you three doing here, then?"

The man slammed his shovel into the mud.

"We the gravediggers."

Amon took off his hat and placed it over his heart.

"How many?" he asked.

"Four. A family—momma, daddy, little girl—and a man named Paul who tried to save 'em."

"I'm so sorry."

"My brother," one of the other men said. "Paul."

"Garver making any plans to retaliate against the Klan?" Davis asked. "Last thing we need is a damn race war on our hands."

"Weren't no Klan," the first man said.

"Who then?" Amon asked.

"Ask them boys in the back seat," the big man said.

"Hush now," came a cracked and breathy voice.

The third man stepped forward from the darkness.

"Y'all saying too much to this man," he said, and the saying seemed a great labor.

"Mr. Garver," Davis said. "Where's the rest of your people?"

Colston Garver ignored him, walking gingerly toward Amon.

Amon could see the deep burns on the bottom half of his face. The skin around his mouth and chin was barely hanging on.

"Ranger," he said and nothing more.

"Yes sir," Amon replied.

"Rangers killed a bunch of black folks in Redtown."

"Yes sir, they did."

"Rangers saved a bunch of black folks in San Augustine."

"Yes sir, they did that too."

"You in the war?" Garver asked.

"No sir, I was not."

"You are now," Garver said. "You want to know who did this, you ask the Fenleys. They know."

"Where are the others?" Amon asked. "Where are the people?"

"Somewhere safe."

"We can help you, Mr. Garver," Amon told him. "We can help all of you."

Garver motioned to the other two men, and they took up their shovels and walked past the car and disappeared into the woods. Amon thought to follow them but decided against it.

"How many people live in the Neck?" Amon asked Davis.

"Fifty," the deputy answered. "Sixty, maybe."

"And they can just disappear somewhere?"

"Garver's probably got them down in Reklaw. Colored town in the next county over. It ain't like they're hiding in the salt caves."

Amon frowned.

"Salt caves?"

"Mud, oil, hot springs. There's all sorts of shit under this ground, Ranger, including miles of caves covered in salt. Been used as far back as the Caddo."

Amon felt the urge to lift his foot, as if he might be crushing something valuable. Instead, he toed the earth with his boot. The smell of the smoke was heavy on the air and the air was still.

Night birds called in the cold. The rain had given out, and for a moment it was a rare, cloudless sky. Stars emerged cautious, like curious spectators to some caged oddity, turning white rock roads blue in the dark. Casting shadow onto shadow and taking their every measure. Shaping them black in the night.

"You want my theory," Davis said, already climbing in the car, neck and chin near buried inside his coat, "some sad sonofabitch figured it would take setting the whole woods on fire just to get warm."

26

Jesse sat the porch after Sarah was abed and looked out at the knobbed and leafless oaks that stood heavy among thick tracts of lank yellow pines. Dark and cold and quiet.

"Gonna sleep out here?" Eliza asked, coming outside and closing the door behind her.

He looked past her at the door. At the cracks.

"Not gonna sleep at all," he said.

He'd told her everything there was to tell and now he waited for her response.

"What do you plan to do?" she asked. "Stand guard on the porch all night, looking down the road? Who are you even expecting?"

"Maybe the Fenleys. Maybe whoever it is that's after them," he said. "I hadn't thought it all the way through, but that's about how far I got."

"And if nobody comes? What about tomorrow?"

"Like I said, I hadn't thought it all out yet."

"What about me and Sarah? What about when we go to the market? Somebody gonna be there huntin' us?"

She shook her head and crossed her arms against the cold.

"This thing the Fenleys want you to do, is it something you could live with?" she asked.

"It's something I already live with," he said. "Something I'll die with. But I got no place left to put more of it, Eliza. No room at the inn."

"If there's another way, tell me," she said. "Tell me and we'll do it."

"I can figure something out."

"And Frog and Squirrel? Even if you pay Hollis's debt, you think they'd let you turn them down, just like that?"

She was pleading now.

"I'd figure that out too," he said.

She closed her eyes and sighed, then opened them again and leaned back and opened the door to the cabin and looked in and listened. It was quiet.

"I quit on God," she told him in a hushed voice, bringing the door back closed. "Maybe you didn't know that. But I did. Back during the war and the flu and all. After . . ."

Her words trailed. Jesse didn't know what to say.

"I wanted to call her Grace," she said. She put her hand across her chest as if in allegiance, and she held it there with her eyes closed for a while and then opened them and went on. "I let Daniel name her Edith, of course, after your mother; but in my heart, she's Grace. That's alright, isn't it? To call her that? What difference does it make what I imagine her as? What difference does any of it make?"

"You can call her whatever you like," Jesse said, and he'd meant it to be comforting, but the tone came out strange.

She turned away and was quiet for a time and when she turned back there were tears in her eyes, but her jaw was tight and she would not let them fall.

"I will not bury another child, Jesse. I will not say another prayer. I will not beg Him for mercy again. Not after all He took from me. Do you understand? The mill is closed. The hogs are diseased. And all it would take is for her to get one fever, one bout of the flu. I know you and me—I know we don't love each other. Not in that way. I know it. But you're my husband. I'm asking, as your wife, if you'll do this."

"I'm not gonna turn bootlegger just because money's hard to come by," he told her. "I can find work."

"Where? Where can you find it?" she challenged. "There's no more bonus bonds coming, Jesse. Your war buddies are getting ready to march on Washington, and we know how that's gonna go."

Jesse shook his head.

"Think of Danny," she said, then hesitated, pushing the guilt away. "Sarah is all that's left of him. She's your family. Whatever you promised yourself, whatever you swore, go back on it. Do this now and make your peace after. Even if it means—"

"Get inside," he told her. "Now."

He heard the low thrum of the coupe's engine as it passed along the logging road and he heard it lessen, slowing at the turn and revving up again, and now he could see the headlamps at the top of the trail, gutting the black night as the car navigated the slow passage down through the pines.

He stepped inside the house and pulled the deer rifle from its hooks above the door frame.

"Keep it closed," he told Eliza and nodded and shut the door.

He flipped up the lever on the gun and pulled back and looked in the chamber and then slid it back into place. He was trembling. His breath unsteady.

The lights grew brighter as the coupe jostled across the yard and up toward the porch. The car stopped and the engine idled and Jesse held one hand up against the bright beams, and there the scene became frozen for a time. He steadied his breath. Took inventory. The weight of the rifle. The long pale bars of light falling across the porch behind him, and his shadow among them. The door opened and Yancy Greaves stepped out. Jesse could barely see him in the dark.

"Don't shoot, Cole," he said, chuckling. "Just bringing something by for you."

Yancy opened the back door and struggled to haul something heavy out of the seat.

"Squirrel was worried you weren't gonna take him seriously," Yancy said, grunting. "He hoped this might help convince you not to make that mistake."

Jesse heard something thud onto the ground and then the doors closed one after the other and the car backed up in the yard and turned around and a minute later was gone from sight.

Eliza came back onto the porch and Jesse looked at her and unhooked the lantern and took it with him down the steps and across the yard. He could see the body before the light was on it and he thought it might be Hollis, but it wasn't. He held the lantern out of front of him and passed it over Max Doughtry's body like some sort of ritual blessing and stood there a while without saying anything.

When he came back up to the porch, he told Eliza, and she nodded her head.

"They're seeing if you'll go to the law with this," she said. "They're making you choose right here, right now."

"They are," Jesse nodded.

"Well?" she asked, expectant.

Jesse was a long time standing.

"I'll stay here," he said at last, "in case any more trouble shows up. You go fetch Hollis from Old Moss's place. Two shovels are better than one."

She started down the trail then stopped and turned back.

"Thank you, Jesse," she said and then went on.

He waited until she was out of sight and went around to the rain barrel and loosed the spigot and splashed a trickling of near-frozen water onto his face and shuddered.

He could hear the church bells ringing in that far-off country. Not a memory—but a part of himself still there to hear it strike.

27

Cigar smoke spired, twirling through the lantern light, and drifted up toward the black of the ceiling. Squirrel leaned back in his chair and shadows covered his face so that when he exhaled, the smoke seemed to materialize from out of the dark.

"You gonna earn your pay this week, Deputy?" He asked the man sitting across from him.

"Shoot, I might be in line for a raise."

The speak was crowded with men of means and men of muck alike, and the sound of music and the sound of loud drunk voices, and it all sounded like money to Squirrel.

"Let's hear it then," he said.

"Zev Blakewell," the deputy told him, leaning forward over the table.

"Am I supposed to have heard of him?"

"He wouldn't be very good at his job if you had."

"What's his job?"

"Fixer."

"Fixer."

"That's right. Pure muscle for them that can afford the service. Railroads before the war. Oil companies after. There's reason to believe he

was behind all that trouble outside of Houston a few years back. De-
veloper come in wanting to buy out some little piece of the swamp, but
there was a handful of coonasses down there who wouldn't sell. Then
all of a sudden . . . You know the rest."

Squirrel nodded.

"Still nary a body one's been found," he said.

"That's right. But there were others, locals in the area, who said they
saw our man down there in the thick of it."

"How'd they know it was him?"

"He ain't hard to miss."

"For fuck's sake, boy, I'm tired of playing twenty questions. Just tell
me. Speak."

"He wears a black mask. A prosthetic. Like all them other poor bastards with holes in their face after the war."

The deputy drank and nodded at a woman as she passed by and
smiled.

"Blakewell was a marine," he said. "He was with Lloyd Williams's
outfit at Belleau Wood, charging through one of them godforsaken wheat
fields with German machine guns spraying every which way. Blakewell
caught a string of bullets in the jaw. Pretty well blew the bottom half
of his face off. If that weren't enough, a mortar round went and landed
not five feet from him. Should've killed him stone dead right then
and there."

"Would that it had've," Squirrel mumbled.

"I talked to a fella I shake dominoes with every now and again,"
the deputy went on. "Said he had a cousin up in the panhandle who'd
served with Blakewell. Said when the mortar hit, his cousin swore he
seen the man's soul leave his body. Now, I ain't much for voodoo and
the like, but—"

"Get on with it," Squirrel said, unamused.

"Alright. Well, he was sent to medical in Amsterdam, and that's
where the official record runs dry. He was in the military for another
six or seven years, but nobody knows what he was doing or where he
was at. Everything's classified or redacted. And most of the oil company

stuff is hearsay. But it all lines up. Man in a black mask shows up, folks get hurt. Property gets damaged. Livestock and livelihoods under the gun. And always some corporate interest on the back end."

"A fixer," Squirrel repeated. "For some heavy hitters."

"The heaviest."

Squirrel sucked his teeth and looked thoughtful at the drifting smoke.

"I can't tell you who he's working for," the deputy said. "Not yet, anyhow. Could be that he's out on his own."

"I already know who hired him," Squirrel said, still lost in thought.

"Oh," the deputy said, confused. He drank again and wiped his mouth with the back of his sleeve. "You sure it's alright if folks see us in here talking?"

"What I don't know yet, is how the Ranger fits into all this."

The deputy looked around the low-lit room and tried to find the girl who'd smiled at him.

"You think they're working with each other?" he asked.

"That's what you're supposed to tell me."

"Well, it's a hell of a coincidence, both showing up at the same time," the deputy said. "I'll give you that. But the Ranger don't seem like the type."

"What type does he seem like?"

"I don't know, something awful," the deputy shook his head in disgust. "Like righteous, maybe."

Squirrel let go of a slight smile.

"Fair enough," he said. "But keep an eye on him anyway."

"Yes sir."

"And nobody in here can say they saw you, because then they'd have to say they were in here too," Squirrel told him. "And how could that be, when nobody's ever been in here in their life?"

The deputy nodded and finished his drink.

"Is that dark-haired gal working?" he asked.

"Who, Laura? She's pouring drinks."

"I meant—"

"I know what you meant. Here's your twenty dollars," Squirrel said, sliding two ten-dollar bills across the table, then pulling one back. He poured from his personal bottle and filled the man's empty glass. "I'll send her over."

The deputy raised the glass.

28

A gray dawn, and the sun cloaked in such darkness that the day appeared only a lesser shade of night. The hoarfrost clung to winter pastures, and rimes of ice outlined fences and branches and shaded tracts of road. Jesse sat the porch with Hollis and Old Moss and drank coffee, their shovels behind them on the boards.

The ground was cold and hard, but they built fires to soften the soil and they buried Doughtry in a shallow grave and vowed to never speak of it and gave thanks he had no family.

"You boys ought to just kill them bastards," Moss said.

"Shit," Hollis scoffed.

"What?"

"It ain't that simple, old man."

"Sure it is."

"We ain't killing nobody," Jesse told them both. "But we are gonna have to work for the Fenleys. At least for a while. Until I can figure something else out."

"And if somebody's waiting in the road with a Thompson?"

"Well, we just turn right on around and drive the other direction."

Old Moss shook his head and spit.

"Things used to be different when your daddies and granddaddies was growing up around here," he said. "Somebody like the Fenleys tried to come in, they wouldn't have never got a foothold. You hear me? Not so much as an ill word spoke and they would've been dealt with. Them was the old ways."

Moss reached into his boot and fished his hand around.

"I never did care for Max Doughtry, but he was always good for a nip," he said, pulling out a flask and jostling it in front of them before pouring the contents into his coffee.

"You stole whiskey off a dead man?" Hollis asked.

"He ain't gonna miss it none."

"Come on, Hollis. We'd best go see the Fenleys before they come looking for us."

"I'll walk with ye," the old man said. "Hadn't heard them old waddies talking at the exchange in a few weeks. Better go on in there and see about the news."

They went together, the three of them.

They made town by midmorning and Jesse and Hollis went into the insurance office and Moss watched them and then went on.

They walked in and there was a little lobby with two chairs and an oddities table between them that held a stack of pamphlets and a bowl of hard candies. The man selling insurance leaned on the other side of a short counter that came out from the back wall. The small room smelled like kerosene and lilac.

"They ain't open yet," the man said, judging that they were not in the market for a policy. He was hunched over a book with a jar of glue next to him.

"They are now," Jesse said.

"You're Jesse Cole," the man said, and it wasn't a question.

"Far as I know."

"I'm Dizzy. Dizzy Alderman. You probably don't remember me but—"

"I remember you," Jesse said, flat.

"Oh. Alright. Well, they said you'd be coming by. Go on back."

Jesse waited a few seconds for his eyes to adjust to the lack of light. When they did, he saw Frog and Squirrel staring at him from the corner booth.

He nudged Hollis.

They crossed the room and sat and Squirrel motioned for the barkeep and held up four fingers.

The man, who looked somewhat familiar to Jesse, hurried to the table and set a bottle and four glasses in front of them. He began to pour the first glass, but Squirrel shooed him away, taking the bottle himself instead.

There were empty glasses on the tables and bottles scattered on the floor. Cigarette butts overflowed the ashtrays.

"Looks like y'all had a hell of a party last night," Hollis said, grinning.

Squirrel ignored him.

"Welcome, Cole," he said, pouring, "to your first day on the job."

"What do you call that little adventure we already went on?" Jesse asked.

"A trial run. Drink up."

All but Jesse drank.

"I want every dollar you promised me," Jesse said. "And I want it up front."

Squirrel brought a canvas duffel from under the table and pitched it onto the seat next to Jesse, who didn't bother looking down.

"And how long until my debt is clear and I start getting paid," Hollis added, quickly finishing his drink and reaching for the bottle.

Squirrel jerked the whiskey out of his reach.

"You don't," he said to Hollis. "You're done."

"Done?"

"You owed us money. You made a run. More importantly you brought us Cole, here. Consider your debt paid and your drink on the house. Now get out."

"Hold on a minute. We're a team, me and Jesse. You can't just cut me loose."

"Is that right?" Squirrel asked, looking at Jesse.

"I only came to you to help him out, Squirrel," Jesse answered. "You know that."

"And now he's been helped. You have my word. But what about you?" Squirrel raised his eyebrows. "I asked around. I know you owe the bank. I know you got people to take care of. And we both know the mill ain't coming back anytime soon."

Jesse swirled his drink and watched it rock against the sides of the glass like a caged ocean. Trapped and angry.

"Get out of here, Hollis," he said, barely audible, barely a whisper.

"What? C'mon now, Jesse, we're partners."

"It's for your own good," Jesse told him. "I'll catch up with you soon. Just get out."

"How sweet," Frog said.

Hollis was dumbstruck, but he didn't argue further, retreating to the wall, where he slid it a few feet open and squeezed through.

"You'll take the speaks and private orders between here and Rocky Ridge Road," Squirrel said, using his finger to trace the empty table like an invisible map. "Yancy and the Schaffers handle everything west of that. We got two or three decent still hands out at the farm. Few more folks around, here and there. Never want to have it all in the same place. But you don't need to worry about all that. Your job will be to pick up the crates, deliver them, and collect."

"And get shot at," Jesse added.

"And get paid," Frog growled.

"We pay granny fees to the local law," Squirrel interjected. "Occasionally feds come through, but they've seemed to dry up lately. It's only this new bunch that's a threat."

"You know who they are? Who's backing their play?"

"You ask a lot of questions, Cole," Frog said, leaning forward.

"You just hadn't took to me yet, is all," Jesse deadpanned.

"Easy, Brother," Squirrel told Frog and then turned back to Jesse. "You'll have to forgive him, Cole. He's got more reason than most to want you as far away as possible."

Frog stood, angry, and swiped the bottle from the table and stalked off into another corner of the dark room.

"What reason is that?" Jesse asked.

"Here's the keys to the coupe out front," Squirrel said. "Consider yourself orientated."

He slid over the keys and a piece of paper.

"What's this?" Jesse picked up the paper and looked at the names and addresses.

"Your first round of stops," Squirrel said, finishing his drink. He watched Jesse's eyes as the recognition settled in them. "And the reason my brother always looks like he's planning out places to bury you."

Jesse's eyes lingered on the last address.

"Stick to business," Squirrel said. "My brother is a jealous man."

Before Jesse could respond, Yancy Greaves slipped through the false wall and came in quick strides to the booth. He looked at Squirrel and then at Jesse. He bent and whispered in Squirrel's ear. If the news was upsetting, Squirrel didn't show it. His face stayed absent of any emotion. His eyes stayed fixed on Jesse.

Yancy straightened and waited for a response.

"Just now?" Squirrel asked, calm. Almost bored.

"Yes sir."

"Alright. Call a meeting for tonight. Right here," Squirrel said. "You too, Cole. You're a part of this now."

And so he was.

As Jesse left the building with the canvas bag slung over his shoulder, he wondered if the last ten years had just been a chance to catch his breath. Despite all his vows to the contrary, Jesse found himself again in the middle of a violent conflict between warring parties. And he thought perhaps Hollis was right, that everything should remind him of war because war is everywhere at once and for all time.

Yet war wasn't the only thing from his past that he would be forced to reckon with. He looked at the address again and climbed into the car.

29

Amon woke expecting to find his father, but instead it was Cora who had touched his shoulder. The sun was already up.

It had been well after midnight when Davis dropped him at home, and what sleep he had managed was wholly inhabited by dreams and within them were dreams that ran deeper still. Layers of imaginings, one below the other, in an endless descension of subconscious conjuration. Down and down and down eternal, until there was no light and Amon could not find his way back in the dark.

"I let you sleep," Cora said as he lay there, only his eyes moving. "Seemed like you caught a rough one last night."

"Where's Joseph?" he asked.

"In yonder, in the kitchen. He saved you a bite of sausage and spread some jelly on it. There's no bread left or flour for biscuits. But he's real proud of his breakfast, so make a show of it if you can."

Amon nodded.

She left the room, and he dressed in the natural light and took his gun belt from the side table and put on his hat. His dreams lingered. Gypsies on horseback, galloping through green hills with colorful sashes flowing behind them and bright, shining jewelry that reflected the sun. Phil Werskey drinking coffee and the coffee spilling out from the holes in his chest. Joseph behind a glass wall and Amon screaming for him, over and over. Screaming. Desperate. Dead men in the water and dead fish in the trees. Children throwing a severed head back and forth over a building. "Whoops," Phil said, dabbing at the coffee with a handkerchief. Smiling. "Better clean that up."

Amon shook away the bizarre visions. He walked from the room and stood in the space between the kitchen and the den where the wood stove was ever at its burning.

Joseph was there on a rug nearby the stove. He was still in his undershorts. He wore a white cotton shirt and red child's cowboy hat with white stitching. In his hand was a wooden revolver with a hammer that clicked when you pulled the trigger. The boy felt the vibrations on the floor and looked up at Amon and shot off a few rounds.

"I'm running late for work," Amon said, exaggerated. "But, boy, am I hungry."

He rubbed his stomach and shook his head.

The boy grinned. He scrambled up from the floor and ran to the kitchen. He stood on pointed toes and reached up to the counter and brought down a plate and took it across the room to his father.

Amon looked at the sausage patty with wide eyes. He picked it up and took a great big bite and closed his eyes in satisfaction as he chewed.

"This is a mighty fine breakfast," he said, nodding at Joseph. "But it might not be enough."

He set the plate down and turned toward the boy.

"I might need to eat something else," he said, raising his arms up by his head.

The boy shook his head urgently, but he was smiling.

Amon chased him around the room and grabbed him and pinned him on the small couch and tickled his sides and kissed his cheeks.

"Take care of your mother," he said when they'd finished their game. "And say a prayer for your father."

Davis was waiting at the annex, and when Amon walked in, the deputy handed him a cup of coffee.

"Figured you might need some extra getup after last night."

Amon took the mug and looked at it and looked up at Davis.

"Thank you," he said, unsure. "Where's Boyd?"

"Draggin' ass right behind you," Boyd said, coming in and flopping down in his chair with a great sigh.

"Tied one on last night, did you?" Davis chided him.

"Conducting a personal investigation," Boyd said, grinning.

"Investigating how drunk you could get," Davis said. "I guess you done heard about the Neck."

"Yeah, I heard. I imagine Garver and the rest of 'em just want us to stay out of it."

"Tends to be the case," Davis concurred.

"Colston Garver told us who set the fire," Amon interrupted. "He said it was the Fenleys."

Boyd looked confused.

"Y'all went out there?" he asked, frowning.

"You ain't the only one had a big night," Davis said.

"Y'all good buddies now or something?" Boyd asked.

"And Garver didn't say it was the Fenleys, Amon. He just said they know who done it."

"*Amon* he calls him," Boyd said.

"Well, either way. It's past time I had a talk with the men I'm here for," Amon said. "Deputy Davis, care to drive?"

Davis nodded and the two of them headed out.

"There they go," Boyd called after them. "Laurel and Hardy."

Davis drove.

Amon rode with one arm propped against the door and the other hand resting on his pistol.

North of town they turned onto the logging road that cut through the hollow.

They drove on into the winterscaped country.

Whitebark branches, bare to the world, threshing against the gray sky with every whimper of wind come down from the north—every cold gust that passed across the field and went muffled into the dense pines that lined the forest in scattered rows. Tree line black in the morning mist. Crows, buzzards, and the like circling high above the dead and soon-to-die. Fallen stalks of dead sprangle grass, brown and bent in some seasonal sorrow.

Amon noticed a thin column of smoke coming up from the trees off to his right. Then another. And up ahead on the left, and further up the road.

"They know we're here," Davis said, noting Amon's concern.

"The Fenleys?"

"Everybody. And they want us to know they know," Davis told him, shuddering. "Spooky folks in these hollows."

They left the sedan at the turnoff to the Fenley farm and approached the homestead on foot. The house was set at the rear of the pasture a few hundred yards in, and Amon turned several times to look back at the car as they moved further away.

They came on the house from the southeast and the sun came with them, breaking through the clouds just enough to spotlight a black cat as it leapt from the porch and disappeared under the house.

There was neither noise nor movement within.

They ascended the porch and Davis looked at Amon. Amon nodded, and Davis raised a boot and kicked out and near brought the door off its hinges as it flung open.

"What in the hell are you doing?" Amon asked as he ducked down and drew his pistol.

"You nodded at me," Davis said. "I thought that meant we were going in."

"It meant knock on the door, not blow it in."

Davis shrugged.

"Sheriff's deputy," he called, then added. "And a Texas Ranger too."

No response.

The house was small—three bedrooms, a den, and a kitchen—and it didn't take long to call it empty. Amon stood in the kitchen. There was a pan of bacon on the stovetop. He eyed it, thoughtfully. He took a step and reached his hand over the pan and let it hover there and felt some heat still rising from below.

"Is there water on this property?" he asked. "A creek, maybe?"

"Out back a ways," Davis said.

"Show me."

They walked out of the house and around to the back and entered the woods a quarter mile from the creek. They picked their way through the layer of underbrush and Amon thought he could see a few traces of a path here and there but none of them lasted long.

When at last they reached the creek, there were mud-sculpted footprints and dried ruts near the slope of the bank, but nothing else.

"This here's Buck Creek," Davis said.

"How far does it go down?"

"All the way to the river."

"Well," Amon said. "Let's start walking."

"What?"

"Whiskey's still half water," Amon told him, heading off along the creek.

Once more into the vines and scratching cedar branches, they moved slowly south.

Another long mile and then up a ridge above the creek and they could see down to where the trees opened into a small clearing and there below them was a mangled still site.

When they reached the still, it was in pieces. Copper drums overturned, piping pulled apart, and wooden stands hacked and splintered and piled atop smoldering fires.

"Don't look like this thing's in much shape to make whiskey," Davis said.

"No," Amon crouched down and felt a piece of copper coil and sniffed the air and stood.

He walked further into the woods and stopped on a low ridge and looked down where the trickling creek wound southward and a wooden post was driven into the mud near the water. He slid down the short embankment and traipsed through the sludge and stood at the edge of the creek. There were boot prints all around.

"You think the Fenleys spied us coming?" Davis asked. "Busted up their own still?"

Amon shook his head.

"No," he said. "I think somebody else beat us here."

There were shell casings in the mud and Amon looked back where he'd come and then continued on to the other bank.

"Got something?" Davis called.

There were stalks of broken winter grass and a dead man laying on his side. A few yards away, another body.

"Two dead," Amon said, following what looked to be a blood trail that went back east toward the road. "Looks like someone made it out."

He returned to the creek bed and he and Davis followed the flow of the prints for a while and then turned back.

"Come in from the south," he said. "Went back out the same way."

"Figure it's the same bunch that played hangman and set the Neck to kindling?"

Amon nodded. He looked at Davis.

"I'm gonna need to bring in some more hands for this. That gonna put a bee in your bonnet?"

"Nossir." Davis shook his head, emphatic. "I know I was a prick the other morning. And I'm sorry about it. I just didn't know if I could trust you is all. Meaning no offense. It's just, there sure does seem to be a lot of lawmen nowadays that don't have much count for the law."

Amon studied him. Davis looked sheepish, almost embarrassed.

"I appreciate your saying that, Deputy," Amon told him. "Truly, I do."

"Just wanted you to know I'm on board," Davis said. "You ain't gotta worry about me."

"And Boyd?" Amon asked. "Should we be worried about him?"

Davis considered it.

"He's not much for conversation," he said. "But I imagine he's alright when it counts."

"Good. Because we're fixing to be dead center in the middle of a whiskey war, and we'll need all the help we can get."

30

He was there by midmorning, but it was almost noon before he could bring himself to get out of the car. The old house had changed very little. Smaller, perhaps, than he'd remembered. Though it seemed the world itself had shrunk since his childhood, so he dared not blame the house.

He went slowly up the path. A box elder tree stood naked in the yard, and a sparse brown garden butted against the east side of the house. Jesse took a few steps toward the door and a fat, bushy fox squirrel squawked at him from the edge of the slat-board roof. He stared up at it and the door opened in front of him.

"Don't listen to him," Ada said from the doorway. "He likes to bark, but he ain't got much bite."

Jesse looked at her. He swallowed the flood of memories.

"You got a pet squirrel?" he asked, unsure of what to say. Unsure of anything at all.

"Can't afford dog food. I take what I can get."

"Well."

She had aged everywhere but in her eyes, which burned green, yet she was still every bit the beauty he remembered. Her dark hair fell in waves across her shoulders and her pale skin had been made paler still by the gloom of winter.

"Come inside out of the cold," she told him, and he followed her into the house.

"Crates are there against the wall," she said, pointing. "I'm working on next week's batch, so you'll have to do the loading yourself. Most of this is going out near Stewart's Mill. Squirrel wants you to pick up his sugar while you're out there."

"His sugar?"

"We can't exactly walk into Mott's every morning and ask for all the bags of sugar he's got."

"You get it from the sugar mill."

"You always was a bright one," she said.

He stood just inside the door and watched her move into the kitchen and take up a large pot of corn mash and reposition it on the wooden counter. She felt his stare.

"What?" she asked.

"I didn't know what to expect," he said, and he wanted to say more but didn't.

"Best not to expect anything," she told him. "Least that's the way I see it. Life don't care much for our expectations no way. Hand me that bowl. And try not to dip them fine chin tassels in there."

Jesse's hand went to his beard, and Adaline winked at him.

He picked up a bowl filled with an herbal powder he couldn't place. He passed it to her, moving closer. His body needing to be near hers.

She dumped it into the vat and began stirring.

"What is it?" he asked.

"Orris root," she told him. "From the Dixie Iris in my garden— what I could save before the winter. Keeps things from starting to smell. We ain't all got the acres to hide a still on, so I gotta be careful. Raisins, maybe some apple, that's the smell you want. I only make small batches. Brandy. Some special orders. Still, too much stench in the air, folks might get suspicious."

"Neighbors would turn you in?"

"Not straightaway. But I've done had a couple of fellas try holding it over my head. You know how it goes. Give me a bottle and I won't say nothing. Give me two bottles. Give me something else, maybe."

"What happened?"

"Frog talked to them. Talked pretty loud," she told him. "Had a Texas Ranger come by here the other day. I had to spray so much perfume in the air I thought I might gag on it."

"What'd the Ranger want?" Jesse asked, and he wondered if he was asking questions to keep himself from having to answer any.

"Wanted to know if Frog killed Charlie."

"Did he?"

She looked at him.

"Charlie had plenty of people that wanted him dead."

"Well, I'm sorry about it. About him," Jesse said.

"Yeah," Ada said, thoughtful. "I am too."

She lifted the big pot from the counter and took it to the stove. He saw her forearms strain and the veins in her neck. She brushed past him, and her hair smelled like soap, and he'd thought at first that none of this was real, but he realized now that it was something more. Something hyperreal. As if the last decade had been a strange dream from which he'd only just now come awake.

"I guess I'll have to marry Frog now," she said, and he wondered if she was testing him already. "I mean, if things keep on how they are."

"Is that what you want to do?"

"When have you ever got what you wanted, Jesse Cole?"

He shrugged.

"After a while, *want* don't factor into the way we think," she told him. "It don't even play no part."

She looked at him and he felt afraid. Naked. Like she could see every flaw. Every fear. Everything he wasn't. And worse yet, everything he was.

"I—" he started and then stopped.

"You what?" She asked.

"I didn't know you were back," he lied.

"About two months now," she said. "And I'm glad to be home. But if that's all you're gonna say to me, then you'd best start loading these crates. Squirrel is prickly about staying on schedule."

He began loading the crates. Each trip in from the car, he looked at her, and each time she ignored him. When he was finished, he thought about saying goodbye, but instead said nothing and turned to go.

"Jesse," she said, and he stopped. "I saw you once, a few weeks back. You and your family. Y'all were over at the butcher's and I was across the street."

"Alright," he nodded.

"I got a hundred questions I want to ask you."

"You can ask them," he told her.

She shook her head, and they stood there in the quiet until finally she sighed.

"God, do you remember when we were kids?" she asked.

"Sure, I do," he told her.

"Guess we ain't no more, though, are we?"

He didn't answer and shut the door and stood there on the porch. A few minutes later, she heard the car's engine and let out a long breath and closed her eyes.

31

The car jostled down the rut-strung street and onto the logging road and turned north toward the highway. The afternoon sun was at long last melting away the frost and the forest glimmering gemlike in its light, and all at once there was an orange tint to the country.

He'd thought about her. Days and years. But the seeing is always deeper than the thought. There was some small part of him, buried deep, that twitched—a coma patient moving a toe. The boy he'd been, signaling silently for help.

He drove on.

Jesse traveled to Stewart's Mill a few times a year to sell hogs. Hours each way, with Jesse walking and Cecil drawing the wagon of carcasses, the two of them like a pair of Florentine *becchini*. But now the road flew by as if it were being pulled out from under him, the engine's low-throated whine echoing somewhere off in the trees.

He could see the small town ahead. A few old buildings, the sugar mill, then, to the north, miles of rolling hills and dense forest.

Most of the little shacks were clapboard or sheet metal. A few were red brick. Vines ran down the length of nearly every building Jesse passed. He stopped at a fueling station where a sign hung from the door that read No Fuel.

Inside there was a small mercantile section stocked with automotive odds and ends. Some canned goods in another aisle. There was dust on the shelves and the stocked items had not been touched in months. Years, perhaps.

Jesse studied a porcelain dog, white with black spots and black ears and holes in the top for salt or pepper to come out. He lifted it and turned it over and set it back down in the outline of dirt that had gathered around it on the shelf.

A woman stood behind a counter with a rag over her shoulder like some sort of pioneer town barkeep. Two older men were at a table in the corner playing checkers.

Jesse looked at the woman. She had dark curly hair, cut short. She was tall.

"Ma'am," Jesse nodded.

"Sir," she said back, and he couldn't tell if her tone was combative or just loud.

"Is Mr. McAllister about?"

"He's out back," she said, and one of the checker-playing men chuckled.

"I've got some business with him."

The woman shrugged.

"Fine by me," she said. "Good luck."

Jesse was puzzled. He thought to ask the woman if he'd offended her, but instead he turned to go.

"Don't make him walk all the way back there, Lou," one of the men said. "It's too cold for all that."

Jesse stopped.

"Harold McAllister's been dead six years, son," the other man told him.

Jesse walked back to the counter and leaned forward. The woman stood unapologetic and unimpressed.

"Listen," he said, whispering. "I've got a shipment from the Fenleys in Enoch. The paper just says McAllister and gives this address. Help me out, here."

The woman stepped back and shook her head.

"I'll help you," she announced. "First, tell Frog and Squirrel they ought not be using ink and paper. Revenuer gets a hold of you, they get a hold of your little list too. Second, don't assume a woman can't smoke, drink, fight, or fuck just as good as a man."

"I don't think that."

"And yet the thought never crossed your mind that *McAllister* might have tits?"

"I take it you're Harold's daughter?"

"Elouise," she said without extending her hand. "Your money's in the envelope."

She pointed to a thick paper envelope at the end of the counter.

"Alright, well, you think you could do me another favor?" he asked, hesitant. "There's not another address on here, but there's two more names: Dutton and Dawson."

"Dutton," one of the old men raised his hand.

"Dawson," the other one did likewise.

"Your money's in the envelope," they said in tandem.

"Seems like you run a tight ship, Miss Elouise," Jesse told her.

She shrugged and tilted her head to the side and sized him up.

"Things loosen up here in the evenings," she said, switching the towel to her other shoulder and leaning forward on the counter. "You could come by later and find out."

Jesse was trying to process the woman's invitation and the old men were both chuckling when the entire building began to shake. Glassware rattled and the porcelain dog fell from the shelf and shattered.

If it was the apocalypse, it was over quickly. The world came still again in a matter of seconds, and Jesse ran to the window where the old men were staring out.

A few blocks down the street, the sugar mill was engulfed in a thick cloud of smoke and flames were roaring up the side of the structure.

"That was my next stop," Jesse said to no one in particular.

"I don't think they're taking deliveries right this minute," one of the old-timers replied as he hopped a black checker around the board.

32

Amon navigated the car slowly through the slick clay sludge. A mix of red dirt and black soil, pine needles and dead oak leaves. The barbershop apartment was only a few blocks from the annex, but he turned on the heater anyway.

It was still cold in the car when he wheeled it into the alley and turned off the switch. He opened the door and there was sudden movement near the cluster of trash cans. A gray fox with a red belly and white ears moved quickly, hugging the north wall of the alley, a dead rat jostling lifeless from her jowls. Her two kits followed close behind, their fur softer and a lighter shade than the mother.

The heavy clouds rolled beneath the sun like the closing of a great tomb, and the day darkened, and the shadows fell across Amon's face as he climbed up the stairs.

He kissed Cora and hugged his son and went to the bedroom and took off his hat and pulled off his gloves and his gun belt and laid them all on the bed. He walked to the bathroom and stood over the sink and splashed cold water on his face and used his wet hands to slick back his hair. He could spot the gray strands where there had once been brown.

His father's hair had gone gray, then white—like the ghost of the hair. The ghost of the man.

Toward the end of his career his father had taken to working alone. No partners. No backup. He didn't trust anyone to do the job the right way.

Amon saw his father's face there in the mirror. Scowling.

"You think I look like you?" Amon asked his reflection. "How about now?"

Amon hooked a finger in both sides of his mouth and pulled it into an exaggerated smile.

"There's something you've never once done in your whole god-damn life," he said. "I won't make your mistakes. I won't be afraid to ask for help."

"Supper's on the table," Cora called as he came back down the hall.

"I'm gonna run downstairs to Bennett's shop for a minute," he told her.

"You just walked in."

"I know, but I need to make a phone call. See about getting some more men out here. Things are heating up in a way I don't too much care for."

He'd only just come from outside but already it was colder, and him without a coat. He hurried down the stairs and looked briefly across the street at choppy river before ducking into the barbershop to find some warmth.

Mr. Bennett had a mustachioed client smocked up and ready to work on.

"Ranger," he said, nodding and cutting at the air with his scissors like some pretend barber at a sad theme park.

"Mr. Bennett," Amon responded. "Mind if I make a call?"

"You help yourself to anything you want, friend," Bennett told him. "Don't let nobody ever say W.C. Bennett ain't a friend of the law."

Amon wasn't impressed.

"You cut Squirrel Fenley's hair when he comes in here, don't you?" he asked.

Before Bennett could respond, the man with the mustache started laughing.

"Don't let nobody ever say W.C. Bennett ain't a friend of the dollar," the man mocked. "No matter where it come from."

They both looked to the barber to see his response, but Bennett shrugged it off.

"Hair grows on the just and the unjust alike," he said.

Amon went to the little room in the back of the shop where the phone was mounted and dialed the operator, who put him through to Wolfe.

"Somebody is moving in on the Fenley brothers," Amon said, glancing over his shoulder. "Deputies here say it's a man named Blakewell. Mercenary of sorts. And it's getting bad. Whole communities are burning. Mills exploding. Men hanging dead in the trees. And, all due respect to the local law, they don't have the manpower or the experience to even approach something like this, let alone put a stop to it. And that's not considering they may be in on the hand."

"Ranger Atkins," Wolfe said his name and followed it with a deep breath. "There's a depression on, in case you haven't been made aware. Oil town riots all over the state. Race relations as bad as they've been since Billy Yank freed the slaves. We are spread thin as it is. Your request for additional resources or, rather, additional men is beyond what I am willing or able to provide. This is an election year. I need my men where voters will see them, not hidden in some backwoods outhouse."

"Sir, there are fifty or so people who have been made homeless in the middle of winter. That in itself is a humanitarian crisis."

"Those are fifty colored people, are they not?"

Amon was quiet.

"And coloreds don't vote," Wolfe went on. "Or are discouraged from voting, by the hillbilly ilk they continue to live among. Besides, the reports say the negro community of Revrag has joined now with those in Reklaw. No one is freezing to death in the streets, despite your hysterics."

Amon was near shaking. He gripped the receiver so fiercely it dug into the skin on his palm.

"Sir," he said, steadying himself. "The murder of Charlie Cooper cannot be a priority at this point. There is little evidence, less cooperation, and a much more serious and imminent threat here."

"If you're asking to be relieved of your duty, I'm happy to oblige," Wolfe threatened. "If not, stick to your purview, Ranger. Use the resources you have."

Amon did his best not to slam the receiver back into place, but Bennett still gave him a suspicious look as he walked back through the front of the shop.

"Everything alright back there, Ranger?" the barber asked, holding up his scissors and comb on either side of his client's head. "Last time I rattled down a telephone thataway there was a gal on the other end who'd up and decided she was better off with some politician from Redtown."

Bennett was working on an undercut for the mustached man who tilted his head at the barber's admission.

"Have you heard the one about the politician in hell?" the man asked.

"I believe I have, but tell it again," the barber said. "Have you heard it, Ranger?"

"I appreciate you letting me make a call," Amon was saying, but the man had already begun.

"So, there's this politician who dies and goes to the pearly gates," the man started.

"How'd he die?" Bennett asked.

"What?"

"What happened to the politician for him to die?"

"Shit, I don't know. It don't matter how he died. He's dead. I thought you heard this one?" the man said, then fell back into the telling. "Anyhow, he's at the pearly gates, and Saint Pete says, 'Alright, haas, we're gonna give you the choice of where to go, but before you decide, you've gotta spend at least an hour down in hell.' Well, the politician is scared out of his mind, but they send him on down to hell and when he gets there all he sees is the softest green grass hills, white sandy beaches, and most beautiful women. There's folks playing baseball, playing music, eating the finest foods, and drinking the finest wine."

Bennett started to laugh.

"I do remember this one," he said, and the man looked annoyed. "But go on and tell it so the Ranger can hear."

"So, this politician has the best hour of his whole life. He don't even want to leave to go back to Saint Peter, but he does and he tells him, 'Bud, send me to hell, there ain't nothing that could possibly top it.' So, Saint Peter snaps his fingers and the politician wakes up in the middle of an inferno—nothing but fire and people burning and demons dancing around. And the old boy says, 'What's going on here, this ain't what it was supposed to be like.' And the devil himself comes up and says, 'Yeah, well, earlier we was just campaigning—now we've done been elected.'"

The two men were wheezing with laughter and Amon gave them a smile and nod.

"What about the congressman and the pope?" Bennett asked, catching his breath. "Have y'all heard that—"

There was a gunshot so loud and so close that Amon reached for his pistol to return fire, but it wasn't there. He'd taken off his gun belt upstairs.

No.

Bennett jerked with the scissors in his hand.

"Where'd that come from?" he asked.

The mustached man had a peculiar look on his face. He reached up and touched his neck.

"Lord God," he gasped. "I been shot."

"You ain't been shot," Bennett told him, showing him the scissors. "You been poked by a pair of snippers. Barely broke the skin."

They both looked over to where Amon had been standing, but the Ranger was gone, and the door was swinging closed.

Amon bounded up the steps, taking them three at a time. He burst through the door to the apartment and scanned the den and the kitchen and, seeing no one, he ran to the bedroom.

Cora was there, on the far edge of the bed, sitting with her back to the door. She was rocking and crying and cradling Joseph.

"No," was all Amon could say.

His legs turned to wobbling, and he leaned against the wall. Cora turned at the noise, and Joseph slid from her lap and walked over to

Amon to inspect what might be wrong. Amon gasped. As suddenly as his breath had been taken, it was rightly restored.

"Joseph," he said and touched the boy's face.

"It went into the ceiling," Cora said, wiping the wet from under her eyes. "I wasn't watching him. He—it went into the ceiling."

Amon moved quickly to the other side of the bed and picked up the revolver and emptied the cylinder of the remaining bullets. The barrel was still hot. He took the empty gun and holstered it and put the gun belt around his waist and fastened it with such sincerity he half believed he might never remove it again.

Joseph came and stood nearby and made a fist and circled it in front of his chest.

"I know," Amon nodded. "Me too."

33

Jesse stopped the car in front of the insurance office then thought better of it. He drove two blocks down the street and parked in the alley and the car backfired when he cut the engine and the sound muffled what he thought might have been a gunshot. He froze, his hand still on the switch. He listened. Nothing.

When he walked out to the street there was no commotion. No one waving a gun. No one running scared. Still, he looked over his shoulder several times as he made his way up the thoroughfare.

He slipped inside the darkened insurance office and through the passageway to the speak.

The Fenleys were holding court in their usual booth and Yancy was there with the Schaffers and two other men and Jesse pulled up a chair without invitation.

Frog glared at him.

"How'd you get along, Cole?" Yancy asked. "I can just about smell the burnt sugar on your coat."

Jesse passed him the envelope and Yancy tossed it onto a pile of others between himself and Squirrel.

All were quiet.

Squirrel took the shot of whiskey in front of him and closed his eyes for a few extra beats and then addressed them.

"Blakewell and his boys busted up our still this morning," he said. "Killed two men. Roughed up another pretty good. Y'all already know what else they've been up to. The Neck. The sugar mill. Thomas and Dotzel. They're strong-arming our buyers, daring us to respond."

"So let's hit the bastards," Hank Schaffer said.

"We will," Squirrel nodded. "But first thing is to bring on more hands. To that end, Jesse Cole has come aboard. Horace and Nick Clayton too."

Squirrel pointed to the two men at the table who Jesse recognized from veterans meetings years ago.

"What about Hollis Wentworth?" Yancy asked.

"What about him?" Squirrel asked, angered by the interruption.

"We need everybody we can get, don't we?"

Squirrel sighed but seemed to be thinking it over.

"Hollis ain't cut out for this," Jesse said, jumping in quickly. "He ain't got the brains or the balls. He's as liable to shoot one of us on accident as he is to be any sort of help."

"There you have it," Squirrel said, nodding at Jesse. "Now, we got storehouses and inventory to last us a short while. But short ain't long. We need to get that still rebuilt first thing. Frog's going down to Beaumont for a few days on a supply run. He'll be back with plenty of sugar and corn. Your job will be to make sure everything is set up and ready at the new still site when he gets back."

Heads nodded around the table.

"As for hitting back," Squirrel added. "I'm gonna go on a little hunt."

"Alone?" Eli asked.

"I kill Blakewell," Squirrel said, "and whoever he's working for will slink away into the darkness."

"And you don't know who that is?" Jesse asked. "The person he's working for?"

Squirrel looked at him and Jesse tried to get a read.

"All I know is Blakewell is a problem. And I'm going to solve him."

"And the Ranger?" Eli asked. "What about him?"

"Until we're sure if he's part of this, he's off limits," Squirrel said. "Kill a Texas Ranger and every lawman in the state will have an excuse to come flooding into the county. We don't need any help finding trouble right now."

Again a round of nods.

"Alright, so where's the new site?" Hank asked.

Squirrel nodded at Yancy.

"The quarry," Yancy said.

"The quarry?" Hank was surprised. "A little out in the open, ain't it?"

"No," Jesse shook his head. "He means the caves."

"That's right, Cole," Yancy was grinning. "There's a half dozen. Few of 'em go nearly a mile deep. And a freshwater spring right there to siphon from."

"A fella can see a long way down that old rock-hauling road too," Horace Clayton added. "From a military standpoint, it'd take one hell of an effort for anybody to sneak up on you, unless they were to take the creek trail all the way from the river."

"From a military standpoint," Jesse said. "It seems like a good place to get pinned in."

"Only if there's somebody left to do the pinning, Cole," Squirrel said, and with that the meeting was over and the drinking began.

Jesse was on his way out when Horace Clayton called him over.

"Sit and have a drink with me, Cole," Horace said.

Jesse sat in a red upholstered chair with mahogany feet.

Horace poured a half glass of bourbon and offered it to Jesse.

"I don't drink much anymore," Jesse told him, but accepted the glass all the same.

"Good on you," Horace said, sincere. "I can't hardly shut my eyes without it. For a while there I thought me and Nicky might be keeping these boys in business all on our own."

"That much, huh?"

"I'll cork the whole thing for good just as soon as somebody shows me something better," Horace submitted while raising his glass. "Makes a scared man brave and a smart man stupid."

"You want to be stupid?"

"Lord yes. Hadn't you seen how happy all these dumb bastards are? They don't know the first thing about any of it. 'We won, didn't we?' 'Couldn't be that bad.'"

Horace shook his head and drank.

"I guess there were some good things though, yeah?" he asked. "Three square meals and free cigarettes don't sound too bad right now, the way things are going."

Jesse took down the bourbon in his glass and shrugged.

"Not worth it," he said.

"Well, maybe not. But that's what we're doing here, ain't it?"

Before Jesse could answer, Horace's brother, Nick, came up and clapped them both on the back.

"Y'all get started without me?" he asked.

"Little bit," Horace said. "We ain't knee-walking, but we've tipped a few back. Let's have another."

"Another," Nick repeated.

"Ain't nothing for a stepper, huh?"

"You said it."

Hank and Eli Schaffer joined them. The bottles began to fall away. Twice Jesse stood to leave but twice he sat back down at the behest of one of the men. Good men with little else to sustain them, he thought, but then he thought the whiskey may be softening the edges of his empathy.

Finally, the party began to break up.

"I'd better walk away before I have to crawl," Hank said. "I want to get out on the town. See if I can't sniff out that little moll likes to hang around the café."

"You keep on and you'll have to make an honest one out of her," Nick said.

"No sir. That's what the money's for. I pay her not to follow me home."

"You don't mind it?"

"What?" Hank asked.

"You know . . ."

"Look, she's looser than ashes in the wind. But that's fine by me. Shit. If I could get paid for it, I would."

"I ain't never thought of it that way," Nick admitted.

"I've seen your pecker, little brother," Horace chimed in. "There ain't no reason for you to think of it at all."

Jesse laughed. The whiskey burned his throat and felt warm in his stomach. Rot gut, Danny had called it.

Jesse was thirteen when his brother dragged him outside after supper. Danny had hidden the bottle under a pile of pine straw and leaves just past the edge of the wood line. He uncovered it and held it up with great care, as if it were an ancient relic not meant to be handled.

"Where'd you get that?" Jesse asked.

"I was hunting a fish trap in Moss's barn and come across it sticking out of a coat the old man just throwed in a corner and about buried under all that shit he's got in there."

"Have you drunk any of it yet?"

"I had a swallow or two there in the barn, but I figured I'd best wait until tonight after Daddy's gone to work and Momma's gone to sleep. Then I'll really get into her."

Jesse looked at the bottle with a sort of wonder. Their parents did not drink alcohol or even allow it in the house. But he'd heard whisper of its powers. And now Danny, by some miraculous happenstance, had the elusive elixir here in his possession.

"Can I smell it?" Jesse asked.

Danny shook his head.

"Just wait until later tonight," his brother said. "You can do a lot more than that."

There was little recollection of the night, but an unmistakable memory of the next day's pain. The combination of the hangover and their father's belt had been ferocious. Whatever magic the bottle held had dissipated, trickling slowly into nausea and a pounding skull.

"Was it worth it?" their father asked, and while Jesse shook his head in shame, Danny had been the one to answer.

"You want the truth, Pa?" his brother laughed and then winced in pain. "I think it might have been. It hurts like hell now, but for a while there I don't believe there was anything better. Could be that's a trade I'm willing to make."

Jesse thought about his brother and put back another shot of the Fenley's whiskey and then left by the false wall and through the darkened insurance office and out into the cold.

He drove the coupe home and killed the switch and climbed out of the car. His head was buzzing, but he didn't mind it. He looked up at the night sky. Clouds upon clouds.

Hidden beyond the atmospheric drapery, that cosmic stage held millions of starlit players ripe for the wishing, but such hopes would be stayed until spring. For the stormy, cloud-drenched winter had so shuttered the lights of the night sky that he wondered if there were any stars left at all—or if they'd abandoned their posts, thousands at a time, moving on to some other more worthy world.

He went inside.

Sarah was asleep in the chair next to the radio. Eliza had covered her in quilts. The broadcast was playing soft string music, and Jesse stood and listened and looked at the girl and then leaned down and clicked the radio off.

He fed the stove and then went to the back bedroom.

He sat on the edge of the bed and the thin metal frame whined under his weight. He took off his boots and unhooked his suspenders in the front and shrugged out of them. He untucked his shirt then paused and took a breath. He twisted in toward the bed and leaned over to where she pretended to sleep. He traced two fingers along her neck and shoulder. He hooked the top of her nightgown and pulled it down until her right breast spilled out. She recoiled. He did the same, slower.

For a minute they were both quiet.

"Sorry," Eliza said, and he believed her. He believed she wished things were different, believed she was truly sorry with how it all turned out.

He rose quietly. He picked up his boots and his clothes and carried them out. He redressed in the dark in the living room and opened the door to the porch and went out.

34

They sat that night at the small kitchen table and Cora drank tea and Amon drank coffee. Joseph was asleep on the couch in the adjacent living room. The stove was the only thing dividing the two areas of the apartment and both man and woman watched the sleeping child from a distance.

"Do you think there's a difference between good luck and a miracle?" Cora asked, keeping her voice low despite the obvious.

"You remember the Coffer twins from back in Fort Worth?" Amon said.

"Sure, I do," she said. "Those two red-headed boys nobody could hardly tell apart. Used to switch places in class. Even on dates, I heard."

"Yeah, well, I imagine it's something like that. Luck and miracles."

They were quiet for a while.

"I called Daddy," she said.

He looked up at her.

"Cora—"

"No, don't 'Cora' me," she told him. "This is no place for our son."

"I can't just leave," he said.

"I'm not asking you to," she said. "But *we're* going."

He looked at her. Wounded.

"I've stayed by your side, Amon," she said. "Every step of the way, I've stayed. But it's too much. You see that, don't you?"

"I know it's getting worse," he told her. "More guns out there now than I've ever seen. And firing more rounds. There's criminals set on breaking the laws, and laws that are creating more criminals. I worry for the future, Cora."

She waited, but there was nothing else.

"Is that it?" she asked. "The world is awful and you have to fix it?"

He was quiet.

She studied his face. The forever frown that began at the corner of his eyes.

"It wasn't any bootlegger or bank robber that could've killed our son, today," she said.

"It's my fault, I shouldn't have left it on—"

"It's not that you left your gun out," she said, imploring him to see. "It's that this is your life. Our life."

"What would you have me do?" he asked.

She waited. Closed her eyes.

"Daddy said whenever you're ready we could go up to McKinney and you could work in his office."

"I can't quit, Cora," he said, and even though she'd expected him to say it, it still hurt to hear.

"Why not?" she asked. "You'd make more. No more worrying about where meals are coming from. We'd be able to put down roots and get our son away from all of this."

He shook his head.

"You don't understand," he said.

"Then make me," she snapped.

He grimaced at the harshness in her tone, but he knew she was right. Somewhere in some far reach of his heart he knew she was right about everything.

"I was five years old when I decided I was gonna be a Ranger," he said. "A.E. Benson had come to my grandfather's funeral. A.E. was probably the most famous lawman in the state at the time, and old men and little kids alike were following him around. All but tugging at his sleeves. After the service he told some stories about my grandfather and some stories about ranging.

He told us that he wanted to go into medicine initially. He spoke Spanish well enough and had practiced what they called 'border-country medicine' since he was a teenager, stitching folks up after a fight or tending a fever or what have you. He said the worst was on Friday nights they'd have these dances in Zapata. They'd always end up in a brawl. Folks stabbed with broken glass or knives. Sometimes somebody shot. He got tired of sewing everybody up, so one Friday he went and bought up all the Chandler's candy tablets he could find—"

"The laxatives?" Cora asked.

Amon smiled and nodded.

"And he went to the barn where they were gonna have this dance and he put them out in little dishes on all the tables. Looked like they were mints or candies or something. Anyway, A.E. said that night nobody got stabbed. They all went home early with something else to do."

"And that made you want to be a Ranger?"

"Not the story," he said, still smiling, but this time at something far away. "Not A.E.'s exploits or his popularity. It was the way my father looked at him, listened to him like, like—I don't know. Like he was happy. Or proud. I can't tell you exactly, I can just tell you that I knew right then."

"And?"

"And what?"

"Did your father ever look at you that way? The way he looked at A.E. Benson?"

Amon shrugged.

"When you were pregnant," he said, "I knew it was a boy. I know how that sounds, but I did. I knew it would be a boy, and I knew I'd be gone his whole life, just like my father had been."

"But you aren't gone," she reminded him.

"No," he said. "I overcorrected. Instead of being away from my family, I'm dragging the two of you with me. Forcing you to live one step above a hobo. And I tell myself it's because of his condition—that I wouldn't want to leave you alone with that burden. But that's not true. It's far more selfish than that. I don't want to feel guilty. To feel like I'm turning into my old man."

"Amon, you're not your father. You—"

"No," he said. "I'm worse. I'm hiding behind my family. Telling myself I have to protect you, when in truth—even if you left today—I wouldn't stop. I couldn't."

His words trailed off. She didn't push him for more. She could see the pain inside him pour out onto his face.

They sat together in the relative silence. The fire in the stove popping and crackling. The wind passing through the alleyway.

After a while, she stood and walked around behind his chair and draped her hand soft across the front of his shoulder. He took it and held it there against him.

"We're leaving," she said, soft. "We'll be gone by the end of the week."

35

There was a slight glow to the night. A soft, sad light cobbled up out of the liverish moon, pulsing there behind reefs of thin, ragged clouds. Ragged twilight. Trees and shadows of trees and night creatures set about their hunting and everything cold. The whole country. Cold.

Jesse stood the porch with his hands in his coat pockets and listened. Birdless song of the night.

A twig snapped. Something shuffling in the trees. There was no light to the porch, but Jesse crouched down anyway. He waited.

More harried leaves, and he could see the shape of a man hunched over at the base of a slender pine. Jesse squinted into the black until his vision became clearer.

"Moss," Jesse hissed. "What'n the hell are you doing out there?"

The man jumped back from the tree and froze and looked up toward the porch.

"Shit fire, Jesse. You scared the hell out of me. I didn't wake y'uns, did I?"

"You better hope not," Jesse said. "Keep your voice down."

"Right. Sorry," Moss said, holding his hand up in apology.

Jesse came off the porch and was walking toward him.

"What are you doing?" Jesse asked again.

"Harvesting," Moss said, grinning. "Follow me home. I'll show ye."

They took the path through the woods and Jesse headed for the old man's cabin, but Moss waved him off.

"Got some critters been staying warm in there," he said, as if it were a normal encumbrance. "The smell ain't too friendly. It's like Gloria done started a hostel. Anyway, I'm making camp in the barn."

Jesse shook his head, but sure enough there were remnants of several fires in the open bay of the barn, and Moss set about making another one.

Jesse took a lantern off its hook and walked around the barn.

There was a wooden board with marble holes. Old blankets. Paperbacks. A shave bowl and a blade. Small mirror on a smaller stand and a wooden ladder up to the loft. The whole place was a mix of hay and mud and sawed trimmings.

"I've knowed you since you was a baby," Moss said, and Jesse turned back toward the new fire.

"You have."

"And I ain't one to go telling folks what they ought to do."

"You're not."

"Alright, then I want you to know I'm serious when I say messing with them Fenley boys," Moss shook his head. "It ain't something I'd advise."

"Yeah, well, you can only decide between what's there in front of you. Money's gotta come from somewhere."

"Money," the old man spit angry into the dirt as if he would rid himself of such a word. "Paper checks and paper bills."

They were quiet for a while.

Jesse watched the fire. Moved closer to it.

The crackling of the pine logs and the haze of smoke drifting up to the night sky, proposing itself to the firmament, and there bearing witness to the cascading of stars as they fell, one by one abandoning the empyrean from which they were first forged in that time beyond all time.

"I seen Ada today," he said.

Moss frowned.

"Did you, now?" he asked.

Jesse nodded.

"Stood right there in her momma's old house like not a thing had changed," he said.

"Do you know what Frog Fenley would do if he caught you thinking what you're thinking?" Moss asked.

"That ain't what I'm thinking."

"Sure you are. And thoughts lead to actions. And actions lead to getting caught. You think you could get the drop on him. You're wrong. Maybe you just question it. A coin flip, you think. Well, I'd say to ask Charlie Cooper, but you can't, and there's your answer."

"I appreciate the concern," Jesse said. "I'd better get back. Eliza wakes up and me gone, she'll spin herself up into a funnel cloud."

The old man crouched curious over his fire and studied the writhing flames and tilted his head to either side as if he'd have the world burn straighter.

"Let me at least feed you some," he said.

He went again into the darkness, or to the edge of darkness, and returned with an iron pan he held with brown scraps of a cloth that had once been white.

He pushed the pan halfway into the fire and used it to drag a cluster of coals just separate from the main body, and the pan rested there on the glowing embers.

He then produced from the depths of his tattered coat another strip of cloth, this one folded around a troop of oyster mushrooms. He unwrapped the cloth and held the fungi beneath his nose and smelled.

"Harvesting," Jesse said.

The mushrooms looked plastic to him, like white prop flowers that might be worn by jugglers under the big top.

"*Pleurotus ostreatus*," Moss told him.

He pulled out a pocketknife and opened it and dumped the mushrooms onto the stump and knelt next to the stump in ritual. He began to make small subtractions from the mushrooms.

"Jest cut off some of these nasty bits," he narrated, "and we'll have us a good old feast is what we'll do."

When each piece had been trimmed to his liking, he threw it in the pan before him and the mushrooms sizzled and smoked and the old man nodded vigorously and let go strange, gleeful giggles.

"A good old feast," he repeated, then he looked across the fire at his guest. "You fancy a drink of something, Jesse?"

"I don't see the sense in stopping now," he said.

Back into the boundless coat and out Moss came with a pint bottle and tossed it over the flames and into Jesse's lap.

"Get ye a nip. Warms the blood. Makes the food taste better."

Jesse took a pull, then swirled the bottle and took another.

"Moss, my old friend," Jesse said. "I'm fixing to be right back in the middle of it. And this time, I do believe my luck is gonna run out."

"I didn't never know you to have much luck to begin with, Jesse," Moss said. "You always struck me as the sort of fella who would cut cards and draw a two."

Jesse laughed at this, and it felt good to laugh.

"Yeah, well, you may be right," he said. "I guess I thought not dying young had been good thing. Now I'm not so sure."

"Ah, it ain't that bad," Moss said.

"What ain't?"

"The world."

"I used to think that too. Hell, I always figured the world for a good place," he said, "until I got out in it."

"It all depends on where ye standing," Moss said. "The same river that goes through cities goes through places nobody's ever took a piss in. Think about it that way, and the wonder of life'll never be far from ye."

Jesse shook his head.

"I don't believe that," he said. "Maybe in the old grandfather times. But there ain't nothing left these days that hasn't been pissed on."

"You sound like Danny boy, now," Moss told him.

"Yeah?"

"Your brother loved so deeply there ought to be another name for it.

He cared so much for this place and the people in it. And over time I think that broke him. I think it was all just too much. He kept his heart open to anything and anyone, but that meant letting in all the bad too."

"He said something like that to me once," Jesse nodded. "He said the world was a shit place full of shit people, and that was all the more reason to love it. I didn't understand it back then. Maybe I still don't. It seems like my whole life I've only ever loved one thing."

He tossed the bottle back to Moss.

"You seen her?" Jesse asked him.

"Who?"

"You know who."

The old man sighed.

"Yeah. I seen her in town here not too long ago," he said and leaned over and spit again. "Don't look as good as she used to, you ask me."

"Yes she does," Jesse said.

Moss nodded.

"I know it," he said.

Jesse stood and, as he did, he felt his head swimming and it felt nice. He told Moss goodnight and started back toward the trail.

"Say, Jesse Cole," the old man called just as Jesse reached the edge of the firelight.

Jesse stopped. He gave a partial turn toward the fire so that half of him stayed shadowed, the other half coppered by the glow of the flames.

"If the world was a good place," Moss said, "it wouldn't need good men."

36

1918

*They gather under the ceiling of a two-story building with partial walls.
There is rubble all about them. Bodies of soldiers and bodies of villagers.
Women and children.*

 "Anyone here a captain? A lieutenant?"

 "I'm a sergeant."

 "Alright. You have command."

 "Germans retreated east. Abandoned the village."

 *"We'll pursue until we can see the back of their lines. Then we'll make
camp and wait on the rest of the goddamn army to catch up."*

 "Should we check the town?" Jesse asks.

 "For what?" the sergeant replies.

 "I don't know. People, I guess."

 *"If they survived, they don't need us. If they didn't, they need us even
less. Let's get out of this shithole."*

 *They come into the road in a loose double-file march. They head
east through the town and through the destruction and there are buildings collapsed but laundry still hanging, toppled wells with buckets
stacked neatly beside them. It's as if the village was being constructed in a*

dream and the dreamer awoke too quickly, startled, and left his creation in ruins.

"Stop," Jesse says.

He leaves the road and moves toward a small shop that still has a door. He tries the knob, but the door will not open. There is a hole where a window once was and Jesse climbs through it, punching away glass with the butt of his rifle. The others are shouting at him.

"There's a boy in here," he calls to them. "He's hurt bad."

"Leave him," the sergeant says. "Let's go."

The boy is young. He is small. Ash and dirt cover the shop and cover the boy as he sits with his back against an empty pastry case. His eyes roll in his head and his head rolls on his shoulders. There is a large section of stone ceiling covering his legs and his waist. His shins and his feet stick out from beneath. Jesse looks up and sees the gap in the roof where the s tone fell.

"I need help," Jesse calls.

"We're moving, soldier," the sergeant says. He motions and the men follow. A few look back, but none turn. Only Hollis breaks rank. He shuffles to the empty window and peers inside.

"Help me, Hol," Jesse says, straining to move the stone. The boy is gasping for air, then going still, then gasping again. His feet twitch.

Hollis climbs through and grabs the side opposite Jesse and together they move the great stone and Hollis looks quickly away from the mangled scene beneath. The boy looks down and seems not to register that the mash of skin and bone and blood belong to him. His face shows only curiosity. He mumbles something in French.

"He don't look too good, Jess," Hollis says.

"We'll wait with him."

"What?"

"Until the rest of the boys get here, we'll set right here and wait."

"He's gonna die, Jesse."

"Not alone."

Jesse gives him water from his canteen and the boy chokes on it and grimaces.

"*You don't have to stay,*" *Jesse tells Hollis.* "*You can go on and catch up with that bunch that just lit out.*"

Hollis shakes his head and takes a seat in the rubble next to the boy.

"*If you're staying, I'm staying.*"

37

Amon had the fire going and the coffee on by the time Davis and Boyd arrived at the annex.

"Morning, boys," he said.

Boyd grunted and went for the coffee.

"What's the word from Austin?" Davis asked.

"There's no help coming, so we gotta press the issue," Amon told him. "And I think I know how."

"Let's hear it," Davis said, eager.

"This other bunch that's causing all the trouble—who are they targeting?" Amon asked and then answered his own question. "Fenley allies. Suppliers. Drivers."

"Sure, alright."

"So, we need to find whoever's next. Offer them safe haven if they talk. Testify that the Fenleys murdered Charlie Cooper and we'll protect you. That's our deal."

"What if they don't know anything about the Cooper murder?" Davis asked.

Amon ran his hand across the back of his neck.

"We just have to hope they do," he said. "As openly as Frog and Squirrel have operated, surely somebody knows something."

"And what about us?" Davis asked. "How do we know who's next on Blakewell's list?"

Amon nodded at the question, pacing the boards of the small office.

"Well," he said, "maybe we don't. Maybe we just convince somebody we do."

"The Taggerts," Davis said, epiphanic.

"Yeah?"

"The old man won't talk, but I'd bet the house that his son will."

Amon nodded.

"Let's get after it then."

"Hold on a goddamn minute," Boyd said, interrupting. "I hate to piss all over your very fine parade, but y'all are so caught up in this I think you're missing the bigger picture."

"Which is?" Davis asked.

"Let's say you do find somebody who knows something—somebody who can tie the Fenleys to Charlie Cooper's murder or some other dastardly deed. Let's say you arrest them both. What happens to this place, then? From what I can gather of this other bunch, we'd be making things worse, not better. Fires and bombs and hanging men from trees. That's the side y'all are taking?"

"We're not taking sides," Amon said. "We're eliminating one threat before we move on to the other."

"The Fenleys have been dogging us for years, Boyd," Davis said. "This is our chance to actually jam them up. And somebody must think it's a good idea, or they wouldn't have sent a Ranger down here."

"Yeah, and what happens when they call him back to Tyler or wherever else? Leave us to clean up the mess?"

Amon listened to the two of them go back and forth. Something bothered him, but he couldn't puzzle out what it was. He looked over his notes as the two deputies argued about which criminals to pursue first. *Somebody must think it's a good idea.* He walked to the back of the room near the empty cell and took the phone off the rotary stand and was soon patched through to the Austin office.

"Wolfe," he said. "It's Atkins."

"I already gave you an answer, Ranger."

"No, I've got a different question."

"What is it?" Wolfe asked, ever agitated.

"Where'd this Fenley case come from?" Amon asked. "Who kicked it to us, to the Rangers?"

"Far as I know, the local law, sheriff down there sent it up the pipeline. You know how these small counties are. Strapped for resources, they say. Usually just lazy or dumb, or both."

"Do we have a transcript?"

"We have a case file."

"No, I'm not talking about that. I'm talking about the very first phone call or letter or whatever sent us down this road."

"I'd have to look," Wolfe told him.

"Do that. I'd like to know."

"What's this all about?"

"I don't think they needed a Ranger," Amon said. "I think they *wanted* one."

Amon hung up and walked back to his desk and picked out one of the small field notebooks and shoved it in his pocket and headed for the door.

"Where you going?" Davis asked.

"Taggert's."

"You want me to come?"

"No, I've got another stop to make. Be gone all day. Best you stay here in case the seed I plant in Coy Taggert's ear starts to bloom early."

"Hey, Ranger," Davis said, and Amon stopped and turned back. "Keep your eyes open out there."

Amon nodded and touched his hat and was gone.

38

He'd dreamed of her that night. It was the first time in months, years, that his visions were not filled with whistles and barbed wire and fields covered in thick fogs of mustard gas. Instead, it was only Adaline. They lay on their backs on oversized creek boulders and looked up through the wickerwork stylings of oak and pine, and the cypress accompaniments that stretched out over the water from either side as if they longed to touch. It was the last time he'd held her hand in his and the last memory from some far away life.

He woke without opening his eyes, willing himself to fall back asleep, to find her again in that land of dreams. *I would sleep forever,* he thought. But the muted light of another winter's dawn had broken, and the house was awake, and he knew such a thing could never be. He pulled himself up. He could smell the coffee as he dressed and in time could hear Sarah playing the violin. A sad song.

He walked into the kitchen and poured his coffee and took it and stood before the girl and watched her play. She sat on the blue settee nearest the window and held the instrument out with her left arm, moving the bow across the strings with an intention both urgent and full of care—a delicate demanding. Her eyes were closed, and her face seemed to dance with the melody, leading it on some notes, following on others. She drew from it a music magnificent. Resplendent sounds that played off the walls of the cabin and lingered there like the heat from the stove fire.

He leaned forward, hanging on every stroke of the bow. Sarah had created her atmosphere, and they were both caught within it, breathing her melody. Marveling.

When she was finished, Jesse set his mug down and clapped, and the girl gave a half bow.

"Lord, girl, I thought y'all had turned the radio on," Jesse said. "Where's your momma?"

"Outhouse," Sarah said, pushing past his question and focusing on the admiration. "You think I'm getting good?"

"I'd say you passed up good a few miles back and hadn't bothered to turn around."

"There's a music school in New York for the best players in the world," she said. "You think I'm good enough for that?"

"I think there'd be riots in the hallways if they didn't let you in."

She smiled, and he could see her imagining such a life, far from the mills and mines and hardwood hollows. The smile faded.

"Momma wouldn't let me go though, would she?" The girl asked. "Even if I were to get in."

"Oh, I don't know," he lied.

"Yes you do."

"Well, she loves you. And she worries about you."

"I can't stay here, Jesse. Not for my whole life."

"I know it."

"You could talk to her for me," Sarah told him. "You could make her understand."

"Talk to her about what? New York?"

"About anything. About me going to school with other kids instead of at home. Or about going into town some by myself."

He sipped his coffee to buy time. He could feel something changing in himself. Or maybe, changing back to what he used to be.

"Alright," he said. "I'll talk to her."

"Thank you, Jesse," the girl all but squealed. "Thank you, thank you, thank you."

"I can't promise nothing," he warned her.

"I know," she said, and he stood there staring at her. "What?"

"Nothing," he told her. "I just used to know somebody that wanted to go to New York. A singer."

"Was she good?"

"The best."

"You want to play me one?" she asked him, holding out the instrument.

"Nah, there's no sense in ruining a good thing," he said.

"Who do you think I learned from?" she scoffed. "Why don't you teach me something new?"

Jesse shook his head.

"It's been a long time since there was anything new you could learn from me."

"Please," she asked. "Just one."

He looked at the girl's face and her pleading eyes and there saw such desperation. Such a strange blend of passion and paranoia for the world and for her place in it. As if she was afraid it was all passing her by.

He could not give it to her, the world—its joys and catastrophes and indifference toward each. But he could give her this.

"How about we do one together?" he asked.

He went back up the hallway and returned with his banjo and sat in the chair beside her and began to tune it.

She beamed with happiness. A broad smile, but she wouldn't speak. Wouldn't dare spoil it.

"Bonaparte's Retreat," he said and winked at her and she sat up straight and arched her bow arm and tried to relax her face but she was still smiling.

They were only a few notes in when a car horn sounded outside.

"Stay in here," Jesse said, and the girl's brief euphoria was snatched away.

He went outside and saw the truck in the yard and saw Eliza coming from around back of the cabin. He held his hand up to her.

"It's alright," he said. "Go on inside with Sarah. I'll see what he wants."

As Jesse approached, the truck began to move toward him, and he could see Frog staring through the front windshield, hunched over the steering wheel, and for a second he thought the big man might be aiming to run him down. But Frog turned and made a short loop and brought it again to a stop, this time facing away from the cabin.

Jesse stood by the driver's window and Frog looked at him and shook his head and pointed to the other side of the car. Jesse walked in front of the car and Frog watched him, and when he opened the passenger door, Frog told him to get in and he did.

He closed the door and Frog started down the drive.

He didn't speak until they'd reached the blacktop.

"Went to the quarry before sunup," he said at last. "We could hide the cars back around that big rock face. Set up in the two alcoves. The caves are plenty big enough for everything else."

"So, you think it'll work?" Jesse asked.

"That's what I just said, ain't it?" Frog growled. "My brother wants everything ready to make a hundred-case run when I get back."

"A hundred cases?" Jesse guffawed. "That's impossible."

"If it was, he wouldn't have said it."

"How many still pots is that gonna take?"

"A hundred cases worth," Frog said, flatly. "If my brother says something, we do it. Asking questions is just wasting time."

Frog's giant frame loomed over the steering wheel, and Jesse looked at him and then looked away. Out the window he could see swaths of dark clouds like falling curtains, and somewhere far to the south lightning walked silent along the horizon, but there was no rain.

"Something else," Frog said.

"A trunk full of gold bars?" Jesse said.

"I don't like you, Cole."

"I would've never guessed."

"My brother said we needed you, so here you are," Frog gave him a side-eyed glance. "But I'm telling you right now, if you so much as look at her, it better be me you're thinking about."

"Look at who?" Jesse asked.

"I don't care if you killed the goddamn kaiser hisself," Frog said. "I'll break parts of you that you didn't know could break."

"Is that what you told Charlie Cooper?" Jesse asked.

Frog tightened his grip on the wheel.

"I didn't tell Charlie Cooper a goddamn thing," he said. "He was dead when I got there. Dead when I loaded him into the car and drove him to Enoch. And dead when I dumped his body."

"You don't strike me as someone that cleans up other people's messes," Jesse said.

"We do all sorts of things for the people we love. Ain't that right, Cole?"

Jesse didn't answer.

"I didn't kill Charlie," Frog said. "But I would have. In a heartbeat. Just like I'd kill you."

"I'll keep it mind," Jesse told him.

They continued on in silence until they reached the Taggert spread and Frog stopped the car.

"The old man has a truck waiting on you," Frog ordered. "There's all kind of shit to haul out to the quarry."

Jesse got out and stood just inside the open door.

"You drive safe, Frog," he said. "I can't hardly bear the thought of something bad happening to you."

39

Amon was at the Taggert spread by midmorning. The day dark and darker still. The sun locked away in some clouded tower. He saw the soldier, Jesse Cole, at the turn-in. Cole was driving a heavy-duty pickup and he nodded at Amon and Amon frowned but raised his hand in greeting. Perhaps the Taggerts did not trade exclusively in illegal ventures. Or perhaps there was a reason Cole was hesitant to speak with him at the hotel café.

The mouth of the driveway was narrowed such that the two vehicles were only a few feet from one another. Amon cranked his window down and Cole did the same.

"Car trouble, Ranger?" Cole asked.

"Something like that," Amon said. "You?"

"On my way to help a buddy haul off some scrap metal and the like," Cole said, talking loud over the grumbling truck.

Amon could smell the exhaust, could see it drifting there in the cold.

"You thought any more about my offer?" he asked.

Cole looked at him and then looked forward toward the road ahead.

"From what I heard, there's somebody out there who wants the Fenleys worse than you do."

"I've heard that too," Amon said.

"Any idea who that somebody is?" Cole asked.

Amon gave him a careful look and the two of them sat there with the engines running.

"I can protect you," he said. "You work with me, and I'll get you out from under all this."

He watched Cole's face for a reaction, but there wasn't anything there. Not even a hint.

"I don't know what you mean, Ranger," Cole said and put the truck in gear.

Amon nodded.

"Good luck with your buddy, then," he said, resigned.

"Good luck with your trouble."

Cole pulled away and Amon watched in the rearview as the truck turned out onto the road and headed off. He could hear the great growl of the engine and somewhere, he thought, the muffled pealing of a lone bell. But once the truck was gone there was no other sound and he rolled up his window and continued on.

When he pulled into the yard there was no one else about, though plenty of cars sat with open hoods or up on blocks.

He opened the door, and the wind blew it shut, and he opened it again and got out. He put his chin down and crossed his arms against the cold and walked toward a burning trash pile where Coy Taggert was stooped over and trying to pry open the mouth of a cur.

"Give it here, you dumb sumbitch," Coy demanded, and the dog growled, and Coy growled back.

The dog's eyes cut to Amon as he approached and when Coy turned to look the dog took advantage and raced away from the fire and under the porch of the house.

"Goddamnit," Coy bemoaned. "There went a half sack of tobacco."

Amon frowned.

"Will he be alright?"

"Who? The dog? Yeah, he'll be fine. I'm the one who ain't got no chew."

"Are you Coy Taggert?" Amon asked.

"I am. And yonder comes the fella you want to talk to."

Amon looked up and saw Ansel walking toward them from the garage. Black smoke from a burning tire hid away half his figure.

"You don't know why I'm here," Amon said, "how do you know who I need to speak with?"

"Don't matter why you're here. That's still the fella."

"Help ye?" Ansel called, still several yards away.

Amon waited until he'd reached them to answer.

"How's business, Mr. Taggert?" he asked.

Ansel eyed the man. He looked past him at the car parked in the yard.

"Tax man?" he asked.

"No sir," Amon said.

"Well, it's alright. What's it to ye?"

"It's come to my attention that you and your son, and possibly others under your instruction, have been outfitting vehicles for bootleggers so as to disallow law enforcement from spotting them on the road. Furthermore, you're making repairs, hiding cars, burning them perhaps," Amon nodded toward the fire, "and otherwise aiding in the continuation of a criminal enterprise that grows like a scourge on this county."

"I know ye," Ansel said. "That new boy up at the sheriff's office."

"Not a boy, Mr. Taggert. An officer of the law. A Texas Ranger, at that."

"Uh huh. Well." Ansel spit.

"You're aware, are you not, that I could arrest you and your son and at the very least keep you in jail until your trial, which could be months from now?"

"It ain't against the law to tinker on them cars. You ain't got nothing on us, Ranger. We just businessmen with a little ole shop out in the woods. We can't help who comes to get work done. Times is tough. Who am I to turn away a dollar?"

"You're welcome to stick to that story. But I doubt Zev Blakewell and his bunch will care much about what would or wouldn't hold up in court. They're out for the Fenleys and anybody that has anything to do with them. I imagine you'll get a visit here real soon, and by then my offer will have expired."

"I'll ask ye to get on off my property, Ranger. Unless you intend on cuffing us."

"Yes sir," Amon said and turned and looked at the younger man. "It's your funeral, son."

The seed planted, he got back in the car and weaved through the back roads he was growing more familiar with until they spilled him out onto the highway, where he headed west toward Nebat City. As he drove, he flipped the pages of his notebook and read through his own scribbling.

The road ran northwest alongside the winding river. Cold fog overtop the water like a phantom highway for the dead. A turn here or there and you'd lose sight of it, but always it returned.

It was afternoon when he arrived, and the same secretary told him the sheriff wasn't in and she didn't know when he'd be back. She said she'd take a message, but as Amon spoke, she didn't write anything or seem to be listening at all. He left the office and started up the car and made the block and then parked again, this time across the street, catty-corner from the sheriff's office, facing away, and he sat and watched in the rearview as folks came and went.

A storm gathered while he waited.

He could not remember the last day without rain, and it felt as if he'd been bone cold for two weeks straight.

Cars, wagons, and wooden buggies lined one side of the street, several of which appeared to have not been moved in months. Maybe years. Dead leaves came loose from them and from other places and washed down and collected in the door coves of long-shuttered shopfronts.

The rain fell slant, dancing riotous upon the tin roofs of the county. The river swelled. Children saw their own ill-formed reflections in puddles of mud like funhouse mirrors. A cat passed bow-backed through the alley, its paws soft and quick on the cold ground. Amon could hear the river running and some had gathered on the bridge to watch it rise.

He climbed out of the car to take measure himself. He opened his umbrella and walked across the street to where the world dropped into the river. There were stone carved steps from the sidewalk down to the banks and he followed their descent to the small wash between the edge water and the bottom of the retaining wall.

He walked the stunted shoreline and all about him were the remnants of a blind and recurrent Nature. Empty liquor bottles and Youngs Rubber condoms littered among the rocks and sand, and there were rusted fishhooks and torn jug lines and the bones of fish and the bones of legged creatures. The carcass of some small animal with blood abounding but it was too cold for flies.

He knelt and loosened a rock from the wet mud and picked it up and held it in the palm of his hand and felt its weight. It had been shaped by the water but was apart from it.

He tossed the rock toward the middle of the river and his eyes followed its long aerial arc and then it hit the surface, a faint plinking, and was gone. There were short, quick ripples and those soon gone as well, and then there was only water and darkness and neither cared for the rock nor were they determined by it. For surely they had seen great boulders, even the great mountains and ranges of earth, cut through and torn away by little more than the wind and the water and the passing of time—time which cannot govern the wind nor the water nor the dark of night. Time unconditioned.

He could sense his own time's diminishing. Cora and Joseph would be on a train in three days. He had seen in his wife's eyes that there would be no delaying her decision. He knew it was for the best, yet still the thought of being away from them unnerved him. Not only did he fear for them both as a husband and a father, but also he feared what he may become in their absence. At what point had his father's obsession taken such a sinister hold?

Amon watched the river and the place where the rock had been swallowed up and he was a long time standing and then he turned and climbed back up the stairs to street level.

A man came out of the butcher shop with his arms crossed over his apron and stared disapproving at the water beyond.

"Will she flood?" Amon called to him.

The man spit into the storm and stood for a while yet, as if the answer required a great deal of thought.

"Only if the water gets higher than the bank," he said, as a mix of stinging rain and great stones of hail began to pepper the roofs of the cars.

Amon turned back and here he saw the sheriff, red-faced and holding his hat, hustling down the sidewalk and into the office.

A minute later Amon had crossed the street and walked into the office and again was met by the apathetic secretary.

"He still ain't here."

"I just saw him come through the door."

"Well, you can't go back," she told him, stone-faced.

"Sure I can," he said, stepping around her desk and heading down the short hall.

"He's in a meeting," she called after him.

"He is now," Amon confirmed.

Sheriff Cheatham was loosening his belt before sitting down when Amon came through the door.

"Ranger Atkins," the sheriff said, "I wasn't expecting you."

"Sorry for barging in," Amon said. "I just had a quick question for you."

"A quick question and you come all this way?"

"Well, you got a hell of a guard dog on your phone out there."

Cheatham beamed with some sort of pride.

"Wouldn't trade her for ten deputies," he said.

"So I've heard," Amon said, flipping open his notebook. "I was hoping you could tell me why it is you kicked Charlie Cooper's case up the ladder in the first place. I should've asked last time, but it didn't occur to me. I just assumed you were shorthanded."

"Well, yessir, that we are," the sheriff nodded vigorously and pretended to look at something on his desk.

"Right, but why Charlie Cooper's case in particular?" Amon asked. "There've been other crimes, other murders even, that seem like they'd be more important. I mean, by all accounts Charlie Cooper was just a dreg of society. Did I get that right?"

"You mind me asking where this is coming from, or where it's headed?" Cheatham asked.

"It's just something you said," Amon told him. "I wrote it down here, but again I didn't think much of it at the time. You said, 'If y'all want the Fenleys out of the way,' we'd have to come up with something better. What did you mean by that?"

"I don't recall saying that—not in those words," the sheriff stammered. "But I imagine I just meant the Fenleys are a plague on this county. Be good to have them gone."

"It would," Amon agreed. "No doubt about that. But you could've arrested them anytime. For any number of things. You didn't have to wait for a murder. And you damn sure didn't have to call in the Texas Rangers."

"What are you getting at, Atkins?"

"I don't know yet," Amon said. "But something's not right here, and I'm gonna find out what it is."

Cheatham pushed his chair back from his desk and shook his head.

"Well, I sure am sorry you made the drive," he said, sighing. "But I got nothing for you in that direction. We stay busy around here. And a murder is still a murder, lowlife or not. Just figured you boys could help bring some justice to it."

Amon nodded and smiled but he didn't speak and he didn't move to stand. He just sat and watched the sheriff in his uncomfortable squirming.

"Anything else I can help you with, Ranger?" the sheriff asked at last.

"Nossir, that'll do it," Amon said, and he slammed his notebook shut and Cheatham flinched in his seat.

Amon passed back by the secretary and knocked on her desk with his knuckles as he went by.

"You have a wonderful rest of your day, ma'am," he said.

She rolled her eyes.

He crossed the street in the rain and went into the diner and flashed his badge at the girl behind the counter.

"You all mind if I use your telephone?" He asked.

"Nossir, it's right through yonder."

Amon walked around the counter and through the kitchen to the back hall between the janitor's closet and the bathroom. There was a little stool with a rotary atop it and he picked it up and thought for a while and then dialed the operator and gave her an Austin number.

The line rang.

"Hello?" a woman answered.

"Hi, Aunt Beatrice, it's Amon."

"What? Amon? Well, I—what are you doing, honey?"

"I need to ask you something," he said.

"Why sure, darling. My goodness, I ain't heard from you since your Uncle Bobby's funeral."

"You still working for McCallum?" he asked.

"Oh, no, I retired two years ago."

"You got any friends in your old office?"

"I imagine I do," she said, her tone growing more curious. "What is it you're needing, nephew?"

"I need a campaign contributions report."

"For who?"

"Nebat County sheriff, name of Cheatham."

"Well, you know that's public record, Amon, you could just call Jane's office and ask."

"I know it is," he switched the phone to his other hand. "But I don't want nobody to know I'm asking. You understand?"

She was quiet for a few seconds, then answered.

"I understand," she told him. "I can call up there in a minute."

"Don't call, Aunt Beatrice," he warned her. "I need you to go to the office. In person."

"Why come?"

"Wire taps."

"What's wire taps?"

"It's what they'll have on all their phones in that office. Let's them listen in to anything you say. It's how they busted Roy Olmstead up in Seattle."

"Oh my."

"Can you get up to the office today?" he asked her.

"Well, yeah, I guess I can," she said. "But the report is only gonna have the names of folks who give more than fifty dollars."

"I know. The man I'm looking for would've done a good deal more than that."

"Where can I call you back?" she asked.

He gave her the number for the annex and thanked her and hung up the phone.

40

The woods were still, save a lingering gust of wind somewhere in the treetops. Subtle and soundless, the swaying of the pines like maladaptive kelp. The leaden sky bereft of clouds. An eerie and unmoving calm.

Jesse drove and Hank Schaffer itched at the dry skin around his mustache and sang.

"They say there's a war, they say there's a drought, they say save ye money, they say take it out. They tell ye anything from the day you's born, but they can't tell ye nothing when you drinking that corn."

Hank laughed.

"You ever hear any of that Peach Williams?" he asked.

"No," Jesse said, distracted by the unpleasant task before him.

"Well, he's a damn good'un," Hank said, and he looked at Jesse for a few seconds then spit tobacco juice onto the floor of the truck. "Word round the campfire is that the Frog ain't too keen on you joining up."

"Yeah, I ain't too keen on it either," Jesse replied. "So I guess we got that in common."

"I don't believe that's all y'all got in common," Hank said, grinning.

The driveway was all but washed out from the rain and Jesse fought the truck, an International Harvester from the back of Taggert's lot, until the ground leveled out in front of Hollis Wentworth's barn.

"Stay here and let me talk to him," Jesse told Hank and climbed down from the cab.

He went up onto the porch and used his boot to sweep away a loitering collection of glass bottles from in front of the screen door. He opened the screen and used the side of his fist to beat on the wooden door within, and he could hear Hollis shuffling around inside.

The door cracked open.

"Jess?" Hollis asked, sleepy eyed.

"I need a favor off you," Jesse said.

Hollis perked up.

"What sort of favor?" he asked, opening the door fully. "I'm ready. Or I can get that way quick. Where we headed?"

"I don't need you, just something that belongs to you. The turtle sub you got in the barn."

Hollis looked confused.

"Well, it don't work, Jess. It just sinks straight down," Hollis told him. "Granddaddy never could get it right."

"Yes, Hollis, I know it don't work. I'm not trying to spy on the British with it, I'm gonna use it to make whiskey."

"A still?"

"That's right."

Hollis crossed his arms.

"You want the turtle but not me?"

Jesse nodded.

"And what if I say no? I mean, hell, that's my family history right there."

"Hollis."

Jesse looked at him. They stood there in silence.

"I guess that's why you brought Hank, yonder," Hollis said at last.

"I figure it'll take three people to get it in the trailer."

Hollis could not hide his disappointment.

"Well, let's go on and get it over with," he said and walked off toward the garage.

Once the great wooden shell was loaded in the back of the Harvester, Jesse and Hank climbed back in the cab and Hollis lingered at the driver's door.

"I could make a good hand, Jess," he said. "Even just at the still site. I'd rather be on the road with you, but I ain't picky. I'll take what I can get."

"It's better this way," Jesse said. "I'm telling you."

"Listen to him, Wentworth," Hank said. "Knowing you, you'd end up lost in the back of them caves somewhere and never seen or heard from again. Now close that door, we're letting the heat out."

"The caves?" Hollis asked.

"Just leave it, Hollis," Jesse told him. "We'll talk later."

Jesse put the truck in gear, and it lurched forward and creaked and groaned under the weight of its cargo. Hollis watched truck and submarine alike go trundling down the drive.

"A goddamn 'Thank you, Hollis' would've been just fine too," he called after them, but he knew they couldn't hear.

By the time Jesse drove to the quarry and unloaded the submarine hull, a storm had moved in from the west. It caught him on his drive back into town. Sleet and rain and through the windshield the world was rendered in a wet, meandering unreality. The dark green trees turned darker still. A whitetail herd crossed the road in front of him, one at the time, like they'd been placed in ranks and told not to break them for anything—even for the sundering of the earth itself.

He parked the car and went up to her door and knocked, unsure of what he'd say if she opened it.

When Ada answered she was already in her nightgown, and he tried not to stare. She stood there and looked at him and then turned back inside and left the door open behind her. He took a few steps after her and stood in the doorway.

"You gonna close that," she asked, "or just let the whole winter come in behind you?"

He moved quickly to shut the open door, and with its closing a picture fell from the nearest wall.

"You want a cup of coffee?" she asked.

He picked up the photograph and stared at it. Ada in a simple white dress. A man in a dark suit.

When he didn't answer, she turned and looked at him and at the picture.

"You know we got married a month after we met?" she asked.

He followed her into the kitchen and set the cracked frame on the counter and mumbled an apology.

"He was one of the first people I met in Nebat City," she said. "Showed me around. Seemed to know everyone and everything. I should have seen it then, but I didn't."

"Seen what?"

"That nothing made sense to him if it didn't have an angle. He owed all over town. Some places more than others. Had girlfriends, naturally. Just a low-class con man, but I was too angry to think clear at the time."

He put his head down.

"I don't imagine you came here to talk about Charlie," she said. "Did you?"

"No," he said. "I don't know why I came."

"I do," she said, and she stepped toward him, her hand reaching out.

A wave passed through him. A subcurrent.

She touched his cheek.

"You're ready to take this pelt off your face," she told him, then stepped back and grinned. "Go sit down in the kitchen. I'll get my razor."

Soon he was seated in a wooden chair opposite the stove and she was pouring hot water into a bowl.

"Let me just tuck this towel in," she said, wrapping the white cloth around his neck.

She worked free the top two buttons on his shirt and they both looked down at her fingers as they moved.

He hoped she would not hear the dryness in his throat as he swallowed.

"I never figured you for a beard," she said, and he was thankful for the break in silence. "All them years, you never even wore a mustache."

"Me neither," he said. "But then it grew on me."

She stared at him in amused disbelief.

"Good Lord help us," she said, shaking her head. "Are you proud of that?"

"I'll admit it's not my best work. But it's far from my worst."

"That I can believe," she said. "Now hold still so this don't get everywhere."

She lathered his face with cream and held his head back with one hand. She used the other to pass the razor along his cheeks in slow, straight lines.

"I heard y'all are moving everything out to the quarry," she said, and she sounded almost disappointed. "I guess we're still in business."

"I guess so," he said.

"Don't talk," she told him. "I'll mess up."

He closed his eyes and there, in such darkness, he felt her fingers in his hair, smelled the shaving cream on his neck and on her hands. She bent near his ear and he could hear her breathing, her mouth slightly open as she focused on her work.

"I'm supposed to go out there tomorrow and start helping," she said. "Be good to get out the house some."

Her voice, even now, seemed like something from long ago. From far away.

Each time she leaned over he could hear the water lapping in the bowl as she rinsed the blade, and each time she returned to him he felt relieved. *Would that this might last forever*, he thought. But it was over in minutes.

In truth, he knew, it had ended long ago.

"I'm sorry, Ada," he said, standing as she removed the towel.

"What for?"

"All of it."

"Is that right?" she asked with a sad half laugh. "So, if I'd come to your doorstep, any of them years—just walked right up and asked you to come with me—would you have? Because I would've left him in a heartbeat. I would have left everyone and everything. But you never came."

"I didn't know," he said. He'd long imagined this conversation, but now that it was here, he couldn't think of what to say.

"Didn't know," she said. "All that time we spent together, you thought what? I was lying?"

He shook his head.

"I don't know what I thought," he said. "Maybe that I was protecting you in some way."

"Well, a lot of good that did," she said, harsh.

"What happened?" he asked. "I know I don't have any right to ask, or to know."

She closed her eyes and crossed her arms over her gown. What little light through the window was fading.

"You left," she said. "I cried for a week or two. Maybe more. Then I got angry. I decided I wasn't going to go to New York. I wasn't going to be a singer. In fact, I decided I would never sing again. Like I would *show* you or something. I was young and dramatic."

She stopped and looked over at the framed photographs and shook her head.

"Things changed when Momma died. I didn't think I had tears left to cry, but I did. Started the cycle all over again."

"I was sorry to hear about Edna," Jesse said.

Ada shrugged.

"It seemed like half the county was in mourning, the other half was in the ground," she said. "Then one day a man showed up at the door and said he was a friend of a friend of a cousin or some such story and that he was looking for a place to rent. Did I know of anywhere. I told him, sure I do. This place right here. Comes furnished."

"A week later I was in Nebat City, trying to work up the courage to get on a train after all. That's when I met Charlie. I told him I was going to New York, and he said he was too. Just needed to wrap up a few business deals. Twelve years later, we were broke and busted and never had made it north of the Red River. I kept telling myself there was still time. I was still just a girl, in my mind. But then one day I looked up at a mirror and this wrinkled face was looking back."

Jesse wanted to grab her and pull her to him. To hold her face in his hands and tell her she was beautiful. That she was still that girl. That everything was his fault, but he'd fix it. He'd fix it all.

Instead, he stood quiet. He watched her eyes as the last few years of her life replayed in her head. She shook them away.

"Charlie was a sonofabitch," she said, as if she'd just come to such a verdict. "He used me. The rent money from this house came in the mail each month and each month he was there to tell me about why he needed it. This scheme or that. If I said anything against it, or even questioned him, well—men are bastards."

"He—"

"Yeah, he did," Ada said. "But I stayed anyway. He might have been using me, but I was using him too."

"How?" Jesse frowned.

"So long as I could blame him for being stuck in Nebat City, I didn't have to blame myself for being too scared to go," she told him. "I blamed you for a while too. Since it was supposed to have been the two of us together. I figured it was your fault I hadn't ever prepared myself to go alone. I would make up my mind every so often—you know, this was gonna be the day. I can't tell you how many times I packed my bags. Even made it on the train once, but I got back off before it started out of the depot. I'd get these episodes or something, to where I couldn't breathe. Where my thoughts weren't my own anymore, and everything I looked at felt like I was looking through somebody else's eyes. It felt like I was dying. Maybe I was. But I'd always go back. Always end up right back where I started."

She looked to Jesse but he was quiet and she closed her eyes and sighed.

"What are you doing all this for, Jess?" she asked. "It's one thing to honor your brother, but it's another to become him. You used to not do a damn thing unless it pleased you. Unless you saw something in it."

"Hollis needed help."

"Hollis Wentworth is gonna need help for the rest of his life. Why does it always have to be you doing the helping? And Eliza and the girl? Now Frog and Squirrel? What do you get out of any of this?"

"I get to see you."

"Jesus Christ, Jesse."

"What?"

"You're lying. If not to me, then to yourself," she told him. "You can't live your life for other people. Whether it's me or Danny or anybody else. What do *you* want?"

"When we were seventeen, I wanted a handful of acres on the side of some mountain somewhere. A good creek for water. Enough trees to where we could walk naked when the weather was good. And three or four little ones growing up around us."

"And now?" she asked, fighting back her emotions.

"I want to want that again."

"But you don't."

"I think maybe I forgot what it was like to want anything at all," he said. "All those years, I told myself you were happy. Married. Moved on."

"But you never thought to check."

He shook his head.

"I guess not," he said. "I figured you'd just listened to me when I told you not to wait."

"I think it's best if you leave," she said. "I don't feel much like company all of a sudden."

He wanted to protest, but he didn't. He left her there, sipping her coffee and looking across the room at something so very far away.

The night was early yet, and he passed a handful of cars on his drive home. Headlights coming down off Harmatia Hill like synchronized souls falling from grace, burning the dark there before them, and then gone, into the trees, and the curtain of night again drawing shut.

41

Frog hated the ocean. The audacity of it. Vast and open and wave on wave of some unknown form, insisting itself upon the coastline in a minacious manner. And somewhere out there in all those deep, ill-contained fathoms, monsters lurked eternal in their plenitude of darkness.

The big man looked out at the bayou and the moss-hung cypress trees grown up along river where it spilled into the sea.

He shuddered. Turned away.

"Hurry the fuck up," he growled at the warehouse hands as they loaded and packed down the back of his truck and the trailer attached to it. "I don't want to spend another night in this salt-rusted sack of shit."

The shipment had been delayed by storms. Impassable waters. He'd been stuck in Beaumont for two days, drinking and sleeping in a small room above the warehouse that had once been used an office. He knew where his brother was—what he was doing—and he worried for him. Squirrel was smart, capable, but he wasn't a fighter. That was Frog's job. He was the muscle. He was the one who should be at his brother's side, and yet here he was, marooned in a water-pocked bay town where ship horns and seagull chatter replaced the sound of whispering pines.

He thought of Squirrel, and of Adaline. Of Jesse Cole there with her. His breathing quickened. He knew she still loved him. He could see it in her face the day he told her Squirrel wanted to bring Cole on. He didn't press her. There was no need. Let her love him. As long as she was loyal, Frog didn't care. To him, loyalty was all that mattered. He wanted to trust her, the way he trusted his brother. Maybe he did. But Cole on the other hand . . .

"Faster, goddamnit," he hollered and grabbed two hundred-pound bags of corn and threw them in the trailer.

He drove as fast as the heavy load would allow, the trailer swinging wildly behind him as he sped around the winding curves of the Big Thicket. He stopped for gas in Lufkin and was gone again. He approached Nebat County from the south, just after midnight. His pulse began to normalize. He was back where he belonged.

Just before the county line, his headlamps spied an overturned car in the road. It was laid on its side with the roof facing Frog's approach. An anxious-looking man waved him down.

"Thank God you come along," the man said with a relieved laugh. "You're the first car in nearly two hours."

"What happened?" Frog asked, his annoyance evident.

"Oh, yeah, Sully took that last turn too fast," the man said, pointing to his companion, who loitered around the vehicle. "Car went up on two wheels, seemed like a hundred yards, then finally tipped all the way over."

Frog spit out the window, and the man had to jump back to avoid it hitting his shoe.

"Sorry about this," the man said. "If you can help us turn her back right, we can push it out of your way. Let you get on up the road. We couldn't get it ourselves, but you seem like a pretty big fella."

"Shit," Frog said and threw open his door. Again the man had to jump back.

Frog walked toward the overturned car and the night was cold and silent and he could hear ice leaves crunching underfoot like the shattering of vest-pocket porcelain. He stopped and looked back and the man was still standing by Frog's truck, smiling.

"You coming or what?" Frog asked, gruff.

"Be there directly," the man said and brought a pistol out from beneath his coat.

The man near the car pulled out a Thompson and held it in both hands.

Frog closed his eyes and took a quick breath.

Shit.

42

The frost came sharp into the forest and the northern winds pressed down on the land and brought with them rare snow flurries and frozen crystals of rain, and across the fields and into the orchards great reefs of ice formed, and ice hung from the frozen trees and the old fences, and sheets of ice appeared along the roads.

Jesse stood on the porch and tried to gather himself, but he could not. Something raged inside him. Or yearned. He could not tell which or the difference between.

"You shaved," Eliza said as Jesse came through the door of the cabin. He nodded.

"Where's Sarah?"

"Already asleep."

"You need to let her go to school," he said.

He hadn't even taken his coat off.

"What?" Eliza asked.

"And to town. And to New York City if that's where she wants to be."

Eliza looked equal parts mortified and confused.

"Where in the world is this coming from?" she asked.

"I know you have some plan in your head of how to keep her safe," he said. "Of what's best for her. But she needs more than that. She deserves more."

"I'm her mother, Jesse," Eliza said, reeling. "I think I *know* what's best for her."

"You keep on like this, and you'll lose her," he warned, his voice growing louder.

"What did she say to you?" Eliza asked. "What's happened?"

The fear poured out of her. Her trembling hands, frantic words.

"Nothing's happened."

He tried to calm himself. He hadn't expected to say any of this and seeing her there, terrified—her worst imaginings taking hold—he felt guilty.

"Nothing's happened," he repeated. "I just— She's too smart for this place. Too curious and talented and wonderful. I don't want to see her get stuck here. Anywhere near here."

Eliza had a strange but relieved look on her face.

"Alright," she said cautiously. "But she's only fifteen. She hasn't even finished school."

"You won't let her *go* to school."

"I can assure you the curriculum she is learning here is just as rigorous as whatever they're teaching at the Enoch schoolhouse."

She took a defensive posture. Chin up and out.

"It's not about her studies, Eliza," he said, gentle now. "You know it's not."

"We have time," she said, and he could hear in her voice that she would not be moved, that the conversation was over.

Jesse made his rounds the following morning. Two speaks, a few houses, and one funeral home for deliveries. Even the dead deserve a proper send-off. Especially the dead.

More and more, he had been turned away. The fear of the Fenleys had been in large part supplanted by Blakewell. The masked man and his black-clad associates, haunting the hollow.

There was no pork left. His lunch was a tin plate of sliced and salted tomatoes and a half-full thermos of haricots. Everything was cold, and he ate in the car.

He came down the logging road from the north and there was the turn that would take him home, but he didn't take it. Instead, he pulled along the roadcut and sat with the car idling for a long while, choking exhaust out into cold damp air.

You remember when we were kids? He heard her voice. Saw her face.

He put the car in gear and drove on.

He made the quarry by late afternoon. The operation was up and running. The Fenleys had called together every corn cooker in their employment—the men hauling hundreds of feet of copper and pounds of steel by the cold, blue moonlight, and there they looked a band of merry thieves from some old storybook. A picture staged for the taking. There were men stoking fires beneath a series of stills and others cleaning piles of unassembled copper piping, spitting on Raschig rings and spiraled tubing and wiping them down with tattered pieces of cloth. One of the men was stirring a great iron pot of sugar and corn and boiling water. Whorls of copper like mutant plants sprung cochleate from the barrels. The Schaffer brothers, Hank and Eli, were crouched in perfect symmetry on either side of a drip jug as the foreshot came trickling down from the cooling barrel. They looked up as Jesse approached.

"What say, Jesse?" Hank asked. "Didn't know you was coming out today."

"Hadn't planned on it," Jesse said. "Anybody heard from Frog or Squirrel?"

"I was hoping they had gotten some word to *you*," Eli said.

"Nossir," Jesse said. "No word yet."

Horace Clayton stood from a small fire he was tending and crossed his arms.

"We've done been turnt away at half the stops, Jess," Horace said. "Why in the hell are we cooking up all this new hooch with nowhere to sell it?"

Jesse scratched at the ghost of his beard. The thought of a mutiny had its appeal. But he wasn't ready for all that. He needed more time with Adaline, then he'd figure out how to deal with the Fenleys.

"Because we were told to," he said. "We've got our orders. Let's see them through."

"Sir, yessir? Is that it, Jess?" Horace spit. "We're putting ourselves in all sorts of trouble for these boys and here they've done and disappeared on us. Left us holding the bag."

"I'm not too inclined to keep driving around trying to deliver whiskey to folks who don't want it, on behalf of them that ain't nowhere to be found," Nick said. "Could be that Blakewell and his boys have already got to them. Hell, could be that they've decided to move on. Go back to Tennessee somewhere."

Yancy Greaves walked out from deeper in the caverns and shook his head at the lot of them.

"Listen here," he commanded. "Cole ain't in charge. I am. Now, I'll give you sonsabitches a pass this time. But the next ill word I hear about Frog or Squirrel, I'll have you repeat it for them as soon as they're back. Until then, we got an order to fill. Don't matter where it's going or where it ain't. Squirrel said a hundred cases, so that's what we're gonna do."

Yancy pushed through them, stalking off toward the mouth of the cave.

"Where you headed Yance?" Eli Schaffer asked.

"There's a handful of bunkers in the hollow," he said. "If we empty them out, there might be enough groceries to keep us cooking until Frog makes it back. Meantime, y'all just keep that fire going."

Yancy left the quarry, and the others continued their work.

Jesse wandered further into the cave until he found Adaline crouched over a fire and studying the contents of a cast-iron pan that sat on a short grate above the flames.

"What are you doing here?" she asked without looking up.

"What's that?"

"I had some citrus put back," she told him. "A few oranges, lemon, what not. Canned them at the end of the summer. This is the juice. Once I get it simmering, I'll add it to a barrel—maybe two—and it'll give off a good dark color. Little bit of a brandy taste."

"Sounds good," he said.

She stood and crossed her arms.

"What do you want, Jesse?" she asked him. "I don't have it in me to keep hauling up the past."

"You're right," he said. "I was lying. I felt an obligation to my brother. That's true. And I'd heard you were married. That's true too. But even with that, I wanted to see you. To come take you away, just like you said."

"Why didn't you?"

"Because I was too chickenshit," he said. "Because all I could think about was how different everything was—how different I was. I figured if all I did was focus on everybody else, I wouldn't ever have to face myself and the things I did."

"What did you do?" she asked.

"I can't tell you. At least not yet. And I know that's not fair and I know it's not all about me. You've seen your share of trouble too. I know you have. I'm not asking for your forgiveness. But I do want to get to know you again, Adaline. If you'll let me."

She sighed. She wanted to tell him that it wasn't all his fault. That even if he'd come straight home to her, things might have already changed. The plague. The war. Nothing felt the same. Nothing felt right. She wanted to tell him that whatever he did, he had to do—whatever he was ashamed of. And most of all, she wanted to tell him she still loved him. Not the way she had. No. How could she? Who can withstand time's cruel slaughter and still love with all the certainty and sincerity of youth? No, her love was guarded now, but it was still love, and he was still the one, and she wanted to tell him, but she didn't.

"Come help me with this syrup," she said instead. "We'll start there."

And in the shadows, they worked. Jesse, Adaline, and the others huddled around small fires near the mouth of the cave like hyperborean mendicants. The cold and clinical passing of the stars above them, louring down in the dark. Stars dead and alive but shining all the same, unmoored from the tyranny of time and distance. And yet time the only true discernment. Time, brief and everlasting, and its passing bringing us closer to that collective reckoning which we alone must come up against. Alone must undergo.

43

Yancy and the deputy stalked through the woods in the early evening and Yancy blew into his hands even though he had gloves on.

"It's colder than a penguin's pecker out here," the deputy complained. "And I don't remember this being in the job description."

"Gotta pull your weight somehow, haas," Yancy told him. "Seeing as how you've give us jack and shit on Blakewell and his mystery backer."

"And you think dragging my ass out here to dig up bunkers of booze is gonna help?"

"Four hands are quicker than two."

Yancy stopped and looked around.

"This one here, I believe," he said and patted a yellow pine with his gloved hand.

He squared himself to the side of the tree and took four steps away from it and then gave a quarter turn and took ten more. He dropped to his knees and started rooting through the dark wet leaves.

"You're supposed to be doing some of this shit too, you know," he told the deputy.

"Looks like you're managing."

Yancy found the cold wet rope and followed it a few feet on his hands and knees and then stood and yanked at it. The rotten wood door came completely off the hidden cellar. The deputy peered over the side into the dark catacombs and counted the crates.

"That's a hefty load," he said.

"It ain't just bottles," Yancy told him. "There's all sorts of supplies packed away. They don't call him Squirrel for nothing."

Yancy checked the equipment and logged a few inventory-related details in his notebook. At the end of each week, he turned the notebook in to Squirrel, who checked it against his own ledgers. The Fenleys, despite their well-earned rabble-rousing reputation, ran a tight ship with little leakage.

He and the deputy crawled down into the bunker together and hauled up the crates of liquor and additional bags of corn, barley, and yeast.

When the hole was empty save for mud and spiders, Yancy tossed the broken lid back overtop it and looked up through the treetops.

"That rain may hold off yet," he said. "Maybe let's roll us one and take a little break before we carry this shit back to the truck."

"You won't catch me telling a feller to get to work," the deputy said. "You ain't above sampling the wares, now, are you?"

"I don't imagine it would hurt nothing to open one of them little ones down there. Just wet our whistle some while we smoke."

"There's a man knows how to enjoy life."

"Yeah, well, I ain't no preacher," Yancy said, twisting the cork out of a bottle. "But you gotta be careful with this mess. Call it an occupational hazard, a man being around all this drink all the time."

"Can't argue that. Shit, I used to think my old man was the sole reason they passed the Volstead Act in the first place. Mean drunk, that one."

"Yessir, I've known it to happen. You grew up in Sevier County, didn't you?"

"Just south of there, in Little River."

"You ever know a fella named Garrett Holcombe?" Yancy asked him.

"Sure I did," the deputy nodded, smoothing two rolling papers flat against his thigh. "Hadn't heard the name in years, but I remember him."

"You didn't happen to hear the story of his wedding, did you? When he married that little Handy gal from up Dallas way?"

"No, I don't guess I have."

"Boy, it's sure a good'un."

"Well, hell," the deputy said, "go on and tell it."

"Alright, so, this gal, Katherine was her name. Come from some banking bunch up in Dallas, I think. Her folks had a big spread up in Arkansas where they'd go during the summer. That's where Garrett met her. He was working for a timber outfit up there and somehow or the other they ended up courting. I don't know that her folks were real happy about it, but she liked ole Garrett sure enough. And after a little while they decided they was gonna get married."

Yancy stopped and took a drink and was grinning and shaking his head as he swallowed.

"Now, she had one of them little ponies—a Shetland—and she'd had it for however long and there was nothing that would do but she had to have it in the wedding. Wanted it to walk down the aisle of the church house and ever'thing."

"In the church?" the deputy asked.

"You bet," Yancy nodded. "And well, hell, Garrett's done about to marry the girl of his dreams, so he says, 'Alright, whatever you want, darlin'. We'll have us a little mini horse in the wedding.' And they talk the pastor into it, which wasn't no small task, and they smooth it all over with Garrett's momma, which was a might harder given as she weren't what you'd call an enthusiastic supporter of this particular union. She'd always figured Katherine and that whole bunch to be a little highfalutin'. But, anyhow, she agrees to it, and here it comes, day of the wedding, and Garrett's brother—you remember ole Lonnie?—so Lonnie's done tied one on early, and I do mean a good and proper drunk, and he sees that old pony tethered out in the lot, waiting on the ceremony to get started."

"Oh Lord," the deputy grunted, he passed one of the cigarettes over to Yancy, the other bobbing up and down between his lips as he spoke.

"Yeah, yeah, you can feel it coming." Yancy laughed and then recomposed himself. "Now, you gotta understand. Katherine, or her parents more like, they've got this whole place covered in flowers. Not just up at the altar, but all over the dadgum place. On the pews, over the door, and in particular all along this big-ass arch they had brought in and put out in front of the church. Well, Lonnie being Lonnie, he walks over to this arch and starts pulling buttercups—and I imagine you've done figured out where this is going—but he's pulling armfuls of buttercups and he's feeding it to this horse."

"Oh Lord," the deputy said, louder this time.

"Right, and I don't know if folks was too busy with the goings-on and didn't see it happening, or if maybe some people did and just didn't know no better. But he gets a whole bellyful of these buttercups in this horse, then goes on inside and takes his seat."

Yancy lit his cigarette and took a drag and then a drink and then another drag.

"Now, I do believe in God," he said, blowing out the smoke, "but I also believe in luck and timing. And let me tell you, bud, they was all against ole Garrett that day—either that or ever' bit of it was with Lonnie, depending on how you want to look at it. Either way, everything's carrying on just fine and the ceremony gets to going and all, and now it's time for that little horse to come in and Katherine's mother is gonna lead it down the aisle."

The deputy was laughing.

"I ain't gonna make it," he said, slapping his leg.

"Hold on, now. Hang with me," Yancy said, holding up both arms. "So, the piano's playing 'Camptown Races' and here comes this little horse and he gets right about to the middle of the whole goddamn church and then—bam, hallelujah, praise the Lord—the flood gates open and there's horseshit flying out of this little bastard at speeds never before recorded. The chapel's filled with the sounds of Stephen Foster and flatulence and folks laughing and the preacher all but cussing. Katherine's crying and her mother's screaming, and of course ole Garrett's so stunned he don't know what to do. And all the while, Lonnie just setting there sipping on his flask, grinning how he does. To this day there's folks in Sevier who swear the pile of shit was taller than the horse itself."

"Good Lord, have mercy."

"I'm telling you He didn't have none that day."

"Did they still get married?"

"Sure they did," Yancy said, walking off a few paces and unbuttoning his pants. "Been married six or seven years, but Katherine still won't be in the same house as Lonnie, let alone the same room."

"What about the horse?" the deputy asked.

"What about the horse?" Yancy repeated, tilting his head back as he pissed.

"I mean, was it alright?"

"Far as I know. I don't imagine they'd have gone on with everything if the horse had died."

"My goodness," the deputy said, easing up behind him. "I hadn't laughed that much in years. Ole Lonnie. I'll be damned."

"I'm telling you," Yancy said, finishing up. "Well, you want to go on and see if—"

Yancy's eyes went cross when the deputy hit him with a log.

44

The cold of the evening spread out before them and the dark of night crept slowly up the edge of the world. Jesse crouched near the pot still and Ada studied the drip on the opposite end.

"Take that fire down some," Ada said, and he pulled a hot log from the flames and looked at it and set it to the side. He took a jar from his satchel and unscrewed the top and poured a splash of water on one side of the fire and watched it for a while and then screwed the cap back on the jar and set it near the smoking log.

"That ought to hold her for a bit."

Once the foreshot had been collected and discarded, Ada filled the bottom of two short glasses with the dripping liquid from the still and passed one to Jesse, who frowned at her.

"You drink the head?" he asked.

"A little bite won't kill me," she told him.

"I'll wait for the good stuff," he told her and handed back the glass.

"Jesse Cole, war hero, bootlegger, lover of women, and won't even take a drink," she said, then tossed back her shot and smacked her lips.

"I'm only one of those things," he said.

"Which one?"

"Depends on who you ask," he said. "Fine. Give it here."

He motioned for the other glass, and she passed it, and he tilted it to the side and the reflected firelight caught and swirled with the liquid.

He drank.

She watched him.

After a while, she stood and held out her hand.

"Come with me," she said, and he did.

They let go of one another as they passed through the still site near the mouth of the cave, and the Schaffers looked up at them and then at each other, but no one spoke.

Adaline led him out into the early twilight and across the old quarry.

It was a strangely beautiful place.

Red, iron-stained rock cut through with layers of rich green glauconite and mineral deposits from the shallow marine shelf that occupied this land so long and so long ago. And when the sea did return to its mother, uncovering the earth below, there were left large drifts of sand and silt. Rock and stone and oil and water, and none of it buried deep enough to hide from the insidious progression of men.

The quarry remained and so too the Sabine Pass where the stone had been sent down river to build the great shipping port that would open East Texas to the world. But the world was uninterested. Resources were cheaper and more plentiful elsewhere, and had Percy Preston not opened the paper mill and reignited the timber industry, Enoch would have faded and died long before the Depression had a chance to pick over its bones.

It had been abandoned for a decade, the quarry.

Gravel trucks sat gathering pollen and rust, their tires low or flat or stripped off altogether. Scaffolds and grinders and wheelbarrows scattered across the yawning pit like offerings to some strange iron god.

She took his hand again, and they walked past the wooden guard shack and into the pit and out past the trucks and she led him to a spot beneath the eastern edge of the quarry wall and there she put his hand against the rock, and it was warm.

"It's like a painting, or a book," she said, pointing up at the moonlit lines of earth and rock above them. "One that tells about everything that's ever happened. Every little strip of stone is the story of a thousand years. More. But it's in a language we don't know. And I don't think, no matter how hard we might try, we'll ever be able to know it again."

"Again?"

She nodded.

"I think there must have been a time we understood things that are lost to us now. Things about the rocks. The water. Maybe even the way to be."

She leaned her back against the quarry wall and looked at him.

"I knew this tinsmith in Nebat," she said. "A tinker. He was a strange little man, but we got along. Charlie didn't like him coming around, but Charlie was gone half the time. Anyway, this tinker had himself a bunch of relics. Swords or bayonets from this battle or that. 'Course I didn't have any money to buy none of it. But I thought it was neat, some of what he had, and I told him so. You know what he told me to do?"

"Rob a bank?" Jesse teased.

She smiled but shook her head.

"No, he told me to go touch an oak tree. Go put my feet in a river. Hell, just pick up some dirt, he said. Those are all things that have been here longer than any godforsaken sword. It's as easy as that, to reach out your hand and touch the past. It's right here in front of you. You understand what I'm saying?"

"I'm trying to."

"When you're young, you don't worry about what's behind you. You hardly worry about what's ahead. There's no true purpose, but there's the promise of one—of a distant future where the meaning of your existence will surely come to light. It's that promise that makes childhood so wonderful. Yeah, if a boy breaks your heart or your grandma dies, it might feel like you'll never get over it. But deep down, you know you will. You know that the secret meaning of everything is just out there waiting on you to grow up. So you do. You do grow up and that's when—maybe slowly over time, or maybe all at once—you find out there's not a purpose after all. And the only thing waiting for you is the dark. You think back on all the things you should have held onto but didn't, and you try to recapture them, those feelings of magic and innocence. A freedom that's forever pending. It was always just ahead, promising that the next chapter was the one you'd be the happiest in. But when you turn back and try to grab those feelings, you can't. They're already locked up in memories. All that's left is photographs and rock faces."

She blinked with wet eyes, the moisture of which gave them a polished gleam. Green caught afire.

"Then what," he said.

"What?" she asked, coming back to the moment.

"Once you realize that, what do you do next?"

"You live with it," she said and let go a soft laugh and wiped her hand across her face. "You don't try to find the light, or change the way things are, you just live with it. If darkness is all there is, then you carve out whatever little part of it belongs to you. Hollow out your own place and do anything you have to do to protect it, to protect yourself. Just survive. That's what you do next. Survive and try to find those little moments where you forget the truth of it all. Little moments where maybe the magic you felt years before finds its way back to you. Let's you know it wasn't a dream."

"What do those moments look like?" he said and moved closer to her and the back of his hand touched hers.

"Could be anything," she said, her voice soft. "A picnic. A good cup of coffee. A kiss."

She was pinned now against the quarry, and he leaned in and kissed her, and she met his lips with a years-long ferocity, and her hand clutched at the back of his head, fingers digging into his scalp.

She pushed him away and they stared at one another.

"Go back," she said, near breathless. "Let them see you. Wait a while before you leave. Don't park in front of the house."

She left the quarry and he returned to the cave. He crouched over the fire from the nearest pot and used its light to read from the Kipling book. His body was electric, but still he waited. He could feel the eyes on him. *A little longer*, he told himself, and he repeated the mantra for nearly an hour.

When at last he put the book aside and stood to leave, only Horace Clayton watched him go.

She met him at the door and they embraced. And if passion is a thing that exists, it existed there, and if it is a thing created or called forth, they demanded it into being. And the youth within them emerged, shaking off the many burdens they'd been buried under, and they laughed and gasped and explored one another as lovers, and in those few hours all was forgotten. All was right.

He dreamed of the house his father was born in. A house he'd seen only the ruins of, but in his dream it was new. The old dog-run structure with its thin pine logs and standing-seam roof made from tin alloy plated to steel sheets. During summer storms the rain would batter down on the metal roof in thunderous exaltation and his grandfather would open the door to the screened porch and the wind would sing through the run and the smell of the rain and the smell of the mud along with it. Leaves in autumn and a single armadillo waddling over-top them could sound like the marching of a thousand men. And in the winter the fire always burning and the smell of cedar or crackling pine and the smell of hot coffee and bacon frying, and the young liz-ards would slip in through the cracks and gather at the window to look at the world they'd left behind. The honeysuckles opening in early springtime like harbingers to the hollow for all that would soon blossom and the sweet fragrance of nature reborn. And in his own childhood such were the seasons, and he could feel each one with great urgency and the days were always full and the nights were never sleepless. He dreamed this, the entirety of his past life, and all of it trickling through the fractures in his mind like through some morose filter, a rotting funnel to the present world, where wood and rain and lizards still existed, but everything was changed, and nothing would ever be—could ever be—as it once was. He woke to the sound of a boy screaming, and even before he opened his eyes, he knew the boy was gone.

He lay awake in the passing of the dream.

Tears came silent, falling like streaking stars across the blue black of night.

45

Hollis Wentworth sat near the window of the hotel's café in his mud-caked brogans and stained trousers and a once-white shirt that had turned a pale yellow. Despite the late hour he drank coffee, and drank in loud slurps and the sound and the look of him brought strange glances from the other patrons.

A man in a bow tie sat at the polished Ellington upright and began to play an airy tune that Hollis knew but couldn't name.

A woman in a dark green dress and green scarf sat at a table by herself and Hollis stared at her and smiled and held the smile until she finally felt his gaze and looked up. He raised his coffee cup and smiled all the wider. She looked away.

The piano carried on and Hollis tapped his feet under the table and each time he did a small flaking of mud came off onto the floor.

A man came to sit at the table with the woman in green and she leaned forward and spoke to him and pointed at Hollis and the man frowned. The man stood again and ran his hand down his suit coat and lifted his chin. He had a thin mustache and, despite the cold weather, wore a straw fedora. He nodded at the woman and then walked toward Hollis.

Hollis set his coffee down quick and stood to leave.

"Hold on there, friend," the man said, and his voice was not unkind. Hollis stopped.

"I was just looking at her," he said. "I didn't mean nothing by it."

"What?" the man asked, then turned back to look at the woman. "Oh, you mean Lilly? No, it's not like that. She's my sister."

"Well, still, I weren't trying to bother her."

"Yes, no, that's fine," the man shook his head and smiled. "I was actually hoping I might talk to you about a business opportunity."

"To me?" Hollis asked.

"Why, yes, to you," the man said, encouraging. "There are several people in this café, but you stood out to me as a man who isn't afraid to do what he has to in order to move up in the world."

The man motioned to the chair and Hollis sat back down and the man sat across from him.

"Now, am I wrong about that?" the man asked, removing his hat, and placing it on the table in front of him.

Hollis straightened himself in the chair.

"I hadn't never been afraid of a little work, if that's what you're asking," he said.

"Indeed," the man nodded. "I could tell right away you're a hard worker. I'm Remy Oswald, by the way of Oswald Enterprises."

The man stuck out his hand and Hollis took it.

"Hollis Wentworth," he said, "of, uh, the Enoch Wentworths."

"Splendid, Mr. Wentworth. Now, seeing as you're no doubt an industrious fellow, what if I were to tell you that for an incredibly low buy-in price, you could be part of a land development group that would see you get a two-hundred-percent return on your investment?"

"Land development?" Hollis asked.

"That's right," Oswald said, his face brimming with enthusiasm. "It just so happens that my associates and I have exclusive buying rights to some of the most sought-after land in all of these United States."

"Whereabouts?"

"Why, the great state of Florida, of course."

"Florida?"

"Absolutely, Mr. Wentworth," Oswald said. "Florida. White sandy beaches, perfect weather year-round, the food, the women . . . well, I suppose I don't need to tell you about it. I'm sure you've visited the Sunshine State many times yourself."

"Oh, sure, yessir," Hollis said. "Many times."

Hollis raised his coffee cup to drink, but it was empty, and he instead slurped at air.

"What about the gators?" he asked, carefully placing the empty cup back on its saucer.

"Pardon?"

"Florida has a bunch of gators, don't it?" he asked. "Or at least it did all them times I was there. Maybe they done run 'em off since then. Have they?"

"Have they what?" Oswald asked, his confusion growing.

"Run the gators off."

"Ah, well, the particular development areas we're investing in are quite gator free."

Hollis nodded and clicked his tongue.

"That's a smart move, Mr. Oswald," he said. "A damn smart move. Gators are nasty business, the scaly bastards."

"Right. So, the up-front investment is negligible. And of course there are tiers at which you can come in, depending on your willingness—"

"I'm willing as hell," Hollis said, leaning forward with eyebrows raised.

"Well, that's good. That's very good. And how much money would you be looking to invest? After the initial one-hundred-dollar buy-in, of course."

"A hundred dollars?" Hollis asked.

"That's correct, that's the up-front. To get your foot in the door. This is a very competitive playing field, Mr. Wentworth. Highly sought after."

Hollis nodded. He looked out the window at the brown river.

"I assure you, Mr. Wentworth," Oswald added, "you won't make a thin dime just looking on."

"I'll level with you, Remy. I got a bunch of money tied up in some other things, here and there. So I can only give you . . ." Hollis emptied his pockets of wadded bills and loose change and counted it out slowly on the table. "Twelve dollars and eighty-seven cents. But, if you're staying a little while, I can sure enough get you the rest."

Oswald picked up his fedora and held it upside down.

"I'll tell you what, Mr. Wentworth," he said, scraping the money from the table into the hat. "Lilly and I are headed up to Dallas to meet with some more investors. Real sharks, these gentlemen. However, because you seem like a trustworthy fellow, I'll take this money now, and then we'll swing back through in a few days on our way home to Florida. How does that sound?"

"That sounds goddamn splendid, Mr. Oswald," Hollis said, grinning.

46

The faint light of the morning and waxwings called out in the hollow by the hundreds, filling ice-glittered trees like unnatural Christmas balls. They belted their song of survival through the forest and the river valley and nowhere in their melody did the notes take on a wistful tone, despite their fallen brethren who lay dead and frozen-winged beneath the very stage from which the chorus was performed.

The bloated river passed in swells and chops alongside the snow-dusted streets of Enoch. It was a Sunday though no bells yet rang and no one was about the town and Death had slipped in and was gone again but His mark remained.

The pawn shop proprietor was the first to see. He opened the door for the whining dog and followed it out into the cold and looked north toward the mill and the forest and then south toward the town and he saw the body affixed at the neck to a thick rope and the rope looped from the hotel balcony and the body tarrying there in the short breeze left behind by the storm.

The man stared for a while and then called in the dog and closed his door and locked it. It was nearly half an hour before he heard a woman scream.

47

Boyd and Davis were tasked with cutting down the corpse and delivering it to Doctor Withers, sequestering the hotel employees, and asking questions. Amon was on the phone to Austin for half the morning. One aide and then another. When at last he reached Wolfe, he was astounded by the lack of concern.

"I don't think you're hearing me," Amon told him. "This is the third hanging since I've been here, and this one was right in the middle of the street."

"And you believe the Fenleys hung this man?" Wolfe asked.

"No, I don't believe that," Amon said, exasperated. "The man who was hanged was Yancy Greaves, a known Fenley associate."

"Then how does this issue pertain to your investigation?"

"Surely you can't be asking that," Amon said. "This town is about to look like the goddamn Somme if you don't get some men down here, and I mean fast."

"We've been over this, Ranger Atkins. I can't spare—"

"Who can?" Amon hollered into the phone. "The highway boys? The feds? Get somebody down here or we're going to have a bloodbath on our hands."

Wolfe was silent.

"Gordon," Amon said, tired, his head hanging. "Who has the play? Why am I here?"

"Are you refusing your assignment, Ranger?" Wolfe asked, his tone flat.

"Christ," Amon raised his voice again. "Why am I here? Huh? What the hell am I doing here?"

Amon begged for answers, but Wolfe had gone, and the line was dead. Amon hung up the receiver and stared at it for a while and might have kept staring for hours on end had Coy Taggert not walked into the annex with his hat in his hand.

Amon stood.

"Mr. Taggert," he said. "I take it you've changed your mind, in light of recent events."

"Yancy Greaves was my friend," Coy said.

He kept his head down but his eyes up, glancing around the small office.

"Where's them other two at?" he asked.

"In town," Amon told him. "Dealing with the fallout."

"Good," Coy said. "I just want to deal with you. Nobody else."

Amon folded his arms.

"Who says there's any deal to be had?" he asked.

At this, Coy's head shot up.

"There is," he said, willing it to be true. "There's got to be."

"Depends on what you can tell me," Amon said.

"Can you keep me safe?"

"You don't have anything do you?" Amon asked. "You just know the Fenleys are losing their war and you're trying to save your own ass."

"They'll kill me," Coy pleaded. "I gotta know you can keep me safe. That's the deal."

"There's not any deal, Coy, unless you actually have something to say."

"We jack up the back ends of their cars," Coy said. "Raise them up so that when they're loaded down with whiskey crates they look normal."

Amon shook his head.

"That's nothing. You understand that? That doesn't help me. I need to know about Charlie Cooper."

"I don't know about Cooper."

"Then you can't help me."

"That deputy's crooked," Coy spouted. "Boyd."

Amon pursed his lips.

"A desperate man would say anything," Amon reasoned. "How do you know?"

"He comes to the shop some," Coy said. "Gambles."

"Not enough," Amon told him.

"I know he's run liquor for them. And I've seen him take money."

Amon was considering this when the phone rang.

"Stay put," he told Coy, and he answered the call.

A woman was crying.

"Is this that Ranger?" she asked through her whimpered sobs.

"This is Ranger Amon Atkins," Amon said.

"I'm done with him," the woman said. "He ain't never gonna leave his wife. He just strung me along, lying the whole time."

Amon frowned.

"Who?" he asked. "Who is this?"

"And the things I done for him—not just in the bedroom," she clarified. "The secrets I kept."

"Ma'am, who is this?"

"Daphne Gay," the woman said. "I'm his secretary."

"Whose secretary?" Amon asked, but he knew it before she answered.

"Sheriff Cheatham," she said, and then there was a long pause. "I can tell you why you're really down here. They set you up. All of them—"

"Hang up the phone," he said. "Meet me at the diner across from the courthouse in two hours."

He put the phone back in its cradle and took a deep breath and let it out.

"Mr. Taggert," he said, and Coy turned from the window.

"What was all that about?" Coy asked.

"Are you armed?" Amon asked, fastening his gun belt and reaching for his keys.

"Huh?"

"Do you have a gun or knife on you?"

"Why, hell yes," Coy said. "I got one of each."

"Take out your weapons. Put them on the desk."

Coy hesitated but did as he was told.

"Now, walk to the back of the room and into the cell on the left-hand side."

"What?"

"If you'd like to cooperate as a witness, I will provide you with safe transport out of Enoch just as soon as I can set it up," Amon told him. "But in the meantime, I need you in that cell."

Coy looked at the cells in the back of the office and looked at the pistol and bowie knife he'd laid on Amon's desk.

"Fine," he said and went solemn into the cell.

"I'll be back for you as soon as I can," Amon said.

"What?" Coy asked and moved toward the door but Amon slammed it shut.

"What about Boyd?" Coy asked. "He'll kill me if he finds out."

"If he shows up, say I booked you in for drunk and disorderly. Ought not be too much of a stretch."

"Well, where in the hell are you going?" Coy called after him, but Amon didn't answer.

He left out from the annex and drove slowly through town and he took measure of each person who lifted their head to watch him pass.

They set you up. All of them.

There was still a small crowd in front of the hotel, so he turned along the backstreet behind it and came up the alley next to the barbershop and parked the car just beneath the stairs.

He waited until there was no one walking past and then he climbed from the car and up the stairs and stopped at the door to the apartment and looked out again to see if anyone was watching.

He nearly ran over Cora and Joseph as he came through the door.

"What are you doing home?" she asked, startled.

"Where are y'all going?"

"Take some air, Amon," she said, confused. "What's happened?"

"You're leaving," he said, shaking his head and ushering them further from the door. "Pack your things. You're going to your father's today. Right now."

"You're scaring him," Cora said, and Amon looked down at his son. Joseph was wide-eyed and clutching his mother's hand.

Amon tried to shake the worry from his own face. He knelt down.

"I'm going to drive you," Amon told the boy, speaking slowly, forcing himself to smile, "to the train station. You're going to go see grandpa—today, instead of Saturday."

Joseph looked up at Cora and Cora nodded.

"It's okay," she said. "Go get your clothes and your toys together."

When the boy had gone, she turned to Amon.

"What is this?" she asked.

"It's not safe here. It never was. I should have never brought you."

She could see the concern in his eyes. Even more troubled than usual.

"We'll go," she nodded. "And you'll come with us."

He shook his head.

"I can't, Cora. Not yet."

"You can, Amon. Truly," she said. "I told you I wasn't asking, but now I am. I'm asking you to come. But if you want me to make a speech, I won't do it. I love you. You know that. And I know you love me too. But your entire life you've been fighting yourself—part of you trying to impress your father, the other part worried you'll turn into him. This is your chance to change the path you're on. Come with us."

"Get your things," he told her. "Quick."

He stepped outside the apartment onto the landing at the top of the stairs and looked toward the street, where passed a bundled family on their way to the church and he watched them go. In their absence there was only the river beyond, and it flowed endlessly, and he watched it too. Minutes later a squared-off wheelbarrow appeared, carrying the body of Yancy Greaves as it lay in an unnatural procumbence, and the man pushing it paused and looked up at Amon and then went on.

48

They woke before dawn and found each other again in the dark. After, they collapsed into the sweat-dampened sheets and when the cold, pale sun labored in the east, they lay together and watched the world around them come to light.

She rose naked from the bed and went to the closet and slipped into a nightgown. He watched her cross the room and go into the hallway and he could hear her singing in the kitchen as she put the coffee on.

"What'll I do when you're far away and I am blue, what'll I do?"

He rolled over and stretched out toward the side table and found her cigarettes with the tips of his fingers and slid them closer and pulled one from the pack. He repeated the routine to grab the matches and struck one and lit the cigarette and laid back against the headboard and smoked and listened to her voice.

"When I'm alone with only dreams of you that won't come true, what'll I do?"

When she came back to the bedroom, she had two cups of coffee and handed one over to him.

"Frog's gonna come back, you know," she said.

"Maybe not."

"No, he will. It's always the worst ones that survive," she said. "Momma used to say there was them the devil himself wouldn't take on account of how evil they were."

He forced a laugh.

"You don't believe in any of that, though, do you?" she asked him. "I heard a lot of fellas found religion in the foxholes."

"Not me," he said. "The things I saw—"

He stopped and was quiet and she sipped her coffee and ran her fingers through his hair.

"The things I saw made me believe in something worse than the devil," he said.

"Like what?"

"Like men," he told her. "Like me."

"Whatever you did over there," she said, "you had to do it."

"No one *has* to do anything. There's always a choice."

"What was yours?" she asked, and she felt him tighten and wondered if she'd gone a step too far.

He drew in a breath and what he might've said was gone with the sound of someone pounding on the door.

"Frog," she said. "Hide. Or crawl out a window. Shit."

The pounding continued and Adaline put out the cigarette and went through the house to the front door. When she opened it, Horace Clayton removed his hat.

"Miss Adaline," he said. "Frog wants you at the quarry this morning."

"Frog's back?"

"Yes ma'am, Squirrel too," he told her and took a step back and looked down the street.

She frowned.

"What is it?" she asked.

"Yancy Greaves is dead," he said. "They strung him up in the middle of town."

"My god," she gasped.

"That ain't all," he told her. "They burnt his house too."

"Nelda?" she asked. "The children?"

He shook his head.

She put her hand to her mouth.

Horace scratched at his thinning hair. He looked unsettled.

"What else?" she asked.

"It's just . . . I'm supposed to collect you, ma'am," he said. "See that you get there safe. Frog run into some trouble on the road. Plus this business with Yancy—Frog thinks Blakewell and his bunch are making a move."

She hesitated.

"Alright," she told him. "Wait in the car. Let me get my things."

She closed the door and Jesse stepped out from the hallway.

"The children," she said.

"Go with him," he said, leading her away from the door. "Convince Frog nothing has changed. Let me get my brother's family on a train. Then you and me, we'll go."

"Go where?"

"I don't know. Dallas. Denver. Anywhere that's not here."

"You'd leave with me?" she asked him.

"Of course I would. I love you," he said. "I've never stopped loving you."

She moved closer to him and reached up and touched his face. He put his hand on hers.

"I can't," she said, pulling away. "I have to stay. I owe people."

"How much? I have money. And I can make more."

"It's not about the money, Jesse," she turned away from him and walked to the kitchen and opened the cabinet.

"What's it about then?" he asked.

She pulled down a bottle and a glass and set them on the counter and uncorked the bottle and filled the glass halfway. She drank it and gave it another half fill and drank that too, then corked the bottle.

He watched her.

She placed both hands on the counter and hunched her shoulders and dropped her head. She could feel him staring. Waiting.

"You're not the only one that's done terrible things, Jess," she told him.

"I don't care what you've done. We'll leave it behind too. We'll leave it all. Everyone and everything."

"And Eliza? The girl?" she asked. "What do you think would happen to them? Frog would never stop looking for us, but even if we stayed ahead of him, lived the rest of our lives on the run, they would never be safe. Are you willing to live with that guilt?"

He put his head down.

She uncorked the bottle again and this time drank straight from it and held it out to him, and he took it and drank as well.

"We weren't supposed to ever see each other again," she said, not looking at him. "Let alone this."

"But we did," he argued. "We're here right now, goddamnit. You can't ask me to ignore that."

"I'm not asking," she told him. "I'll go on to the quarry. You get your family out of here."

He wasn't planning to do as she said and yet his feet were moving toward the back door. The air felt wrong. Too heavy. Like he was struggling against an invisible screen that weighed down the room. He'd only just found her again. Surely this was not the end.

He was standing with the door open, but he didn't remember opening it. Woodsmoke overran all other fragrance of the morning. Gray smoke and gray clouds drifting along a gray sky. Etiolated country. *Where are your green pastures? Where is your still water?*

"You didn't ask me," she said, and he looked up at her.

"Ask you what?"

"What I did."

"It doesn't matter," he said. "Whatever it was, you had to do it."

49

They drove in silence. Attended only by the occasional winter birds, lighting and lifting from telephone wires that swung and wobbled like strange industrial branches.

When they arrived at the station in Nebat City, there was a train departing, and they sat in the car until the platform had cleared a bit.

"Nebat to Dallas, Dallas to McKinney," Amon repeated. "No stops."

Their train didn't leave for another twenty minutes, but Amon insisted they board. There were a few people left at the depot and Amon took in each of them with suspicion.

"Amon, you're a grown man. I won't badger you or pretend to mother you," Cora said. "But all you have to do is come with us. End this today."

"Soon," he said, eyes darting around the platform to see who might be watching, might be listening.

"Why, Amon?" she asked. "What good are two more men behind bars? You're afraid of turning into your father, but even he saw that it had become an obsession. It was too late for him, but it isn't too late for you."

He put his hands on the sides of her shoulders and looked into her eyes.

"I'm close," he said. "The answers are there. I just need to find them."

He bent and kissed his son. Joseph looked up at him.

"I love you," Amon said, holding up his pointer and pinky fingers, and extending his thumb.

The boy mirrored the shape with his own hand and smiled and hugged Amon's waist.

"Go," he told them. "I'll see you soon."

He saw them onto the train and then crossed the tracks and crossed the street and there stood by a bronzed statue of the angel Phanuel, who held a great sword. And hidden among the angel's wings were the faces of the repentant, peering out.

He stood until the train was in motion and stood longer still until it had disappeared, northbound into the pines.

Daphne Gay was there in the diner when he arrived, her eyes still red and puffed from crying. She held up her hand but then quickly lowered it and looked around as if perhaps she'd done the wrong thing.

"Miss Gay," he said, sliding into the booth across from her. "Tell me everything."

"There was a meeting," she whispered before he could even open his notebook. "In the sheriff's office, the morning after Charlie Cooper died. The other men said maybe they could use it to pin the Fenleys with murder. The sheriff didn't think so. He said people in the county supported the Fenleys. That there'd be an uprising if they were arrested. Especially for killing a lowlife like Charlie Cooper."

Amon looked around the diner and the waitress smiled at him, and he gave a quick smile back and she took it for a summons and came over.

"What can I get you, honey?" she asked.

"Coffee'd be fine," he said, and she nodded and put away her scratchpad.

Daphne waited until the girl was gone and leaned across the table.

"The other men said the sheriff was just too scared to go after the

Fenleys," she said. "They argued for a while. And the sheriff said they must be scared too or else they wouldn't be in his office. That's when one of the men, the old one, got really angry."

"Who were they?" Amon asked. "These other men."

"I don't know," she shook her head. "But the old man said maybe they could use Charlie as bait to catch a bigger fish. Somebody that would have every lawman in the state down here if he were to go missing."

"A Texas Ranger," Amon said.

"That's right," she said. "They hoped if you started poking around, the Fenleys would kill you, then they could have the whole country wanting to make an arrest."

"The sheriff liked that idea, but the other man didn't."

The girl stopped talking. Amon looked up and her face had gone from nervous to frightened. He could see her skin raise.

"He had on a mask."

"Blakewell," he said.

"They didn't use names," she told him. "But he didn't think it was a good idea. He said the Fenleys weren't dumb enough to kill a Ranger. So the sheriff said maybe they just get a Ranger down here and the man in the mask could kill him and that would be big enough to pin on the Fenleys and make it stick. But he didn't like that either. He said that left him too exposed if something went wrong. He said even with all that's happened, the Rangers still carry some clout."

She looked away and bit at her lip.

"What else did they say?" Amon asked.

"The other man. The old one. He said there was a way they might could play it," she told him. "He said there was one Ranger who didn't have any clout left at all. That . . ."

"What? What else?"

"That this Ranger had crippled a senator's son. That he had a target on him."

Amon stopped writing and looked up.

"They all agreed," she said. "They'd give you a couple of weeks. If the Fenleys didn't kill you, the man in the mask would. Then they'd arrest Frog and Squirrel for it."

"Daphne," he said, reaching across the table and placing his hand on top of hers. "Will you testify to this? To this meeting?"

She jerked her hand back, frowning.

"No," she said. "I'm telling you this to save your life. They've got people everywhere, Mr. Atkins. Ending things with the sheriff means I'm not safe here, let alone me talking to you. I'm on the next train to Houston. I'd suggest you get out too, while you still can."

50

The temperature crept up. Bright winter sun. Ice weeping from the roofs of the town. The frost fell from the hushed hermetic pines and rags of snow withered and bled invisible into the cold ground.

Inside the cabin, the fire was roaring in the stove near where Jesse stood awaiting Eliza's reaction.

She stared at him. Blank. Then she began to laugh.

He looked at Sarah and the girl looked scared.

"Eliza?" Jesse asked.

"Another Cole ready to abandon us," she said and then laughed again.

"It's not safe here," Jesse said. "For any of us. There's only one way this thing is gonna end."

"You think I don't know what this is about, Jesse?" she asked, and now her face was sharp and accusing. "You're trying to get rid of us. I know who works for the Fenleys. I know who you've been spending your nights with."

"I'm coming with you, Eliza," he told her. "You're just going first. I have to make sure nobody's gonna follow us. I don't think the Fenleys are just going to up and let me leave, but I have to get you and Sarah out of here."

It was the truth, just not all of it. Eliza was right. He was still grasping for a way to be with Adaline. Still hoping he could figure out how to keep them all safe.

"And if we don't go?" Eliza asked. "If we stay here, then what?"

"Eliza, you have to listen to me. Every dollar the Fenley's gave me is in a canvas bag in granddaddy's old trunk. Take it and go. I'll meet you in Dallas at the Trinity Hotel, but you have to leave today."

Eliza's hands were on the knees of her dress, her fingers digging into her legs.

"I won't," she said. "I won't leave my home. I won't leave Edith."

"Momma," Sarah pleaded. "Please. I'm scared."

"Don't be scared," Eliza said. "Jesse's not leaving. Right, Jesse? You won't abandon the only blood you have left in this world. Your brother's daughter."

Jesse stepped back from her. The girl had been right. It was worse than he'd realized—or than he'd been willing to admit.

Sarah began to cry. Sniffling at first and then sobs.

"I'm sorry," she said. "I'm sorry for crying."

Jesse went to her.

"It's alright," he said, putting his arms around the girl and hugging her tight. "It's alright. I'm not going anywhere. I'll figure this out."

He kissed her on the side of her head, near her ear.

"Go," he whispered, then pulled away and looked up at Eliza.

"Fetch Moss," he told her. "Take Sarah with you. Tell him to stay with you until I'm back. I'll go to the quarry and see what Frog and Squirrel found out. See what their next move is."

"See," Eliza said, her smile as unbalanced as her voice. "We'll all stay here together. In our home."

Jesse looked at the girl and nodded. She shook her head, crying.

"Go," he mouthed, but she slid down against the wall and hugged her knees.

When Jesse arrived at the quarry the Schaffers and Claytons were unloading bags of corn and sugar from Frog's truck. The side panel was riddled with bullet holes. The window glass was shattered.

"What happened?" Jesse asked.

Eli hoisted a bag over his shoulder.

"Couple of fellas thought they'd catch the Frog in an ambush," he said. "Didn't know what they was asking for, I guess."

"Kept one alive for a bit," Hank added. "Worked on him for information. The boy never said a word."

"And won't never say another one," Eli said.

"Where's Frog now?" Jesse asked.

"In there with Adaline," Eli told him, nodding toward the caverns.

"And Squirrel? I need to talk to him."

"He's done been here and gone. Back to the insurance speak, I think he said."

Jesse looked toward the cave. He wouldn't be able to get Ada away from Frog. Not yet. He walked back to the car but before he could open the door Hollis Wentworth came walking into the quarry.

Despite the cold, gray shame of the day, Hollis was smiling. Whistling.

"What say, Jess?" Hollis called out, holding up his hand. "You boys mixing up the good stuff? I wouldn't mind wetting my whistle beens I done come all this way."

"What are you doing here, Hollis?" Jesse asked him.

Hollis clapped his hands together and then put them on either hip.

"Well, I've decided to let you use it," he said.

"Use what?"

"Granddaddy's submarine shell."

"We're already using it."

"I know it. And I've decided to let you keep on using it. All you gotta do is give me a hundred dollars."

Jesse's patience was worn and ragged and barely hanging on. He might have to convince Eliza to leave the only place she'd ever known. And he needed to figure out a way to get Adaline away from Frog without the big man staving his head in.

And now Hollis. *Why today, bud*, Jesse thought.

"What do you need the money for?" he asked, closing his eyes.

"I've got myself a little investment opportunity with a fella out of Florida," Hollis said, and his chest swelled, and he looked down his nose at his oldest friend and grinned. "Big money to be made. I might could get you cut in on the deal too, Jess—if Mr. Oswald signs off on it."

"It's a swindle."

"Do what?"

Jesse sighed.

"The man—Oswald, whoever—he's conning you. Whatever he's promising in Florida, it ain't real. And if it is real, it ain't the way he says it is. You understand?"

Hollis looked shocked. He shook his head and took a step back.

"I never thought you'd be one to get jealous of another man's prospects," he said. "Truly, I did not."

"What?" Jesse asked.

"I said I'd talk to the man for you and see what I can do, but first I need the money I'm owed for the equipment I've done and leased to you bunch."

"Hollis—" Jesse started, but Frog Fenley cut him off.

"You ain't getting a goddamn dime, Wentworth," Frog bellowed.

He came lumbering up from the mouth of the cavern. Jesse noticed his limp. There was blood, soaked and dried, on the left shoulder of his shirt.

"I'm providing a good," Hollis said, standing his ground. "I ought to be paid for it."

"And I'm providing you with one chance to get the hell away from here," Frog said. "Don't come back. Don't open your slack-jawed mouth. And if you see any one of these boys in town, you turn around and walk the other way. You get that?"

Hollis clenched his jaw. His chin still up in the air.

"Is that how it is, Jesse?" he asked.

"Cole ain't got shit to do with how it is," Frog boomed, but Hollis kept staring at Jesse.

"That's right," Jesse said, barely above a whisper. "Go on, Hollis."

Hollis grew red in the face. He stood with a nodding head, then his whole body seemed to shake. Before Jesse could stop him, he was charging Frog, who stood in a stunned disbelief. So surprised, in fact, that he didn't make a move to get out of the way. Hollis lowered his head and collided with the big man, but even with the free shot, Hollis simply bounced off and fell to his knees in the mud.

Collecting himself, Frog looked down and Hollis was there just beneath him, wide-eyed and fearful as the realization of his failed attack settled over him.

Frog delivered a single right hand. Hollis collapsed, his nose broken instantly. He moaned something unnatural, and it sounded to Jesse like the strange wailings of a dying hog. Jesse looked away.

Hollis tried to stand but stumbled and staggered and finally crawled away from the scene. Frog returned with the others to the cave, where already the large-batch fermentation was beginning.

Hollis used one of the cars to pull himself up and he leaned against it, crying. The blood had already poured down his face and smeared where he'd tried to hold it. Mud caked the front of his clothes and his mouth hung open in pain.

"Shit," Jesse said under his breath.

He went to Hollis, who was whimpering and moaning in strange successions, and hooked his arm and helped him to the car. He laid him in the back seat and Hollis was now groaning "thank you" over and over and Jesse told him to hush.

"I'm taking you to Doc Withers," Jesse said. "Then you need to stay the hell away from me."

"What?"

"I've been trying for more than a week to keep you from getting beat on by the Fenleys," Jesse barked at him. "I've blown up my whole fucking life over it. And yet here you are, with Frog's fist printed across your ignorant-ass face. And why? All because you couldn't leave things alone. Couldn't just set still for a few days. No, not my pal Hollis. You had to go and let yourself get cheated. Again."

"What's *again*," Hollis moaned, half crying.

"You think Frog Fenley is some sort of card shark?" Jesse asked, turning around and taking another look at the pitiful state of his cargo. "They cheated you, Hollis. It was fixed. You heard Squirrel that day. Everything is fixed. They don't do nothing unless they're guaranteed to win. Don't you get that? You shouldn't have never set down in the first place."

"I'm sorry, Jesse," was all Hollis could manage. "I'm sorry for everything. Just take me home. I don't want to see Withers. Just take me home."

He was crying and his snot was mixing with the blood.

"I need to blow my nose," he sobbed. "But it hurts."

"Don't blow it," Jesse told him, "or a bone's liable to fly out."

He helped Hollis out and got him up to the door and Hollis had stopped talking and stopped crying and went inside without saying anything and closed the door behind him.

Jesse stood there on the porch and he could hear Hollis's haggard breathing just on the other side of the door.

"Jesse," Hollis said.

"Yeah?"

"I know you spoke against me," he said.

"What are you talking about, Hollis?" Jesse asked him, and he was tired in the asking.

"The Fenleys were talking about bringing me on, and you spoke against me. Said I wasn't worth nothing. Yancy Greaves couldn't wait to let me know it neither," Hollis told him. "I didn't believe him. But I guess I do now."

Jesse started to explain but didn't. If Hollis still couldn't see he was trying to protect him, there was no use in wasting the words. He just shook his head and returned to the car and sat there for a while watching the front door and the windows. Nothing moved except the wooden chimes as they clattered into each other at the slightest breeze.

Jesse drove back through the thicket where there were small drifts of snow along the towpath.

He came out on the south side of the logging road and followed it into town and neared the insurance office. He let the car idle in front of the shop. He couldn't see much inside—no one coming or going. He drove on and turned down the alley and parked in the back.

He walked around to the front and ducked inside, and Alderman was there tending to his own bloodied nose.

"Just a warning," Alderman said, tilting his head back and taking a tissue to one of his nostrils. "He ain't in the best mood."

Jesse nodded and slipped behind the wall. The lanterns in the hallway were unlit and the speak was dark and empty save for Squirrel in his corner booth and a short candle stub before him, the flame reflected there in the glass bottle as he drank.

"Come get right, Cole," he said, his face shrouded by shadow.

Jesse dragged a chair up to the open side of the booth and sat across from Squirrel. Squirrel poured a drink and slid it over to him. Jesse declined and slid it back.

"Tell me you found whatever it was you were looking for," Jesse said.

Squirrel passed his hand slow over the candleflame. The light shown along his forearm but no further.

"The only thing I was looking for was a way out," he said.

Jesse frowned. The wax from the candle had gathered and pooled around the base and now it crept out in all directions across the table. A slow-moving plague.

"The last fight I lost was to my brother," Squirrel said, his hand still passing back and forth over the flame like a fire-fueled metronome. "He was trying to keep me from killing our mother. Frog always could throw a punch."

He stopped with his palm just above the candle and the light dancing on the lines of his hand.

"But I told him, once I picked myself up out of the dirt, that even though she didn't do the things our father did, she still allowed them to happen," Squirrel said. "That's nearly the same, wouldn't you say, Cole? To know something's gonna happen and not do a damn thing to stop it?"

"Squirrel, who's hunting us?" Jesse asked. "Folks are on edge. There's bodies turning up."

Squirrel leaned forward and in the soft light he looked more tired than drunk. Like sleep was something he'd been chasing after and he'd just watched it escape for the final time.

"I'm losing," he said. "We're all fucking losing."

Jesse slammed his fist on the table.

"Goddamnit," he said. "You brought me into this to help you. So tell me who we're fighting."

Squirrel looked up. A strange smile on a strange face, and he shook his head.

"You don't fight the devil, Cole. You just do your best to make a deal. Now take a drink or get out."

Jesse stood.

"You're not giving me a whole lot of options here," he said.

"Options," Squirrel repeated, and his voice sounded far away. "There's only ever one option. The rest are just illusions. Just tricks. A facade of choice when no choice exists. It never did. We just do what we have to, don't we, Cole?"

Jesse thought to press him further but could tell by Squirrel's tone and the near-empty bottle that his efforts would be wasted. Instead, he left the insurance office without a plan.

He needed to talk to Adaline again, but Frog would be with her. He thought about going to the annex, talking to the Ranger, and blowing the whole thing wide open. He decided against it. The Fenleys had badges on the payroll. For all he knew, the Ranger's offers had been nothing more than a test of Jesse's loyalty.

He thought these things and more as he walked down the alley and his boots slapped at the hard ground and something was wrong. He stopped, but the footsteps continued. He turned and there were two men following him. He quickened his pace, but before he reached the car two more men stepped out and stood in front of the hood.

"Mr. Cole," one of them said. "It's time you and him had a little sit-down."

"Me and who?" he asked, but they were already shoving him into the back of the car by his head.

51

The red clay soil was soaked with days and weeks of rain. The whole of the earth was not but wet argil, thrown and dripping about the potter's lathe. Ever spinning. Unending rotations of slurry and bole, and awaiting always that hand which might mold it—might sculpt from the mire some worthy design. But on it spun, shapeless and abandoned.

The old man paced the porch with a rifle in hand.

Inside, the woman rocked nervous in her chair, and the girl brought out her violin and played.

> *O soul, are you weary and troubled?*
> *No light in the darkness, you see?*
> *There's light for a look at the Savior,*
> *And life more abundant and free.*

Sarah laid down the instrument.

"I'm going to see if Mr. Moss wants any coffee," she told her mother, and Eliza gave a wary nod.

The girl poured a cup and took it out to the porch.

"I brought you coffee," she said.

"Thankee, Miss Sarah," the old man said and took the cup and drank from it and set it on the wooden ledge.

"You think Jesse's gonna be alright?" she asked him, and she tried to sound only curious, but he could hear the fear in her voice.

"He already come home from one war," Moss said. "He'll come from this one too. Just say your prayers and try to put the rest of it out of your mind."

"I do pray," she said. "But nobody answers."

Moss eyed her.

"Is that all prayers are for?" he asked. "Answers?"

Sarah frowned.

"You ever left Nebat County?" she asked him, changing the subject.

"Sure I have," he said. "Every time I go across the river, I'm in Mamre County. You know, I think the frogs taste better when they come from that side of the banks."

"That's not what I mean," she said. "Haven't you ever been to Dallas? Or Shreveport?"

The old man shook his head.

"There ain't nothing for me in a place like that."

"How do you know if you've never been?"

Moss thought for a minute before he answered.

"A man can touch a hot stove and he'll know that it's hot," he said, and the girl nodded. "But the fella standing next to him can have the same knowledge without having the pain."

The girl considered this.

"You think it's that bad?" she asked.

"Bunch of smoke and concrete," Moss said, shuddering.

"Well, I'd like to see it," she told him. "I'd like to see anything that wasn't covered in dirt and trees."

He looked at her. The hopefulness of youth. The courage and naivety required to test the world—to cut it open and take measure of its merit.

"He told you to leave, didn't he," Moss said.

She nodded.

"I'm going to miss you," he said softly, almost to himself.

"I'm not gonna go," she told him.

"Yes you are," he nodded. "You're already gone."

52

The sunset was sudden and the evening so cold it seemed strange there would have been any sun to set at all. But beyond the low shelf of thin gray clouds the skysill burned amber and gold, and the small woodland creatures found purchase in hollow logs and under wind-formed trees, and whole colonies of bats came rising out from the karsts and caves tucked back into those once-green hills as the country before them fell into shadow.

Amon made the Enoch sheriff's annex just after nightfall. He killed the engine and sat in the dark. There were no other cars and no light from inside the office.

He unholstered his pistol and checked the cylinder and spun it and snapped it back into place. He left the car door open and went quietly toward the front of the building. The door was unlocked, and he eased it open. He took a few steps inside and pulled the door to.

"Coy Taggert," he said, and the man groaned.

"Jest when I get to sleep," he said.

Amon flipped the switch and the lights hummed above him. He looked back to the cells and Taggert was shielding his eyes.

"What say you build that fire up some?" he asked. "These thin-ass blankets must've come from the paper factory."

Amon put several more logs on the fire.

"When do I get out of here, Ranger?" Coy asked. "I thought you was gonna keep me safe, not keep me here like a sitting duck."

"You can go right now," Amon said, grabbing the cell keys.

"What?" Coy grabbed the cell door and held it closed. "Hold on, now. I thought was making a deal."

"I don't know that there's anybody left to make a deal with," Amon told him. "As far as I know, we're both sitting ducks."

"Wait, wait, wait," Coy said. "I can't just walk out of here. Somebody might've seen me come in. They may be out there right now, just waiting to whip my ass or kill me one."

Amon sighed.

"Fine. One night, then. I'll come let you out in the morning," he said. "I'll make a big show of it. Even give you a citation for public drunkenness."

"I'd sure appreciate that."

Amon nodded. The phone sounded loudly through the office and caused him to jump to attention, his heart hammering.

"That phone won't quit ringing neither," Coy said.

Amon went to the receiver and thought for a moment before picking it up but did.

"Atkins," he said.

"Amon, it's Beatrice," his aunt said. "I been calling. I checked on that campaign report for you."

"And?" Amon asked, his eyes on the door.

"I worked with those women for twenty-nine years," she said. "Twenty-nine years I worked, and for them to sit there and lie to my face. Like I wasn't anything. Like they didn't have a care in the world. It's a sad day, Amon, when these women—"

"Beatrice," he said, "the report."

"Right, well," she sounded offended. "I finally got it, but it took some real doin'. I had to threaten Burnedette Bolles with telling her husband what she really got up to on sewing night."

"The names," he said.

"I got 'em here," she told him. "Gerald Dayne give fifty dollars. Arthur Hightower give fifty-five. Hoster Muncy give—"

"Who gave the most?" Amon asked. "Any big donations?"

"Hmm," she said. "Biggest haul was one thousand and five hundred dollars."

"Who?"

"Fella named Percy Preston," she said.

53

The car strung out along the curves of the forest road and onto the farm-to-market that bent through the northern hills. Jesse sat in the back. His hands were bound with coarse rope.

The driver came up to the head of the highest hill in the county and the sky before them was a mix of blue and gray like thin hammered metal, and somewhere beyond those dark edges it was fastened to the end of the world—pulled tight and affixed to an eternal fulcrum that swung it from light to dark and back again.

They were a dozen miles north of the highway when the car approached the gate and began to slow. The gate was iron and arched and had a scripted 'P' on either side. There was a chain holding it closed and a lock on the chain, but the lock wasn't set and the man riding shotgun hopped out and unwrapped the chain and let it fall to the dirt. He opened the gate and they drove through and followed the rock drive for a long way yet, until they came at last to an old plantation house with towering pillars in the front and a large, stately balcony over the porch. There was a circle drive laid before the manor and from its western apex a pathway of herringboned bricks that led to the stone-cut steps, of which there were several and built in a great swooping shape that was wide at the base and narrowed where the steps met the porch.

On either side of the staircase were long, sprawling garden beds filled with an unruly mix of weeds and vines and months-dead rosebushes, the thorned stalks of which had grown diagonal and now rested against the splintered white paint of the porch railing.

The car stopped in the middle of the roundabout. The driver got out and came around and opened the door and untied Jesse's bonds.

"Go on in," he said and waited until Jesse was out and then got back in the car, and along with the other men, he drove away.

Jesse stood alone before the great manor.

He walked up the front steps, where icicles hung from the banister in varied rows like the warped portcullis of some ancient winter palace, and in any one of them Jesse could see his double ascending the same staircase made miniature in its reflecting.

"I wonder," a man said, "what our forefathers would have done in times like these."

Jesse stopped and looked up and Percy Preston was there, covered in a patchwork quilt, sitting in a rocking chair that wasn't rocking.

"Mr. Preston," Jesse said, nodding. He'd seen the old man before, at company picnics where Preston would give a short speech and thank the men for their labor at the mill and their wives for the assortment of casseroles and pies. He was not an imposing figure, even in his younger years. He was mostly bald but for a friar's ring of hair and an orangish-colored mustache. He had a legion of freckles on his skin, the largest of which was nearly four inches and covered much of the right side of his face.

"You're Jesse Cole, yes?" Preston asked.

"Yessir."

"Good. I've been waiting on you," Preston told him. "Please come inside, it's far too cold out here for an old man."

Jesse looked back down the hill as if there was something in the night that might come forward to support his cause, but there was nothing and no one, and he turned then and nodded to the man who rose slowly from his chair.

The foyer was well lit and the house was warm. Affixed to the plaster walls was a series of iron sconces with coal-burning lamps within and the lamps lighting the way to the great room, where a robust fire roared beneath a marble mantel. Atop the mantel rested an iron-stained stone that looked as if it belonged to another age. Another version of the earth entire.

The fireplace had long been lit and the mounds of ashes threatened to bury the andirons that held the burning logs. Two golden lion statues flanked the fire, each locked forever in a carved and gilded bellowing. A well-dressed black man was tending the crackling wood and he looked up as the two of them entered.

"Three whiskeys, Maurice," the old man said.

"Mr. Preston, why am I here," Jesse started, but the old man waved away the words and motioned for him to sit in one of the leather-upholstered chairs arranged catty-corner from the fireplace.

Jesse relented.

The floor beneath them was an intricate parquet design, tessellations of contrasting walnut and oak, and the oversized windows were positioned above three and half feet of tired, buckling wainscot. There was an echoing emptiness to the house—a forgottenness. The balustrade was chipped and peeling, there were cracks in the plaster where wall met ceiling, and even the few hung portraits were tilted one way or the other, as if they were sighing at the decay. Swept into the corner, where the parquet met the baseboards, was a twice-bitten apple, rotted from the inside out.

The old man himself appeared somehow bound to the aging of the structure. His own cracks and fracture lines. He sat in his chair and rested both hands atop a hooked cane and leaned forward, his mouth and jaw moving slowly from side to side but his lips staying closed.

Jesse turned in the chair and glanced up at the bay of windows across the front of the house and looked out and saw only the reflection of the fire centered in the glass, and it looked as if it were burning in some black void, nothing before or behind, just burning, alone in the dark.

They were silent, the two of them, until Maurice reentered the room with a silver tray upon which he carried the three glasses. He served the old man first, then Jesse, and then rested the tray on the mantel above the fireplace with the third glass unclaimed.

"What is it you wanted to show me?" Jesse said at last.

"I knew your grandfather," Preston told him. "He was a good man. Though Plato would argue that's not quite enough."

Jesse furrowed his brow.

"Plato," the old man repeated. "The philosopher. He said knowing good and doing good are two different things."

"That don't exactly seem like a revelation, does it?" Jesse asked.

Preston laughed and the laugh turned to a cough and then he smiled and nodded.

"You wouldn't think so, but then again," he said, and he said nothing else, instead waving his hand around the empty space above him as though to demonstrate some point.

One of the logs in the fire split open from the middle and collapsed with a quick sucking rush and embers exploded upward and then all was settled again and the fire burned as if nothing had happened.

"How's your drink?" Preston asked.

"Burns good enough."

The old man nodded.

"Good," he said. "Go to the desk there."

He pointed and Jesse rose unsure and followed Preston's finger to a short, narrow desk tucked into the back corner, away from the fire.

"Go open the top drawer."

He did.

There were some old envelopes with the tops cut open and the letters still inside, the letter opener itself set next to them. There was a Bible, a book on gardening, and a stack of loose, unframed photographs. Next to the photos was a pistol. Jesse recognized it.

"What the hell is this?" he asked.

"It's what I wanted to show you."

"How'd you come by this?"

"That deputy, Davis, left it in my possession after law enforcement filed their report. Daniel's wife—well, your wife—never came to claim it."

"So, what? You're giving it to me?"

"I am," Preston said. "I, too, had a brother once, taken before his time. It's a difficult thing to justify losing. A shade of one's own countenance, one's own self."

The old man stared at the ancient rock atop the mantel. The fire burned twofold in his eyes.

"Why now?" Jesse asked.

"Call it a show of good faith."

Jesse felt the room grow colder and then the fire roared as the masked man stood next to it and picked up the third whiskey glass.

Jesse flushed out of his chair like a spooked dove.

"Jesse Cole," Preston said, "meet Zev Blakewell."

Jesse looked not at Blakewell but at the old man.

"You're the one?" he asked.

"Oh dear," Preston said. "It's worse than I thought. Squirrel Fenley hasn't told you anything, has he?"

"It sure as shit don't seem like it."

Blakewell laughed and it came out as a strange choking sound. He looked to Jesse like something from a fever dream. Black mask, white skin. Thinly drawn. And his voice seemed as if it were pulled up painfully from a dry well.

"Your employer and I have been negotiating for weeks now," Preston told Jesse. "In fact, adding you to his little roster was apparently supposed to strengthen his bargaining power. He offered money, territory, even a hundred gallons of whiskey to make peace. Still, I was unimpressed by his proposals."

"Listen, fellas," Jesse said. "I'm the paperboy, not the editor. You understand? Whatever y'all want to sort out, you need to do it with Frog and Squirrel. Not me."

"I'm tired of the Fenleys," Preston said. "They bore me. In reality, Mr. Cole, time is not our friend. My sources in the legislature have affirmed the rumor that prohibition will be ending soon. I need to be the only provider of East Texas whiskey long before that happens."

"Why?" Jesse asked. "If it's about to be legal again?"

"Oh, it won't be legal here," Preston assured him. "No, no. We've talked to the church leaders. Made arrangements. See, the politicians in Washington will leave it up to the states. The states will leave it up to the counties. And no county within a hundred miles of this place would ever vote to legalize such a sinful product."

"Only now," Blakewell added, "we won't have to peddle your hillbilly corn liquor. We'll bring it in by the truckload from other states."

"Quite right," Preston agreed. "High volume at cheap costs. We'll bring it in and sell it at a premium. And of course the engine that makes the entire train run: there will be no tax on our profits. Despite what Squirrel Fenley may believe, I don't want his whiskey. I want his customers. His routes. His territories. And Squirrel is no fool. He knows he cannot win. He offered me those things freely."

"Then why couldn't y'all make a deal?"

"Because what I wanted most was his loyalty," Preston said. "And he could not convince me of that."

"What'd you ask of him?"

"Something he wasn't willing to give."

Jesse shook his head.

"Well, I ain't gonna have no part in it."

"You already are part of it, Mr. Cole," Preston said. "That's what I'm trying to explain to you here this evening. I could not come to terms with Squirrel. I hope the opposite will be true with you."

"I can't speak for the Fenleys."

"I don't need you to. I need you to speak only for yourself. Your own desires. I can make you a rich man. Give you back things that have been taken from you. Agree to head my operation, and I can give you anything you want."

"What about spooky here?" Jesse asked, nodding to Blakewell. "Why not have him run it?"

"Mr. Blakewell deals in acquisitions. Once something is acquired, he goes where he is needed next."

"Uh-huh," Jesse said. "So y'all clear out the Fenleys, then I come in and run things for you. Is that the deal?"

"It is if you can prove your troth."

"I can't imagine I have anything to offer you that Squirrel Fenley couldn't."

"Our contracts are blood bound," Blakewell said, but Preston waved his finger and the masked man quieted.

"Before we get to that," Preston said. "Are you interested in the position?"

Jesse knew it was possible that the old man and Squirrel had indeed come to an arrangement, and this could be a test of his loyalty to the Fenleys. He also had a suspicion that if he declined, he would not be leaving the property with a beating heart.

"You wouldn't give me a day or two to think about it, would you?" he asked. "Big decision and all."

"You're afraid if you say no then I'll have Mr. Blakewell deal with you here and now," Preston said. "Is that it?"

"Crossed my mind."

"I assure you that is not my intention. Loyalty cannot be forced by the owner. It must be displayed by the worker. If you are uninterested in my offer, you are free to leave unharmed. Though of course I cannot comment to the length or quality of your life thereafter."

Jesse looked at Preston. The old man was smiling. Pleasant. He seemed almost docile. Blakewell stood by the fire and Jesse noticed his glass was still full next to him.

"I appreciate the offer," Jesse said. "But the truth is I'm leaving Enoch. Leaving Nebat County. I don't want nothing more to do with moonshining for the Fenleys or anybody else. I was just trying to help out a friend and make some money. I never meant to take up bootlegging as a real trade."

Preston clapped his hands down on his knees.

"Ah," he said, "at least we tried. I'll have Maurice bring the car around for you."

Jesse nodded and was walking quickly toward the door when Preston spoke again.

"Probably for the best," the old man said. "You certainly don't want a man with a guilty conscience heading your operation. The mill's production rate dropped nearly ten percent in the weeks after your brother shot himself in our rose garden."

Jesse stopped. The door was there in front of him. He turned away from it.

Preston was smiling still, but it was different now. Sinister.

"I thought perhaps it was the little one dying that had done him in," Preston said. "After all, we know Daniel had dealt with melancholia his whole life. But lo and behold it was your letter they found in his pocket. In the end, he couldn't live with what he'd done to his baby brother."

"What are you saying?" Jesse asked, and he moved quickly toward the old man, but Blakewell slid over and blocked his way.

"What are you saying?" Jesse asked again, shouting around the masked man. "He didn't do anything to me. What did he do?"

He felt unhinged. Come apart from his being, or perhaps come finally into it.

"I'll be happy to tell you, Mr. Cole," Preston said. "But I'll need you to calm down."

"Fuck you," Jesse said, his blood afire. "What are you saying about Danny?"

Preston was slow and casual. He pulled the paper from his shirt pocket and unfolded it, smoothed it out one crease at a time, then handed it to Blakewell, who passed it on to Jesse.

Jesse squinted down at the faded document.

"A draft notice," he said, uncertain, his hands shaking with the rush of adrenaline.

"Look at the name," Preston told him.

His eyes scanned to the top corner of the paper.

Daniel John Cole.

"I don't understand."

"He was a coward and a liar," Preston announced.

"He was drafted too?"

"It was supposed to have been him," the old man said. "Not you. The day he got this, he came straight to me for help. 'Make it go away,' he begged me."

Jesse was shaking his head.

"No, he—"

"I did, of course. I had my old friend at the courthouse, Jerry Hughes, switch your cards. They figured trying to use somebody else would look suspicious, raise too many flags. But a brother? That might work. Might slip through. Get mistook as just an oversight somewhere along the line. No use in looking too close into it. There was a war to fight, after all."

Jesse felt the breath leave him and when he tried to inhale there was nothing there. No air. Just void. He staggered toward the fire and braced himself on the mantel and looked there at the stone. The red stain.

"He tried, naturally, to outsource his lamb," Preston said. "To use a stranger. He pleaded with me on bended knee, but I denied him. It may have been possible. Probably it was. But as I said, there's something sacred about the bond of brothers. Something inviolable. And yet if my power supersedes such consecration, who might stand against me? What majesty there is in such loyalty."

Jesse heard the man's speech like words in a dream. Sounds from another room. Another world.

"He was mine after that," Preston continued. "In full. For me he crushed unions before they could form, maneuvered accounts, even did a fair bit of debt collecting. He was no Mr. Blakewell, but his services were valuable nonetheless. Yet in the end, it was his guilt—his guilt and his cowardice—that caught up with him. He heard the horror stories. He saw the boys that came home and weren't anything like they were when they left. He couldn't imagine what it would be like to face you. So, he didn't. You could've married Adaline Brookshire twelve years ago. Had a family. Had a life. But he took that from you, your own brother.

I wonder if your blood called to him from the ground, the way it calls to me still."

"Why are you telling me this?" Jesse asked.

"Because your brother lied to you," Preston said. "The Fenleys lied to you. Your wife is lying to you. But I will always tell you the truth, Jesse Cole. Even when it is hard to hear. I make my men prove their devotion, but I prove mine as well. The world without is an unsavory pool of dishonesty and drunkenness. But here there can be no lies. Here there is only greed and greed is the truth everlasting."

"Take me back," Jesse demanded, turning again for the door. He could see it there and he focused on it and nothing else. It looked smaller than it had just minutes ago.

Blakewell moved to stop him, but Preston waved him off.

"When you go, so does my offer," the old man said, but Jesse wasn't listening.

He stumbled out onto the porch and down the stairs. Maurice was there in the car and the car was running. Jesse climbed into the passenger seat and put both hands on the dash in front of him.

"Drive," he said. "Get me away from this fucking place."

54

Dear Danny,

     The war is over. The war has just begun. I am not the boy I was when I left, but neither am I a man. I don't know what I am. A monster.

     For as long as I live, I will never forgive myself for what I've done. I don't know how I'll look you in the eyes. You or anyone else.

     You said to make you proud. I failed.

     Would that some army might come up with a single bomb to finish it all. That's where we're headed anyway. Might as well hurry up and get there.

     I'm quarantined on a ship somewhere off the coast. The Lady Flu is rampant.

     I don't know when I'll be home. I don't know what home is.

     If reincarnation is real, I don't want to come back as a bird anymore. I don't want to come back at all.

                              Jesse

55

Amon was nervous. It was a three-hour drive to Stone County and another twenty minutes to the lake. The forest in this country looked more like a swamp. Everything slumped and sagging. The moss and branches and the roofs of the shacks set off from the roadway. Languishing all.

The car crept along on a series of spidering trails near the water until it reached the small cabin—the yard sloping down and disappearing into the pebbled lakeshore.

Night birds, and down they came from the dark trees and swooping low along the water, just above it, their moon-made shadows spiriting across the surface like dark aquatic comets.

He watched them.

He parked in front of the cabin with little idea of what he'd find inside. He knew death was a possibility.

He knocked a few times and waited and heard nothing. He was thinking of breaking down the door, when it opened.

The old man stood in thermal long johns and held a pistol at his side. He was a caricature of an old man. Thin wisps of white hair strewn about his otherwise bald head in chaotic anti-patterns. Grizzled white and gray beard across drooping cheeks. He was soft shouldered and round in the midsection. The only thing left of his former stature was in his eyes. They still burned with cerulean fire. Blue and knowing. Sovereign from the body, from the passing of time.

"What are you doing here?" the old man asked in the same tone he might have taken with a stray dog digging in his garden.

"Just wanted to have a talk with my father," Amon said. There was a stove fire inside and Amon's father poked at it with an iron and lit a kerosene lamp and set it on the kitchen table.

"Where's my grandson?" he asked.

"With Cora and her father, in McKinney."

Amon looked around the trappings of the old man's life and was suddenly sad for him. The cabin was not but a few hundred square feet and it looked to be in a state of perpetual unkempt.

"Finally left you, did she?" his father asked.

"No," Amon answered. "I sent them away. I'm working a case in Enoch. It wasn't good for them to be there."

"It's never good," his father said. "I learned that a long time ago."

"Is that why we never saw you?" Amon asked, and the old man scowled.

"Is that why you're here?" he asked. "To guilt me? Some sort of reckoning?"

"No," Amon shook his head. "It's not that. I—I wanted to ask you something."

"You could've called," his father grunted.

"You don't have a phone."

"Well?"

"I think the Rangers are corrupt," Amon blurted out. "I think they're bought and paid for by bootleggers or senators or God knows who. And I think they're trying to kill me."

If the old man was surprised by this admission, he didn't show it.

Amon waited for him to speak, but instead his father stood and went to the pantry and pulled out a package of salted crackers and brought them to the table with two warm Cokes. He slid one of the bottles over to Amon.

"Of course they're corrupt," he said at last. "They always have been."

Amon was dumbfounded.

"Not every Ranger. Not every Captain," the old man explained. "But in men there will always be the capacity for corruption. All men. Even me. Even you."

"How can you say that?" Amon asked. "After you fought so long against such things?"

"If your son stood here," his father pointed at a spot on the floor and then moved his hand a few feet away. "And three more boys stood there. And I told you to choose who died—the three boys or your son. Which would you pick?"

Amon shook his head.

"That is corruption," the old man said. "Corruption by love, but corruption nonetheless. Love, greed, fear, guilt—our every emotion tilts the scale."

"I learned it the hard way," he continued. "My twisted logic told me that so long as I kept fighting, I would never lose. Fighting criminals. Fighting dishonesty and venality within the agency. Fighting my own melancholy nature. Just keep fighting, I rationalized—but all the while, I was losing. Losing and losing until *I* was lost."

"So would you do it over?" Amon asked him. "Knowing how everything would turn out. With Momma and Dorothy. With me. Would you do it the same?"

His father thought about the questions. Bit into a cracker and washed it down with a swallow of Coke.

"Five hundred and seventy-four," he said after a time. "That's how many men I arrested. Nearly twenty a year for three decades. That's how many bad men I kept from the door."

He knocked on the table with his fist.

"Would I turn those men loose, so I could have held my wife longer? So I could have had a catch with my boy?"

He shook his head.

"No," he said. "No, I would not. And therein lies my own iniquity.

We all choose our own corruption, son. And I stand by my choice. Just like you stand by yours."

"I haven't made a choice," Amon said.

"And yet here you are," his father told him, pushing the package of crackers across the table. "They're a little stale. But they'll still eat."

56

Maurice dropped him back at the alley in Enoch.

"Mr. Cole," he said. "I'm not supposed to say anything, but I'm going to say thank you for what you done for my cousin."

"Who's your cousin?" Jesse asked, but he didn't hear the man's answer, if the man answered at all. He wasn't listening. He wasn't looking.

All could he see or hear was Danny standing there at the door. Jesse had smiled at him. His own hair and face newly shaven in the way of military grunts around the world. Bag slung on his shoulder. Leaving behind not just his life, but a version of himself that would never exist again. And his brother watched him go.

If we can't protect the ones we love, we're lost.

He drove to the cabin and got out and stood looking at the porch, where Moss had fallen asleep with his back against the door, and Jesse thought to wake him but decided against it. Instead, he pulled his coat tighter around himself and ducked back into the trees, moving slow through the woods.

He walked to the northern border of the property, a small clearing backed by pecan trees, where his people had first settled in this county. There were windrows of pines and other lesser trees that had come back

from a long-ago harvest. Nightjars moved in the brush, hunting for insects that weren't there and wouldn't be until spring.

The chimney was on the back of what had been that first cabin,
and the chimney was all that was left. It loomed over the ghost of the
burned house like a grief-stricken watchman whose warrant lay slain
below. Bones of small creatures populated its base and the remnants of
raided nests were scattered about. Vines had grown thick around it and
then died and fallen away.

The short foundation was heavily cracked. The mantel and one side
of the wood flashing had collapsed, but still in large part it stood as it
may have once stood when it served warmth and life and things not
found in these cold, gray days and black, empty nights.

The wind touched the heavy stone masonry and hummed through
the flue with a dull, plaintive sound. A brown and white barn owl
swooped down from an unseen fortress and landed on what was left
of the crumbling hearth. It stared at Jesse with an upturned head and
black marbled eyes.

Danny had told him—some summer night when the two of them
pulled pallets out onto the porch and slept to the moonlit serenade from
crickets and katydids—that he'd read a book on reincarnation. And
that he'd decided it would be best for both of them if they believed in
it from now on.

Jesse, not yet eight years old, had agreed.

Danny struggled with the idea of not existing. As a child, some days
he was convinced the world was beautiful and other days that it was terrible, but one thing he always believed was that he didn't want to leave it.

Though their parents were devout Baptists, Danny couldn't get past
the grace of God. He said Samuel Watkins had thrown a sack of newborn kittens in the river and laughed at them drowning. He said there
ought not be forgiveness for a thing like that.

"I bet Samuel's dumb ass comes back as a shit beetle," he'd told Jesse.

"What will we come back as?" Jesse asked.

"Something with wings," Danny told him.

"Flies have wings," Jesse noted, but Danny was already imagining himself soaring above the trees somewhere, above all the worries of the world.

The owl tilted its head slow from one side to the other. It lifted a foot and then put it back down. Jesse watched it. He took a step forward and the owl braced itself.

"Tell me why?" Jesse asked, but the owl didn't answer.

It spread its wings and pushed off the chimney, ascending into the dark with a nightmarish scream.

Jesse watched it disappear. He shuddered.

He walked back to the main path and to the car and got inside and sat for a time before starting the engine. He left the cabin and drove through the black, starless night where animal eyes glowed in the woods and rabbits huddled cold in their warrens, and in the still dark a red wolf howled at a moon it could not see.

57

At the north end of Main Street, Hollis Wentworth stood over a fire
he'd built inside a barrel drum and warmed his hands. Next to him were
a dozen stacks of split wood and the old pickup he'd hauled them in.
Hung from the back of the truck was a wooden sign with *sale* painted
in sloppy black letters.

The wind kicked up and Hollis shivered beneath his thin coat. His
nose was swollen and aching under a makeshift splint.

"What say, Hollis?" Darby Langford asked. "I ain't seen you since
Preston locked the gates on us. How you been?"

"How's it look like?" Hollis grumbled.

"You doing any good?"

"Naw. I done burned more than I sold."

"Well, it's sure cold enough," Darby said. "Earlier I seen a politician
with his hands in his own pockets."

Hollis nodded.

"That's a joke," Darby told him.

"I know what it is," Hollis snapped.

"What's got you so goddamn sour?"

"Nothing."

"Alright. If you say it. I'm headed in town to see if there ain't a few cans of Del Monte left at Landry's. Joyce is set on making a fruitcake for the party."

"What party?"

"Oh, nothing much, just a little shindig over at the Deaton place. Potluck type of thing."

"I ain't been invited."

"Well, it's mostly Masons and their families, Hollis. You ain't a Free-mason, are you?"

"I'm a free American."

Darby laughed but Hollis did not.

"Have a good'un, Hollis. We'll see you."

Hollis added another log.

A group of laid-off mill workers passed by in the cold. One of them stopped.

"Y'all hold on," he said, sipping from a flask. "Look at this."

They stopped.

"Hollis," he said, "you've got to be the dumbest sumbitch that's ever lived this long. Selling firewood in the middle of a goddamn forest."

Hollis looked at the wood stack behind him.

One of the men shook his head.

"The Lord takes care of the little children and the soft-brained fools alike," he said.

"You know his grandfather was the same way. Dumber'n bricks, the whole lot of 'em."

Now they were all laughing.

"His daddy was alright," one said, "'fore he went and got himself shot."

"Shit, George Wentworth was the laziest bastard ever set foot in Nebat County. Like a goddamn blister: wouldn't show up till the work was done."

"That's my point. Takes some sense to be lazy."

They all laughed again.

Hollis's head was bowed, as if in silent prayer.

"If it weren't for Cole, I don't imagine you'd have a pot to piss in, would you?"

"Way I heard it, if it weren't for Jesse, he wouldn't have a pecker to piss *with*. Would've gone and got it blowed plum off in France."

"Shit, y'all come on and let's get out of here."

Hollis watched them go and leaned closer to the fire.

Hours to come, Hollis stumbled drunk beside the river. The cratered moon hung like a pale horn in that bleak and bitter sky and shone down on the water and the thin verglas on the rocks along the bank. He stared up at it and, in doing so, slipped on the ice and fell squarely on his ass and from there made no move to rise. Instead, he fussed with his boots until he'd freed both of his feet and he stretched his legs out toward the water. He could feel the cold of the river on his toes without them ever breaking the surface. They hovered there, just above the black water.

"The time for baptisms has long passed, Mr. Wentworth. The hour is late."

Hollis scrambled backward from the water and stood, and the rocks were biting cold on his bare feet and Blakewell was there before him.

58

Amon sat in a wooden chair in the short kitchen. Sleep was itself a dream. His pistol lay disassembled on the table before him. He'd removed the firing pin, oiled the chamber, and used a thin feathered piping to clean the bore. He drank coffee and read by lantern light from the book of Isaiah and after a time he reconstructed the weapon and holstered it and put his holster above the cabinet.

There was only one window in the apartment, and it was small and looked down over the alley between the barbershop and the grocery and most nights Amon would stare aimlessly from above, watching raccoons or cats or the occasional drunk as they crossed below. Sometimes a hunter would bring in a deer or some other game to be butchered and Amon would watch as the carcass was dragged down the alley to the back of the store, tongue lolling and blood trailing and lifeless eyes staring up in accusation.

He closed the Bible fully, then opened it to the ink inscription on the inside cover.

For Amon, my son. Do not stray.

He closed it again.

He went into the bedroom and pulled from the drawers what few possessions he had and gathered his clothes from the closet and put everything into a small trunk and dragged the trunk to the door and left it.

Then he went to the cabinet and took down his gun belt and his gun and took the Bible from the table and put them all in the trunk and stood there with his arms folded for a few minutes and then opened the trunk and took the gun back out.

He was holding it in his hand when he heard footsteps on the metal stairway outside. He thumbed back the hammer and stood just inside the door.

"Ranger Atkins," Jesse hissed, knocking again with the side of his fist. He looked down into the alley and out toward the street. He saw nothing and no one. No new lights had appeared.

Amon opened the door and Jesse looked down at the gun and frowned.

"Will I need this?" Amon asked him.

"Yes," Jesse said. "But not right this second."

They sat in the kitchen with Jesse nearest the fire and Amon across the table.

When Jesse had finished his tale, Amon sat quietly and drank from his coffee.

"So what's the plan?" Jesse said, impatient. "Go after Preston? The Fenleys? Call in the cavalry and get all these bastards at once and be done with it?"

"No," Amon said, lowering his cup.

Jesse waited for him to say more but he didn't.

"So? What then?" Jesse asked.

"There's no cavalry to call, Mr. Cole," Amon shrugged. "I'm leaving Enoch in the morning."

Jesse looked away.

"Were you in on it?" he asked. "Somebody paying you?"

"No," Amon shook his head and shrugged. "Just done with this place. Done with all of it. Charlie Cooper, Percy Preston, Merle Nichols, the Fenley brothers—they're all the same. *It's* all the same: a rigged game. You'll never win and the only way to keep from losing is to quit playing altogether. Just recuse yourself from every last bit of it."

"Then let's unrig the sonofabitch," Jesse insisted. "Don't let them use you anymore for their own gain."

Amon nodded, thoughtfully.

"The same way you're attempting to use me now?" he asked. "To help you get out of a mess you got yourself in?"

"I don't give a good goddamn about who makes, takes, or shakes a bottle of whiskey in this place," Jesse said. "But there's about to be blood on the streets. Hell, there already is. You don't want that on your hands, do you?"

Amon gave him a curious look.

"I asked for your help and you denied me," he told Jesse. "Now you come to tell me there's blood on *my* hands?"

Amon laughed.

"What happened to the man who didn't want to get involved?" he asked.

"You're right," Jesse admitted. "I should've helped you sooner. I was wrong."

"You think knowing right from wrong absolves you from being a bad man. But it only makes you worse than the others."

"And you think walking away makes you noble," Jesse replied, standing from his chair. "But it just makes you chickenshit."

"You fought in the war," Amon said. "I did not—as you and others have reminded me. So tell me, what came from the fighting? Peace? Maybe. For a time. But ask Ludendorff about peace. Ask Goebbels or Röhm."

Jesse paced the length of the small kitchenette.

"I haven't fired a gun in more than ten years," he said. "I've had plenty of opportunity, I just can't bring myself to pull the trigger. You understand what I'm saying?"

Amon nodded.

"I've been trying to avoid the fight," Jesse went on, "any fight, for a long time now."

"What's changed?" Amon asked.

"I've finally got something worth fighting for—for myself," Jesse told him. "Not for my brother, or my country, or anything else. Something I want. Something I've always wanted."

Amon could hear the urgency in Jesse's voice—the ferocity of feeling. He recognized it.

"There's something I've always wanted too," he said. "Something worth giving up the fight."

"You won't help," Jesse said, and it was not a question.

"No," Amon told him. "I won't."

"Fine. Go. Be with your family. Tend your garden. Fly a goddamn kite for all I care. But remember something, Ranger: when you're old and fat and laid up in your easy chair. There's nothing worse than regretting what you've done, except the guilt of not doing anything at all."

"I'll keep it in mind," Amon said, and he watched as Jesse walked to the door and opened it and turned back and looked at him and then went on into the cold dark.

59

Morning. Ashen clouds hung low and sullen overtop the pines. A dozen men and three johnboats put into the water and there crept along through the cold fog, and in the miles to come there was the informant on the bank, his hands in his pockets and chin downward tucked like a shamed dog.

The boats angled toward the shore and the man grabbed the bow of the lead vessel and hauled it to ground and nodded at Blakewell, who climbed first over the side. They used the lightning-hacked stump of a cypress tree as a bollard, wrapping the rope around it.

Blakewell studied the crudely drawn map.

"Where?" he asked.

"There," the informant said, pointing quickly then returning his hands to his trouser pockets. "Along that ridge. You can spot the trail from up there. Runs through the woods behind town, then alongside the creek. Doesn't cross any roads. Nothing. Not even a good clearing. It's the only way to make the quarry without being seen."

Blakewell looked at the others.

They came silently from the boats like visitants from another plane. Their movements were effortless, spirit-like, and even the water seemed to quiet beneath them.

They scrambled up the hill to the ridgeline.

The informant could feel Blakewell staring at him.

"What are you looking at?" he asked.

"A pathetic specimen," Blakewell answered, then followed his comrades away from the river.

60

He'd gone to Ada's that night and parked down the street and waited. Frog's truck was there and come morning it hadn't moved. Jesse sat all night and looked at the windows. The door. He replayed memories of himself and Adaline in the river. Memories of his mother. Memories, even, of a tired old hound named Buck his father had once owned. Anything to keep his mind from his brother and his body from sleep.

The sun rose.

He waited a while longer and then drove back to the cabin.

When he walked in there was silence, and in such silence Eliza was there waiting.

She looked the shell of a woman. Dark swoops of desperation beneath her eyes.

The coffee was cold and the fire near gone from the stove and the chill of the outside world seeped in like a cancer, washing over the cabin in a morose antibaptism.

Eliza under quilts and skins in the rocker nearest the window looked out at the big doe that stood alone beneath a willow tree.

"Did you know?" he asked.

She didn't look at him when he'd walked in and didn't look at him now when he spoke.

"Know what?"

"Did you know what my brother did?" Jesse asked.

She looked down at the cabin floor and didn't answer, but it was answer enough.

He nodded.

"So you lied to me," he said. "Used me. Made me believe Danny would've wanted this."

"You already believed it," she said. "It was all you believed. Everyone in town can think, *Oh, Jesse Cole, how wonderful that he took in his poor brother's family*, but it was us who saved you. Us who took *you* in. Gave you a purpose."

"Gave me a lie."

"You were the one obsessed with living up to some promise Danny never asked you to make," she argued. "He killed himself, Jesse. That's it. Put a gun to his head and pulled the trigger, but you spoke of him like he was some saint. What was I supposed to say?"

"Twelve years, Eliza," he said. "In twelve years how could you not—"

"You didn't want me to," she told him. "You wanted to be a martyr. You wanted an excuse to keep you from moving on. Take care of Daniel's crazy widow. Take care of his daughter. But Christ didn't nail himself to the cross, and you can't either—no matter how hard you try."

"What does that mean?"

"She's gone, Jesse," Eliza said, accusing, "Sarah's gone, and you might as well have pushed her out the door."

Jesse went into both bedrooms, as if he needed to see for himself.

"Her violin. A change of clothes," Eliza said, and she began cry. "That's all she took."

Jesse stopped in the hallway. He turned and went back into the master bedroom and into the closet.

He slid the trunk out and opened it and the canvas duffel bag was gone. He closed the lid and closed his eyes. He wasn't sure what to feel, but surely, whatever his emotion, there was no small amount of pride mixed in.

"Bring her back, Jesse!" Eliza was screaming from the front room. "Go after her and bring her back to me!"

He walked to the front of the cabin and looked at her there in the chair and her face was beyond lost.

"I won't," he told her. "You would've kept her here. Lied to her. Twisted her up. Whatever you had to do."

"Bring her back, please," she begged, and she got up, pawed at his arms.

"She's better off without you," he said and flung her hands away. "And so am I."

He left out of the cabin and slammed the door and a piece of the wood broke off behind him.

"Just bring her back to me," Eliza wailed. "Bring my daughter back."

61

Amon took what little was left from the apartment and loaded it into the back of the car and set out just after daybreak. If the weather held, he could make McKinney by the afternoon.

He was only a mile out of town when the doubts started to win. His father. Deputy Davis. Jesse Cole. They all appealed to his own sense of justice. They all guided his hands as he pulled the car over along the ditch.

He sat there, breathing heavy through his nose.

Then he erupted, slamming his hands against the steering wheel until he'd nearly dislodged the column.

He looked out at the dark trees, blue-like in the cold morning mist, and he watched the tops of them bend and straighten in the soughing wind. And higher still, the black buzzards wheeled in great arcing tracks against the gray sky, and he wondered could they see something dead or dying below. Could they smell it? Or was there something inherent that called them to these places of death. He wondered this of himself as he turned and headed back toward Enoch.

He parked outside the annex next to Boyd's car and went up the short steps to the door. He'd pull Davis aside and tell him Cole was willing to help. But he wasn't sure what he'd say after that. Tell him he was sorry for leaving, maybe. Maybe he owed him that.

"Did y'all already turn Coy Taggert loose?" he asked as he came inside, but there was no one in the building.

He looked to the back of the room where Taggert was laid sideways across the floor of the cell and his blood had spilled out and dried around him to where it looked like he'd decided to nap on a burgundy rug.

Amon drew his pistol and kept it raised.

He moved toward the back to get a better look.

The cell door wasn't locked and he went inside and was reaching down to touch Taggert's body when the back door came open. Davis walked in from the rear of the building and didn't even glance at the cells. Amon stayed crouched and still.

Davis stopped at his desk and looked like he might turn, when the phone began to ring.

"This is Davis," the deputy answered and waited while the caller spoke. "Yessir, I watched him leave town this morning with my own eyes."

Amon tried to steady his breathing.

"Nossir, it won't be a problem. I got it all lined up," Davis said and then changed his tone to mimic giving a formal statement. "I came upon Deputy Boyd just as he murdered a key witness, Coy Taggert. Deputy Boyd then turned his firearm on me, at which point I shot him in self-defense."

Davis waited.

"Yessir, I got a cousin in Texarkana who'd be right for it," he said. "That is, if you didn't have somebody in mind."

When the conversation ended and Davis hung up the phone, Amon was behind him.

"Hands in the air, Davis," the Ranger told him. "Turn around slow."

Davis shook his head but didn't turn or raise his arms.

"Now here I thought you'd made a smart decision," he said.

"How long you been working for Preston?" Amon asked.

"Since before he was interested in the whiskey business, that's for sure," Davis told him.

"You killed Boyd," Amon said. "You kill Taggert too?"

"Made for a good reason to get Boyd out of the way," Davis admitted. "Never could stand that sour sonofabitch. He didn't want to cut me in on the Fenleys. Said he didn't trust me. You believe that?"

Davis shook his head again.

"I had to go to them myself and convince them I'd be a good asset. Play both sides of the coin until I saw who was gonna come out on top," he said. "Hell, you can arrest me if you want. Give me some time to relax before the trial where everything gets pinned on you. Trigger-happy Ranger. Or corrupt lawman. Or however Preston wants to play it. All I know is I'll be right back in this office sooner or later, with my feet up on that desk."

Amon began to laugh. He fell backward against the wall. The deputy looked unnerved, but Amon didn't notice. He thought of Merle Nichols and laughed even harder.

"You were never going to let me leave," he said, sighing and shaking his head.

"You going straight-jacket on me, Ranger?" Davis asked.

Amon nodded.

"Alright, fine," he decided. "I'm still not helping you, Jesse Cole, but I guess I'll do this one thing."

Davis looked amused.

"What thing?" he asked, grinning, and Amon shot him once in the shoulder and twice in the head and was already at the back door as Davis hit the ground.

He looked behind the annex and Boyd was laying in the dead grass.

Amon walked out to him and checked for a pulse and there wasn't one.

He went back in the annex and stood and looked at both of the bodies and tapped his finger on the heel of his gun. He collected the casings near Davis and put them in his pocket, then sat and picked up the phone.

"I'll make you a deal," he said, once he was through to Wolfe.

"I don't know what the hell is happening out there, Atkins," Wolfe said. "But if you're thinking of going rogue on this, I'd think again."

"I've got sworn testimony," Amon lied, "that puts several key figures of the state government in league with Percy Preston and his attempt to head an alcohol empire in East Texas."

"Don't do it," Wolfe warned. "It won't end well for you."

"On the other hand," Amon said. "I could walk away. Be done with it. All I'd ask is that you let me be done. Do you have the authority to make that call?"

Wolfe was quiet. Amon waited.

"No. But I'll make it anyway," Wolfe said. "Preston and Squirrel Fenley came to terms this morning. There won't be a war after all. Enjoy your retirement, Ranger."

"I'm not a fucking Ranger," Amon said and hung up the phone and took a long breath and walked away.

He pushed open the door and stood in the cold miraculous morning and stood at the end of one thing and the beginning of another. Monsters had roamed the earth since the word of its creation and they would prey upon it still in the forevers to come, but his was not the soul responsible nor would he allow the guilt of existence to determine the worth of his contribution to it.

Later that day, the *Nebat County Gazette* reported quotations from Texas Ranger Amon Atkins as to the deadly slaying of two county deputies. According to the Ranger's timeline, Coy Taggert, a local auto mechanic opened fire inside the Enoch sheriff's annex after being apprehended for public drunkenness by the two deputies. Both men were shot multiple times by Taggert, but the brave deputies managed to kill their shooter before they died.

"Deputies Boyd and Davis were good men," Ranger Atkins was quoted as saying. "Their deaths, so soon after the death of my partner, Ranger Phil Werskey, have left me mentally unfit to do my job. I'm therefore resigning my badge, effective immediately."

62

Jesse drove back to Ada's. She wasn't home and Frog's truck was gone. He knew where'd they be. He had to get her alone, away from Frog, and convince her to come with him. With Sarah already gone, maybe there'd be a chance.

When he made the quarry it was early evening and the temperature was near freezing. The red dirt and clay were slick under his boots, caking and clotting like some alien blood. He could hear Frog's boisterous voice near the mouth of the cave. Adaline was with him. The Claytons too. He didn't see Squirrel.

"Cole," Frog said on Jesse's approach. "Follow me back here, I want to show you something."

Jesse couldn't help but look at Ada. She gave him a slight nod.

"Alright," he said.

In the caverns of the quarry, where the hidden springs flowed, low fires burned and the Schaffers were hauling a barrel of corn. They looked at Jesse and Frog and looked worried but said nothing and let them pass.

The wind came into the quarry unblocked and unchallenged. It hallooed through the caverns, wherein it sought to gain some foothold, some continued momentum, but found neither.

Frog checked the submarine still with Jesse by his side.

"We're pulling you off the road," Frog said. "No more pickups. No more deliveries. From now on you just cook."

"Sure, alright," Jesse said, and Frog gave him a strange look. Jesse was too worried about talking to Ada and he seemed to miss that he was being demoted.

"I mean, I don't know how to do this shit, Frog," Jesse tried to recover.

"That's why I'm showing you," Frog said. "So pay attention."

"Some people get impatient and start bottling too quick," Frog went on. "They get some of the head in there, methanol, acetaldehyde, and the like. Or they get greedy, leave things going too long, and end up with some of the tail. Turns things all sorts of slimy. But I got it down to a science. I know just when to start it and just when to pull it off.

"Then there's folks who try to hide the impurities with fruits and such. Have things tasting like burning strawberries in your throat. I don't mess with all that. There's only one thing goes in my batch—a stick of cinnamon. Just one. Real subtle-like. That's why they call it Frog's Finest."

Frog stoked the fire beneath an oversized copper cookpot and Jesse could smell the mash mixture within as it began to steam.

Frog stood up and cracked his neck and handed off the fire iron to Jesse.

"Don't let it boil," he instructed, "or it'll taste like slimy piss. And watch that rock on top of the barrel. If it starts shaking, you got a clog. And I know what you're trying to do to me."

Jesse looked up.

"Adaline's mine now," Frog said. "Your place is here. That means, if I see your car anywhere near her house again, I'll kill you before you can start the engine."

Jesse looked hard at the big man. He was trying to find something—anything—that looked like a weakness. He took a step toward him. Frog began to smile.

"That's it, Cole," he said. "Let's do it right here, right now."

Maybe, Jesse thought, *if I can get him tired—*

The world erupted in gunfire.

It was the tunnels and trenches all over again. Jesse could hear the rifles and the shouting and there was fire and smoke, and he and Frog were running back toward the entrance. His heart was hammering at an escape path through the front of his chest.

"Cole," Frog yelled and flipped him a pistol and pulled out one for himself and then hauled a sawed shotgun from his coat. He fired it at the first man they came to and the man fell quickly in a hail of buckshot and they kept moving.

One of the Schaffers was moaning and bleeding with his back against the cave wall and there were two men hacking at one of the giant stills and the liquid pouring out from each wound. Three more gunmen opened fire and Jesse and the Frog scrambled across the slick floor toward any means of cover.

Smoke was filling up the cave and flashes of gunfire were all that could be seen. Purposed or not, some of the alcohol had been lit on fire. Men were coughing and shooting at shadows. It was a hellscape all its own.

Eli Schaffer came running through the smoke, screaming and firing a Derringer. Jesse saw him cut down and men on either side of the passageways exchanged pop shots and insults, bullets whizzing past with high-pitched hums and smacking into the rock and wood with loud cracks.

Frog was fumbling with the lock on a long pine box and looking over his shoulder. When the lid finally came free, he emerged with two double-grip Thompsons and began spraying into the smoke. When he stopped, all was quiet.

Frog barreled into the smoke and Jesse behind him. They spilled out into the quarry and the Claytons were there, Nick with a long rifle and Horace with a Thompson and they were laying down fire toward the tree line.

"They came from the woods," Horace said, his body tremoring from the repeating power of the gun as he shot it.

A trio of men had worked their way around to where the cars were parked and were taking shots from behind the automobiles. Nick Clayton caught a bullet in the neck and slumped over silently with his head against a rock as blood pooled beneath him.

"Ammo box," Frog called to him, reloading one of the machine guns. "Go."

"Where's Ada?" Jesse asked.

"Ammo box, goddamnit," Frog repeated.

Jesse ducked and ran back into the cave and found the ammunition box so near the flames of the burning booze that it was hot to touch. He shrugged out of his overcoat and wrapped it around the box and carried it like a baby.

Once each of the Thompsons had been reloaded, Frog and Horace fired at once, in blood unison, and it weren't long that what was left of the attackers were slinking away back to the creek. Jesse leaned against the rock wall and tried to slow his breathing.

He rolled a body over with his boot but he did not recognize the dead man's face.

He walked slow into the open quarry.

"Adaline," he called, "Ada!" but there was no response.

Horace Clayton was moaning over his brother as Frog implored him to get up and help pull whiskey barrels from the burning cave.

Jesse found her sitting against the bumper of a car. Her eyes were open but there was no life within. They stared blankly beyond the veil toward whatever is at last rewarded, at last revealed.

He knelt next to her and checked her pulse out of some strange formality, as the truth could already well be seen. He leaned forward until his forehead touched hers and he put his hand on the back of her neck and held it there. He imagined if Frog saw him he'd kill him, but he held her all the same.

He held her there in the day's bitter gloaming, the smell of damp pines sweet with soil and spores of algae. And hidden beneath the treetop horizon were those far-off fires of the setting sun, blazing in distant lands where each night named and unnamed gods work to cauterize the wounds of the world.

63

All night the bodies in the quarry burned. All night and into the morning.

Frog had ripped Jesse away from Adaline's body and Jesse had welcomed whatever was coming next, but nothing came at all. Instead, Frog only pointed at him.

"I'm going to find my brother," the big man said, and Jesse could see him holding back a flood of emotion. "But you and me ain't finished. You understand? Mourn her tonight, Cole. 'Cause sooner or later, I'm coming for you."

Jesse didn't respond. He sat on the cold ground across from Adaline while the others hauled bodies to the fire. He sat for hours and looked at her eyes and he would not close them.

When they came for her body he attacked—springing forward and tackling Hank. Jesse swung his fists wildly and they were shouting at him to stop and finally, with Horace Clayton's help, they wrestled him away, but someone who sounded like him was still screaming and wouldn't stop.

As the sun rose somewhere in a world beyond the pines, he watched her turn to ash before his eyes. He stood staring at the flames. He could feel them burning within and he imagined his own bones falling away into dust.

Dreams are like bones, he thought. *You cannot see them, but they are inside of you. They are inside of you until you die and then there is nothing left to hold them.*

The morning came and went and they had been ordered to stay at the quarry but he did not. He walked away and they let him go.

He left the car and went on foot into the forest and cut across the hollow and followed a trickling stream that ran high above the roads. There were clumps of leaves and clumps of mud and his boot kicked something hard. He bent down and dug through the leaves and there found a fogged bottle half-full with whiskey. The bottle was tied to a string and he followed the string through the leaves to where the other end was tied around a pine tree and there was an *X* carved into the bark.

He took the whiskey and left the string and went on through the woods.

Hours to come, he walked and drank and followed the stream until the underbrush around it grew too thick and he descended back into civilization.

He took the logging road, whereby he passed the ghosts of industry and prosperity, and continued on toward the town, watching as the sun sank into its ancestral grave beyond the hills, where countless suns were gone and buried before it.

The logging road was empty, and it had been empty for years. Jesse remembered when the trail was first cut and the traffic never stopped. The earth groaning under the trundling trucks and their gruff engines like low-throated howls rising and falling through the curtains of pine before which they passed. And each truck in the cold and dusted parade with bundles of the long yellowwood logs, felled and bound and jostling behind them like captured soldiers on display.

Now there was only cold, bitter silence.

He came to the top of the rise that overlooked Enoch and stared through drunken eyes at the last of the failing light and the long pink sky and soon it was faded, and the evening gray surrounded him. He wandered on toward the town but found no solace among the living.

Every building he passed held some memory and his memories now tasted of sorrow and ash.

Once his whiskey ran dry, he hiked back up to the crossroads and stood there in somber indecision until a car appeared atop the nearest hill.

The headlamps reflected off the wet road as the car came down out of the hollow, uncovering those things that waited in the dark. Trees. A bar ditch. A scared gray rabbit with pinned ears. And then there stood Jesse and the car slowed and idled next to him and Horace Clayton called for him to get in and he did.

Neither of them spoke.

They drove south of town and onto an old county road and then west, down the long gravel trail that spilled into the quarry, and it was there they stopped at last and Jesse sat unmoving in the passenger seat.

"They want to see you," Horace said. "They're in yonder."

He pointed to the old foreman's shack and Jesse could see the lantern light flickering within and he nodded and climbed down out of the car and walked across the lot and knocked on the door.

He unsheathed his knife. He was sure the Fenleys would try to kill him, and he was ready for the fight. But when the door opened, Squirrel looked down at the knife and shook his head and pointed to the chair in the center of the room where Hollis was tied.

"What is this?" Jesse asked.

Hollis was crying.

"Jesse," he said. "Help me, Jesse, please."

Jesse looked at the other men.

"What's going on, goddamnit?" he demanded.

"Your old pal here told Blakewell about the quarry," Squirrel said. "Even showed him the creek trail that led right to us. It was his men in the woods."

"Is that true?" Jesse asked.

"No," Hollis wailed. "It ain't true. It ain't true, Jesse. I swear."

"How do y'all know it was him?" Jesse asked.

"Jess—" Hollis was crying too hard to speak.

"Horace seen him with Blakewell hisself," Frog said. "Night before it happened."

"That true?" Jesse asked, and Horace nodded at him.

"Saw them talking real quiet-like, down by the river."

"No, Jesse," Hollis insisted. "I didn't tell him anything. I didn't. He asked, but I didn't say nothing."

Jesse's stomach felt sour. He looked down at his oldest friend.

"You talked to him?" Jesse asked. "You talked to Zev Blakewell?"

"He come up on me," Hollis said. "That's all. He just come up asking questions."

"And you didn't tell him anything."

"I didn't, Jess, I swear I didn't."

"Then, what? He just let you walk away?" Jesse asked.

"No, it ain't like that," Hollis said. "He said I was useless to him. Not worth killing. He said—"

"Alright. Enough," Squirrel said. "We brought you here out of courtesy, Cole. But it don't change what needs to be done."

Squirrel handed Jesse a pistol.

"Do it and let's get him buried."

"No," Hollis moaned. "No, no, no."

He was sobbing and the room smelled like urine.

"She's dead, Hollis," Jesse told him, raising the pistol as the floor of the shack appeared to spin beneath him. "The only person who ever loved me back, and she's dead."

Frog's body tensed, but he didn't speak. Didn't make a move.

"I loved you back," Hollis countered. "I loved you back and you threw me aside. Now look at us. Just look at us, Jess."

Jesse's jaw was clamped shut. The pace of his heart felt erratic. He felt the weight of the gun, the weight of the world.

Hollis continued to mumble his innocence, then suddenly he went quiet. He looked up at Jesse and saw there the fear and anguish within him. Hollis closed his eyes. His intensity quieted. He let his body relax.

"We ain't got time for this shit," Squirrel said. "Do it, Cole."

"It's alright, Jess," Hollis said, nodding amid his newfound calm.

"Really it is. You just do what they say, now. Don't worry about me, bud, I'm ready to go."

Jesse's hand trembled. His whole body was leaning forward.

Hollis closed his eyes.

"We sure were brothers, weren't we, Jess?" he asked.

"Yes," Jesse told him and pulled the trigger.

64

The boy is in and out of sleep, and so too is Hollis. Jesse checks the surrounding buildings, but there is no one alive and nothing of use and when he comes back he wakes Hollis.

"Take watch for an hour or two and let me get some rest," Jesse says. Hollis nods.

Jesse sleeps sitting up, his helmet still on his head. The hours pass.

"Wake up, Jesse." Hollis shakes him until his eyes open.

Jesse hears German being shouted in the street. Hollis is holding a finger to his lips.

"Twenty," Hollis mouths, flashing ten fingers twice.

They can hear the men outside and they stay quiet, waiting for them to pass. Finally they do, the voices receding. Hollis closes his eyes and breathes out through his nose.

But now the boy comes awake in the grip of some death-rattling fervor. He is screaming and calling out the names of the dead. Both men move to silence him. The boy picks up Hollis's helmet and swings it wildly at him, connecting with his temple. Hollis stumbles back just enough to catch the lip of a broken table. He falls backward and strikes his head on a stone and Jesse has his hand over the boy's mouth and is trying to keep him from flailing.

He can hear the voices rising again.

"Hush now, hush boy." But even with his hand over the boy's small mouth he cannot stop the noise. His heart is pounding in places far from his chest. His fingers. His head. He can feel it everywhere. He grabs his knife. He ends it. The boy's warmth pouring out over Jesse's hands.

The soldiers are just outside. Hollis touches the blood on the back of his head and Jesse puts his finger to his mouth. Hollis nods. He eases his hand down and pulls up his rifle.

There is machine gun fire outside, but it is not from the Germans. The main body of allied troops has arrived. The soldiers scramble. They are calling out and screaming and waving white handkerchiefs.

Soon the church bell is ringing, and the street is flooded with American troops, but Jesse will not let loose of the boy. Hollis pleads with him.

"We gotta go, bud," he says. "This is our ticket."

Jesse is neither responding nor crying. He just stares at the child's eyes, and they stare back at him. They have taken from one another. The child will hold now a piece of Jesse's soul. And the ghost of the child will follow him. This is the exchange. This is the arrangement. And now they have been witness to it—attendants to the great and unyielding sorrow.

Hollis tries to take the boy from Jesse's arms and Jesse grabs him by the throat.

"It's me," Hollis insists. "It's me. It's Hollis. Your brother."

Jesse turns him loose. Now he is crying, and the bells are tolling and Hollis calls for someone to come help and he hugs Jesse into his chest and kisses his matted hair.

"They're coming," Hollis assures him. "I'll stay with you till they get here. We'll be alright. We'll be just fine."

65

Jesse woke with a pounding head and shivering cold in Moss's barn. He was still in his clothes and covered with an old quilt that had once warmed newborn horses in those first unsure moments of life. He smelled the blanket and tossed it aside and went into the yard.

The frost hung heavy in the trees, fatigued branches bending beneath its weight, embowed like wilting flowers. Evergreens paled against the ice-white sky. Strange, empty sky.

The first limb came down off a cedar tree with a great cracking sound. Dismembered from the source without warning, as if by some internal detonation. It went crashing to the frozen ground, leaves shaking in its wake like wet fur.

Then came a second limb. Then another. Pine and cedar. Frozen fascicles and ice-warped branches and those that didn't break remained overtasked, hanging crookbacked and circumflex in their tired midwinter weeping. Mourning the sun.

"The world's decided to come apart one limb at the time," Moss said, coming out of the cabin with two cups of steaming coffee.

He handed one over to Jesse.

Jesse took it and held it as if it were some curiosity from an exotic land. The night flooded in and he made a strange sound and dropped the cup and steam hissed off the ice where the coffee touched it.

"I killed him," he said, crouching down and hugging his knees. "I killed Hollis."

Moss didn't react.

"I know," the old man said. "You come in here last night screaming and hollering about it."

"I shot him," Jesse said, quieter, talking now to himself, rocking back and forth on his heels.

Moss drank from his coffee and looked out at the wounded woods.

"Hollis understood war," he said. "He picked a side. His choice had consequences."

Jesse looked up at him, hurt and confused.

"I'm not saying it ain't a tragedy," Moss told him. "And it shouldn't have had to be you that done it. But Hollis was a grown man."

Moss looked as if he might say more but he didn't.

"A grown man," he repeated instead, nodding.

"Did you know?" Jesse asked him. "About Danny?"

Moss shook his head.

"You said that last night too."

"I'll never understand it," Jesse said.

"He was a father," Moss told him. "A husband. He was trying to protect his family."

"Not that," Jesse said, shaking his head. "It's not that he stole my whole goddamn life from me. It's that he didn't ask."

"What?"

"He lied to me because he thought I'd say no," Jesse said. "I wouldn't have. If he'd just come to me, I would have taken his place right then. In a heartbeat. I would've done anything for him."

Moss nodded.

"I know you would have."

"But now he's dead. And Adaline too."

"And here you are," Moss said.

"Here I am."

Jesse tried to find the sun through the trees.

"They'll be coming for me soon," he said, speaking his realization out loud. "Preston's boys. Or maybe Frog'll beat them to it, if he decides he wants more blood out of all this. I doubt Eliza will be safe—you might be in trouble too."

"I know it," Moss told him. "We're gonna get you out of here this morning. You can go find Miss Sarah and make sure she's alright. Stay away from Enoch for a while."

Jesse didn't argue or agree. He just stood.

"Well, let's go on and get you packed," Moss said.

Jesse nodded.

"Sure," he said, detached. "Give me a minute. I'll meet you inside."

Jesse went back inside the barn and stood in front of the cracked mirror and saw in its reflection an aging man. The high cheeks of his father. Lines on his forehead and on the backs of his hands. He felt the weight of time as it passed.

He was slower than he used to be, and there was a soft sagging around his midsection, and when he closed his eyes his mother's face was all but lost to him. Yet in the horrific theater of his mind he was still a boy. Still standing in the cabin with his bag slung loosely about his shoulder and his brother there smiling at him, his hand on the door.

He could see that moment more clearly than anything from the last two weeks. Two decades. But this man in the mirror was a stranger to him. His life, his future, even his feelings, were wholly inaccessible.

Only then did he look down and see the pistol in the dirt near where he'd slept.

When Jesse did not come back to the cabin, Moss went to fetch him from the barn. He wasn't there, but next to Moss's shaving kit was a note. "Watch after Eliza if she'll let you," Jesse had written. "And quit naming the pigs."

66

He walked dreamlike to the paper mill and the world was still and the world was cold and he could hear his breath as he went.

The gate was open. The lock hanging there on the chain where it had been split with a pair of bolt cutters. There were tire tracks in the mud but he didn't see any cars. Wasn't looking for them. He walked around to the north end of the mill, where the administration building was, and stood outside of it near the frost-warped rosebushes and looked out at the river. He could hear it running. Swollen brown rapids leaping and spiraling and continuing on and ever onward toward the suck of the sea. The final and solitary resting place of every arc and incurvation. He drew the pistol from his coat.

He closed his eyes and he didn't see her face or any other. He didn't see anything.

The gunshot ripped open the morning quiet and a murder of crows abandoned one tree for the safety of another, cawing their displeasure as they went.

Jesse lowered the pistol and looked toward the building where the shot had been fired.

He waited. Listening. Still he could hear the river. But there was no other sound.

He went up the steps of the administration building and tried the door and it came open. There were voices down the corridor. He followed them, rounding a corner and nearly tripping over Frog Fenley's lifeless body.

The big man's eyes were open and looking up as if he were trying to see the gaping hole where the bullet had come out.

Jesse looked behind him. No one.

He walked to the back door of the building, where it opened to a covered sidewalk. He went outside and followed the walkway to the factory door and pushed it slowly open.

There on the main floor of the mill were five men loading crates of whiskey onto dollies and they stopped when they saw Jesse and no one said a word.

One of the men drew first and fired as Jesse took a quick step to his right, dropped to one knee and squeezed off five shots. He stayed crouched, pistol raised, but none of the men were alive to return his fire.

His heartbeat was slow. His hands didn't shake.

He straightened up.

He caught movement to his left and spun in that direction. Blakewell shot him in the wrist and Jesse dropped the gun and grabbed his forearm.

"Mr. Cole," Blakewell said in his strange, wheezing voice. "Unexpected."

Jesse shook his head.

"Y'all were right here the whole time," he said, wincing.

"The most obvious place," Blakewell affirmed.

"And Frog?" Jesse asked. "He figure it out on his own, or did you bring him here just to kill him?"

"He was invited," Blakewell said. "But not by me."

"Who?"

"Me," Squirrel said, stepping out from behind one of the granite rollers. "Like I said, Cole, I hate losing."

"Your own brother."

Jesse's stomach hollowed. He felt seasick.

"It wouldn't have been my first choice," Squirrel admitted. "But Mr. Preston's contracts are sealed in blood. And in the end, we do what we have to do to survive, don't we?"

"You knew," Jesse said, breathing heavy. "You told us you didn't, but you knew it was Preston the whole time."

"Of course I did, Cole," Squirrel said, feigning offense. "You think anything happens that I don't know about? But if I told my boys they were going up against Percy Preston and half the elected officials in the county, you think they would've stuck around? I wanted to at least see if we could fight the bastards. Turns out we couldn't."

Squirrel shrugged.

"No harm," he said. "I guess I ought to thank you for turning the old man down, though. Gave me a second chance."

"No harm," Jesse whispered, and the room had begun to turn and felt unsteady.

Squirrel looked over at the dead men near the whiskey crates.

"Still," he said, "it's tough to kill someone you love—when all they've ever been is loyal."

Squirrel grinned as the realization washed over Jesse's face.

"Oh, sure, Blakewell here put the screws to your buddy Hollis," Squirrel went on. "Worked on him pretty good. But he never broke. Never said a word. Loyal till the end."

Jesse closed his eyes and tried to stop the spinning.

"Shame how it all turned out," Squirrel added. "But that's the mystery, ain't it? No matter how many times the house wins, folks still can't help but sit down at the table. Speaking of, I don't suppose you're looking for work, are you?"

Jesse didn't answer. His entire body was shaking, and he couldn't tell if it was anger or pain or if there was any difference between the two.

"Yeah, I didn't think so," Squirrel said. "Well, that's a shame. Judging by the mess you made of these boys, you're as good as they say. Would've been a hell of a hand."

Squirrel turned and headed toward the dry end of the mill.

"He's all yours," he said to Blakewell. "And you tell Mr. Preston that Squirrel Fenley's held up his end of the bargain."

Jesse dove for his gun and took aim at Squirrel, but Blakewell was faster. He shot Jesse in the other wrist as he fired, and the gun clattered to the floor. The bullet clipped Squirrel's ear, marking him, but doing little damage.

Jesse knelt near the pistol. He knew it was empty. He waited for Blakewell to finish him, but the shot never came. Instead the masked man stood there, watching, his head tilted to the side as if he were curious what Jesse might do next.

Jesse stood and stared back at him. Then he turned and went for the door.

The cold air hit Jesse hard and he sucked in a breath. His head was throbbing. He was bleeding from both wrists.

He made for the north gate, but it was locked. He leapt onto the fence and climbed it, grunting and gritting his teeth. He dropped down on the other side and looked behind him and Blakewell was there, following at an unassuming pace.

The forest was two hundred yards ahead of him and he ran for the tree line without looking back again.

When he reached the woods, he turned once more to gauge the distance, and Blakewell was still following, taking long strides across the field. Breathing heavy, Jesse pushed further into the woods and stopped only when he heard a single shot.

The sound confused him—a shot that far. What confused him more was the zip and pop of the bullet as it went through his back and exploded from his abdomen.

His hands went up to hold his stomach and he fell forward, face-first into the mire of pine needles and thick mud.

He began to crawl. He could taste the blood in his mouth, could feel his insides sliding, trying to leak out. He struggled to his feet but slipped down again.

He pulled himself up to the trunk of a willow and managed to get his back against the tree and there he sat, bleeding.

He watched Blakewell walk slow through the woods. His shape looming, growing larger. Then he was standing there above Jesse, smiling down like some perverted demiurge of a lesser realm.

"I imagine it hurts," he said. "A bullet in the belly."

Blakewell crouched beside him.

Jesse's mouth was dry. His breath was labored. He tried to cuss the man, but he only wheezed.

Like a dying hog, he thought.

"Sleep well, Jesse Cole," Blakewell said and shot him again in the stomach and headed back through the woods.

Jesse gasped for air. His mouth was dry. There were spots of light surrounding him and he tried to find her but he could not. Not yet.

He strained, pushing himself up. He leaned against the tree. Blakewell was two dozen yards away. More.

Jesse managed his knife from its sheath. He moved just off the tree and wavered for a moment and then found his balance. He brought his arm back and hurled the blade forward toward its target. The knife entered the back of Blakewell's head and burrowed through his skull to its hilt and had it been a half inch longer would have come out through his forehead. He was dead before his knees touched the ground.

Jesse collapsed beneath the tree.

The world sounded of silence and there was a comfort to the darkness, but whatever passage lie ahead he would not go without her.

Jesse.

He heard his brother's voice and he opened his eyes.

A kinglet, with its ruby crown, lit high in the tree above him and warbled a short, shrill tune. Jesse's fingers flexed—digging into the garnet earth as if he might hold or be held by it. He sucked in air and expelled it and the process felt pained and unnatural. He pushed himself over onto his back and made a soft panting noise. He looked up through the branches at the breaking clouds and the blue sky beyond. The bird flittered there among the bald limbs and Jesse watched it as best he could while his vision blurred and darkened and windowed away the plane he so desperately clung to. It came, the bird, to the lowest limb and called out to him.

He could no longer feel the cold of the dirt in his hand.

"Yes," he answered, and he shut his eyes again, and the comfort returned and the warmth of it all.

He listened to the birdsong and dreamed of the spring to come. Of honeysuckle and clover and rich fragrant pine, of maypops and azaleas, monarchs and hummingbirds and whitetail bucks, their antlers rendered in velvet, and all the world awakening at once, reborn in full from the cold and the dark and manifested in such color and wonder and soul-aching beauty. And he knew he could stay there, in that soft, bright tomorrow, if only he kept closed his eyes. And he knew the voices calling for him were full of kindness and he could feel their welcome, and it was everything he'd never allowed himself to hope for. The things he knew could not be true, and yet here they were. And the war and the mill and the sound of guns and the smell of sulfur and the tolling bells and toy coffins were dreams forgotten, and he saw his body and the flowers that covered it and all of them blooming up from within him. And he saw the people he loved, and they weren't people at all but rather brilliant neon happenings, and there he turned slowly in line with them in a swirling rotation of the never before and always has been. And he pulled it all inside of him through his mouth like a great breath. And he felt it filling his lungs, and his heart beat of it without beating at all, and he was not afraid. But still he waited. Still he would not go.

And then came the light he longed to see. The only one he'd agree to follow. She smiled.

His eyes were open, but the branch above was empty, and it still swayed from the weight of the bird now gone.

67

Cora sat under a pecan tree on the McKinney square. Around her, the remnants of a hearty lunch. She watched Amon and Joseph throw a baseball back and forth and the boy felt her watching and turned and waved. She waved back.

There had been little rain since Amon arrived in the weeks prior, but there was a spring shower on the horizon and the warm wind kicked up and threatened to scatter the picnic, blankets and all.

The three of them scrambled to pack their things and ran the short block down Virginia Avenue to their home. They made the covered porch just as the rain began to fall. Cora sent Joseph inside with the basket and blankets and she stood next to her husband and watched the weather rolling in.

Grackles squawked in the nearby trees and somewhere in the distance a trolley car went clacking along its route. Thunder groaned behind the blackening clouds, but Amon didn't hear it.

There would be days when the rain came. When the guilt flooded him with a sorrow he could scarcely contain. He would read the papers and hear of the things happening out there in the dark of the world. Oftentimes he would ask himself if there was more he could have done, more he could still do. But then Cora would touch his arm and smile at him. She would bear their second child. A girl who would wear flower crowns and call him Daddy and giggle from the feel of his beard when he kissed her. Joseph would graduate from high school, then college. Weddings and grandkids and hayrides in the fall and dances in the spring and even the wars to come could not dampen his happiness because they would not be his wars.

And he would do good deeds where he could and try always to hold kindness in his heart. But for the remainder of his days, he would take no part in the misery of the collective. He was a man recused from men and the great sorrow of men. And he saw that it was good.

68

1917

Jesse sits on a rock amid one of the massive outcroppings along Buck Creek. Giant, virid boulders covered with moss and lichen jut out from the shaded hillside and the woods are dark and damp even at noon. There is only a sliver of blue sky visible through a short gap in the pines and the smoke from the mill passes slow and steady within it.

He lays his paper on the rock next to him and from his pouch he tips a short pile of dry cut tobacco. He rolls his smoke and smooths it out between his fingers. He pulls a matchbox from his pocket and slides the drawer free but it is empty.

"Well, shit."

"If a gal strikes a match in the woods, will it burn?" Adaline asks, climbing up the rocks.

He grins at her.

She lights his smoke, and he draws from it and passes it to her and they lie back together on the quillwort and holly fern and stare up at the patch-work canopy, a chaotic assemblage of limbs and leaves jutting and bending in strange, farcical positions. Beyond is the sky, where clouds or smoke or the bellies of birds might pass. And there is more—the sun, the moon, the stars—many things he doesn't know but feels he should.

"Eldridge Wentworth used to tell me and Hollis all sorts of stuff about what's up there," he says to her. "About how there's a whole bunch of worlds like ours, and each one of them is a little different—maybe a little better, maybe a little worse. And we exist in all of 'em, as some sort of version of ourselves."

"So do we know each other?" she asks. "In the different worlds, I mean."

"I imagine in some of them we do."

"What about the other ones?"

"I guess those are the bad ones."

They hold one another, and more, and afterward they bathe in the cool water and dry on the rocks like lizards. They tell each other secrets and make promises they can't hope to keep, but such is their youth and their love and the warmth of the moment.

In the eventide, three deer come to the edge of the creek and turn their noses up and measure the air. There is a pale gold band above the trees, where the sun has only just passed.

"If today was a fish, I'd mount it on the wall."

"What's so good about today?" she asks.

"I got to spend it with you."

"You spend damn near every day with me."

"Well," he considers the fact, "I guess I'd need a big wall."

She laughs and pushes her shoulder into his.

"I love you, you know," she says.

"I know," he tells her.

"And you love me," she emphasizes.

"Oh, I love you alright. Gonna make this a whole lot harder because of it."

"What?"

"They pulled my number," he says.

She stiffens but doesn't say anything. Doesn't take her hand away from his.

"I gotta report to some folks over in Nebat City," he says. "Then wherever they say to go, I guess."

"When do you leave?" she asks. She is crying, but she holds her voice together and will not let it break.

"In the morning. Catching a ride with Hollis and a couple of other fellas."

She shakes her head.

"Right. Well, I guess I'm supposed to just sit here on this rock and wait for you?"

"No"—he touches her face—"you can sit on any of these rocks, it don't have to be this one."

She laughs and wipes her eyes.

"I will," she tells him. "I'll wait for you."

"Don't."

"What?"

"Don't wait for me. Not for one day. Not even for a minute."

"What are you saying?"

"Go to New York. Or go somewhere. Get out of here and go be something. Be somebody."

"But it's supposed to be the two of us."

"It will be," he tells her. "It will be in the end."

EPILOGUE

It was spring in that green country, when the sun was hot but the wind still cool, and the children drank from the river and splashed it on their faces and the water would awaken their spirits as it ran down their chins and necks and shoulders. The creeks were full and cold and the songbirds in the meadows and the wildflowers growing up everywhere, and the children turned their faces up toward the hot sun and closed their eyes and the sun nourished them, fawning over their cheeks like a doting aunt, squeezing them red.

They lay in the sun and in the grass, and the warmth of the midday would hold them and caress their heads, which were filled with great hopes for the future.

When night fell the tempered air was welcome and the flowers swayed in a soft, comforting breeze. The promise of summer and salvation was ever on the mind of all who passed along under the wise old moon. Knowing moon. And even in the moonlight they did not see the burnt man climb down from his wagon.

His movements were strange but efficient and he was quickly inside the gates and on the porch. He looked at his pocket watch with the only eye left to him. His hand was ligament and soft tissue. Red and pink strings.

The door came inches open.

Maurice nodded, then he was gone.

The burnt man nudged the door further and slipped inside.

Percy Preston slept in a chair in the great room, blankets all about him. Who can say what greed came to him in dreams.

The burnt man stood beside the chair and bent over—his tender, malformed face near touching Preston's ear.

"For the Neck," he said, and the old man opened his eyes just as the blade carved into his throat.

When it was done—and it was done quickly—Maurice entered and nodded again at Garver and poured two glasses of bourbon and they stood by the golden lions and the crackling fire and drank up the sun.

———

Moss stopped off at the Cole place and left a mushroom potato casserole on the porch.

The poor woman hardly left the house, but he knew she was alive because every now and then she'd set a clean dish back outside and he'd take it with him if he was passing by. He'd seen her once, too, at the grave site. Sitting on that little bench. Poor woman and the poor world she's left to live in.

Moss, too, carried the burden of loneliness. The burden of guilt. His mind waking him in the night to lay out each of those things he might have done different that day. Or any day prior.

Perhaps there had been too many sleepless nights, or perhaps he was simply tired of telling himself no, but either way, he'd made himself a midnight coffee and made the casserole and fed the pigs and gone out into the night.

He covered the casserole dish with a towel and knocked on the door and didn't wait for anyone to answer. He walked out through the yard and down the trail and a gray-looking pig followed along beside him. He sang to the pig songs of that long ago and thought to himself if only he could get back there somehow.

The walk was long, but it was pleasant in the warming weather and when he reached Enoch proper there was hardly a soul about.

He went down Main and into the pawn shop and Sid was awake still, but the dog was asleep.

"You can't bring that animal in here," Sid said.

Moss frowned.

"Wait outside, Pig Newton," he said, and he ushered the pig out the door and onto the wooden porch boards.

"What'll you take for a pistol?" Moss asked, turning his attention back to the counter.

"What sort of pistol?"

"The kind that shoots."

"I can let go of this Colt for fifteen dollars," the man said, passing over a slender gun with a nice weight to it.

Moss took it and looked it over.

"Bullets?"

"It only has the three in the cylinder there," Sid told him. "I may have a box back here somewhere though."

"That's alright," Moss said. "I don't need but the three."

Sid frowned.

"Well, alright."

"I give you fifteen for it, then what would you give me for it?" Moss asked.

"Huh?"

"I give you fifteen dollars," Moss repeated. "You give me this here Colt. Then I come back after a while and want to pawn it to you. What would it be worth?"

Sid scratched his head.

"I gotta make money on these things, you know," he said, defensive. "There's always gonna be a markup."

"How much?"

"I'd probably take it back for ten, I guess."

"Alright then, let's say we did that," Moss told him, nodding. "Here's the five I'd owe you. And I'll be right back with the gun."

He laid a bill on the counter in front of the befuddled shopkeeper and left through the front door.

He walked down the street to the insurance office and stood outside and waited.

He didn't have to wait long.

He saw a man and a woman leave first, both drunk and whispering. But the second time the door opened it was Squirrel Fenley smoking a cigarette. The top of his left ear was missing.

Like a cut hog, Moss thought.

Squirrel looked over at him and down at the pig and then nodded and Moss nodded back and raised the gun and shot him three times in the head.

He turned and went back to the pawn shop and went in the door and left the gun still smoking on the counter.

"Y'all be good," he said, and he rang the bell on the counter for good measure, which woke the dog and sent it into hysterics.

———

She sat with both hands atop the duffel bag, the bag in her lap, and she looked out at the country as it passed by. Others around her slept or talked or read from newspapers or dime novels, but she was concerned only with the changing landscape. Pines thickets and rolling hills, flat stretches of fields and forests. Mountain ranges and river valleys and great cities with buildings that touched the clouds.

She didn't know if seeing the world would make it bigger or smaller. Perhaps it depended on the nature of those things she might see. But what she did know is that change was ahead—and whatever fortunes awaited, they did so in places not yet discovered.

The unknown frightened her but not nearly so much as the predetermined.

She loved her mother and believed that she would one day see her again. But she would see her own days first, and she would live a life unprescribed.

A woman a few rows up turned and looked at her and smiled and the girl smiled back and as the train clattered across the tracks she began to hum an old tune from the radio.

She pulled her violin case from under her seat and set it next to her and leaned closer to the window so that she might watch the future come into view.

ACKNOWLEDGMENTS

Thank you to Mark Gottlieb, Trident Media Group, and everyone at Blackstone Publishing, including Anne Fonteneau, Sarah Bonamino, Brad Simpson, Bryan Green, Isabella Bedoya, the amazing Michael Krohn, and my design hero, Kathryn English.

Thank you to the two editors, Michael Signorelli and Corinna Barsan, who worked tirelessly on this story.

Thanks also to Owen Egerton, Elizabeth Wetmore, May Cobb, David Joy, Corey Ryan Forrester, Sarah Bird, Christopher Brown, Stacey Swann, Jim Haley, Matt Bondurant, David Heska Wanbli Weiden, Claire Fullerton, Kathy L. Murphy, Mandy Haynes, Robert Gwaltney, Jacob Marquez, Carol Ann Tack, Theresa Bakken, Mark Zvonkovic, Scott Semegran, Chris Mullen, Caren Creech, Wes Ferguson, the fellas at the Weather Permitting podcast, and so many others.

Thank you to Becka Oliver and the Writers' League of Texas, Heather Duncan and the MPIBA, and everyone at the Western Writers of America.

Special thanks to Lucy Griffith and Andy Robinson for your friendship and kindness. I'm not sure I would have finished this one without your unyielding generosity and support.

And thanks as always to my wife, Jordan, who continues to rent me a room.